D1056335

The Switch

DIANE WHITESIDE

HEAT
NEW YORK, NEW YORK

THE BERKLEY PUBLISHING GROUP
Published by the Penguin Group
Penguin Group (USA) Inc.
375 Hudson Street, New York, New York 10014, USA
Penguin Group (Canada), 90 Eglinton Avenue East, Suite 700, Toronto, Ontario M4P 2Y3, Canada
(a division of Pearson Penguin Canada Inc.)
Penguin Books Ltd., 80 Strand London WC2R 0RL, England
Penguin Group Ireland, 25 St. Stephen's Green, Dublin 2, Ireland (a division of Penguin Books Ltd.)
Penguin Group (Australia), 250 Camberwell Road, Camberwell, Victoria 3124, Australia
(a division of Pearson Australia Group Pty. Ltd.)
Penguin Books India Pvt. Ltd., 11 Community Centre, Panchsheel Park, New Delhi—110 017, India
Penguin Group (NZ), Cnr. Airborne and Rosedale Roads, Albany, Auckland 1310, New Zealand
(a division of Pearson New Zealand Ltd.)
Penguin Books (South Africa) (Pty.) Ltd., 24 Sturdee Avenue, Rosebank, Johannesburg 2196, South
Africa

Penguin Books Ltd., Registered Offices: 80 Strand, London WC2R 0RL, England

This is an original publication of The Berkley Publishing Group.

This is a work of fiction. Names, characters, places, and incidents either are the product of the author's imagination or are used fictitiously, and any resemblance to actual persons, living or dead, business establishments, events, or locales is entirely coincidental. The publisher does not have any control over and does not assume any responsibility for author or third-party websites or their content.

First edition: January 2006

Library of Congress Cataloging-in-Publication Data

Whiteside, Diane.
    The switch / by Diane Whiteside—1st ed.
        p. cm.
    ISBN 0-425-20817-6
    1. Sexual dominance and submission—Fiction. I. Title.

PS3623.H5848S95 2006
813'.6—dc22

2005052783

PRINTED IN THE UNITED STATES OF AMERICA

10 9 8 7 6 5 4 3 2 1

Acknowledgments

My deepest thanks go to . . .

Eric, for answering endless questions about the Rangers;

Karen, for making sure that Beth walked smoothly in the ways of both Japan and America;

Clint and Meretta, Tom and Lise, for explaining how soldiers jump out of perfectly good airplanes then go on to do even greater things;

Louise, for describing Tiffany's illness so well; and

Delores, who quickly told me how Sean got out of the Army when I was running hard to meet a deadline.

You're marvelous friends and I couldn't have written Sean and Beth's story without you.

Prologue

Sean Lindstrom jumped out of a perfectly good airplane with a smile: the long-planned raid was finally happening. He always felt more alive at times like this than he ever had in his wife's bedroom.

Experience took over immediately, of course. Not much time to do anything during a low-altitude jump, but at least nobody was shooting at him the way they had in Panama. His squad had all gotten out safely, ready to hit the ground running. A static line jump, so the chutes opened as soon as they exited the airplane.

No moon out, but his night vision was good enough to orient himself by as he looked for the landing zone, a mud bank beside the river scoured flat during last week's floods. That stretch of mud had made the whole operation possible, a covert drop into rebel territory. Nighttime was vital but nobody wanted to land in the middle of unseen trees. Then the mud bank had showed up, one valley away from the hacienda where the last good guys lived, and higher-ups had green-lighted the raid.

He was immensely calm, fully alert, as he came in toward the treetops. Mind and body working perfectly together, preparing for combat. As he looked for the LZ, a flash of light flickered past the corner of his eye. Yellow light, like a fire, high on a mountain. The hills beside the river blocked his view, with only seconds left before landing.

He hit the center of the landing zone perfectly, feet and knees together. Only two men had landed in the trees and one in the water, thank God. Fast, silent action by the rest of the squad saved them, with only a multitude of scratches to show for the adventure. They gathered their chutes and formed up just inside the tree line minutes later, the medic immediately going to work with antibiotics and bandages. It seemed to take forever but actually went remarkably smoothly. Of course, combat experience and lots of practice in night drops helped.

"All here? Good," Sean double-checked quietly. He was in command on this raid, thanks to Lieutenant Benson's close encounter with his son's skateboard just before the squad's scheduled deployment.

They were supposed to meet a local guide the next day but he was from the hacienda's folks. If what Sean suspected was true, the fellow would never speak to an American again on this earth. More than likely, he was chatting to St. Peter even as the unit formed up. "Anyone see something at the hacienda while coming down?"

"A couple of flashes, maybe gunfire," Adam Hepburn, his oldest friend, offered. One of the younger Rangers hissed briefly, as if flinching. "No chance to see much, though."

"Anyone else?" Silent head shakes answered him. Sean made up his mind. "We're supposed to go to ground amongst those hills. I want us up there as fast as possible so we can see what's going on. Cache everything possible, except what's needed for an ambush."

"Yes, sir," they snapped and went to work.

Two hours later and barely an hour before dawn, after visiting some of the worst scenery he'd ever had the pleasure of enduring, Sean and Adam crept up to the hillcrest and looked across the mountain valley. Sean automatically steadied his heartbeat, so he could better study the scene.

Below them lay the river's other branch, a frothing silver stream twisting through the jungle. Like the stretch he'd just crossed, it was running high and fast, full of rainwater and nasty critters. A bridge crossed it at one point, with the small, deserted village of San Desiderio on the mountain flank. Burned fields and shattered buildings showed the rebels' handiwork. A narrow road twisted up the mountain beyond to the old hacienda, where the last decent folks lived— or had lived—in this valley.

Fire leaped from the hacienda's windows and doors, sending a column of smoke and flames into the sky. A boxy shape blocked the flames then rolled clear. Sean focused his binoculars carefully. A truck? No, a very big car. Another bulky shape was silhouetted briefly, and a third. The rebels were behaving according to pattern.

Sean smiled thinly. He'd be delighted to repay those assholes in kind. He handed the binoculars to Adam, waved the squad forward to look for themselves, and took a long swig of water from his canteen. Adam was short and dark, one of the fastest sprinters he'd ever met. He was an urban kid, from a good family in Seattle, but he'd taken to Army life like a duck to water. Hell, he'd even become a Delta Force operator.

After a long survey, focused notably on the hacienda and San Desiderio, Adam handed the glasses back. Their eyes met. Nothing more needed to be said, not between men who'd started out as buddies during Ranger School.

Sean tucked the binoculars away and the squad slithered back to where they could speak quietly. He'd remind the men what the rebels were like now, then move them out. "Miller, what's the raid pattern for the local rebels?"

Gary Miller possessed a degree in Elizabethan poetry from Harvard, plus one of the sneakiest minds Sean had the pleasure of working with. He answered readily. "They prefer to attack just after dark. Kill the men and children first, rape then kill the women. Loot everything portable and torch the remainder. Leave just after dawn."

"And steal all the target's vehicles, to carry the loot," Sean added. "Everyone think that description covers what's going on up there?" He jerked his head toward the hacienda.

"Yes, sir," came the quick answer from multiple throats.

"Anyone think there's a civilian alive up there?"

The response was slower this time but just as steady. "No, sir. Not by now."

"No way can we reach that hacienda before those assholes leave it. But their weakness is those vehicles. They'll have to drive them through that collection of rubble called San Desiderio before off loading them. If we can reach there before they do, then we use Plan A to crush them."

"Plan A, Lindstrom?" Adam Hepburn questioned, dead-pan. Great straight man. Sean would owe him a beer when they got back.

"The one we created first and practiced so damn much, before we received the latest so-called *intelligence*." Sean's voice dripped sarcasm. He glanced around at the intent faces. "Our mission is to ambush and kill those pond scum. It'll be a hell of a forced march, getting down these hills and across that river before dawn, but we're Rangers. We can do it."

The men grinned mirthlessly, their white teeth startling against their camouflaged faces. They didn't even groan. Forced march through a swamp at night and they just nodded. "Hooah, Sarge," one assented from the back.

"Hooah," Sean agreed. Minutes later, they were on their way, racing to kill a passel of murderers before they could disappear back into the swamp.

"Sadist," Adam hissed softly as they started down the hill. "Wasn't Ranger School enough for you?"

"Masochist," Sean retorted and grinned at their oldest joke. Ever since Ranger school, whoever provided encouragement was labeled "sadist," while the other was called "masochist" for enduring the worst the Army could dish out. Sometimes Sean was the masochist and Adam was the sadist. It didn't matter who carried which name, as long as the job got done. He quickened his pace.

The rebels rumbled down the mountainside into San Desiderio an hour after dawn, their stolen cars and truck engines wheezing from exertion. Most of the pond scum were sleeping, their drunken snores barely audible above the engines.

Sean watched, waited, every nerve alert and yet relaxed. He was still sopping wet from the armpits down but that didn't matter. Leeches had found him in the swamp, which was also unimportant. The only thing that interested him now was seeing all the rebels corralled so they could die.

The last truck clattered in, just as the lead truck approached the outskirts on the other side. Sean calmly sent up a flare.

Immediately, a small explosion ripped the air, then a large one as the lead truck blew up. The pattern repeated an instant later when the last truck exploded. The rebels woke up with a start and immediately start firing randomly. But his Rangers, Sean was proud to note, used proper fire discipline. Steady, accurate, careful shots began to drop the raping, murdering assholes. Sean fought, too, all the while watching and giving the few orders needed.

A man jumped out of an old Ford sedan and began to run, silhouetted against a burning truck. His limp and the cigar clenched between his teeth identified him immediately as El Jefe, once a university student but now the rebel leader. Sean squeezed the trigger as coolly as if he was on a firing range. El Jefe crumpled into the mud, motionless. Sean allowed himself the luxury of a small, congratulatory smile.

The firing died down quickly after that, with all of the rebels dead. Mission accomplished and time to move out. They should be able to be picked up the next night and back home a few days later. His son, Mike, would be thrilled. They'd be able to attend that Alan Jackson concert and do some fishing together. Maybe pick up that golden retriever Mike wanted so much.

Tiffany, his wife, would be furious, though; she'd planned to use his bedroom to sort her spring clothing while he was gone. And she was probably trying right now to break into his lockers. Tough. She'd just have to stop snooping. He didn't poke his nose into the things that kept her happy, as long as the family budget stayed balanced. She'd promised to do the same for him, when she threw him out of her bed while complaining of her physical inability—and he'd damn well held her to that promise. It was the least she could do for him.

One day, Mike would be grown up and he could think about a divorce, when his son didn't need a proper home life. But until then, he gritted his teeth a lot and tried to think of Tiffany only as his son's mother, not the bitch from hell who'd used the creases on his uniforms as "cut here" marks. And worse.

It would be too dangerous to dream, especially of a woman who watched him as if he were the center of her universe, not a jerk who had ruined her life with a pregnancy. Because if he ever found a woman like that—someone who made time slow until only the two of them existed—he'd do anything and everything to keep her. Hell, he'd even explore his darkest fantasies for a woman like that. But not, of course, while he was married to his son's mother.

Still, he hummed a favorite stadium rock tune as he led his squad back into the jungle, for the start of the long trip home. A Queen tune about somebody to love.

One

Beth stood on the street corner, waiting for the light to change. Her Savile Row black suit shed Seattle's rain as easily as the London weather of its makers. It also set her apart from the other pedestrians in their serviceable jackets and jeans.

Beth tossed off any envy for their comfort. She'd worn suits for too many years in gatherings where status was measured by one's tailor. This one was more formal than most, especially with the black silk shirt, black hose, and black pumps. It was also perfectly appropriate for hosting a luncheon meeting with Japanese bankers where she had to dress like the Treasury bureaucrat she was.

But her beloved black and gold scarf nestled against her throat, reminding her of other occasions when a woman could wear a formal black suit and be considered all the more female for it. Events that sometimes began in public but always ended in private, with both herself and her lover well-satisfied. Her mouth quirked at the thought, remembering how boneless a sated man could look after he was finally permitted to climax at the end of a long evening's play.

The light changed and she crossed, following the other walkers' lead in dodging the puddles. This neighborhood was old and eclectic, only recently returned to prosperity. Its streets were solid but would probably betray their age later that evening by collecting rivers and lakes, instead of trickles and puddles, from the promised heavy rain.

She'd met Dennis on a rainy night . . .

Beth checked the street number of the closest store and strode briskly on. She'd been told the place was about two blocks down the street from the dungeon, so it should be close. A bookstore just down the street from a professional BDSM dungeon definitely sounded like an escape from work and memories. The dungeon had a good reputation in Seattle's BDSM scene. Any other time, she'd have happily prowled it, searching for partners, but today she'd rather play it safe and visit a bookstore.

Time was precious now, especially for a brief reprieve from the conference. She had spent weeks preparing for its intense discussions on East Asia's banking systems, fiscal stability, and more. All necessary preparations for refinancing hundreds of millions of dollars of East Asian debt. Though in the first horrible weeks after September 11th, she'd found it hard to concentrate on business during the endless round of funerals. Particularly Dennis's.

A shop ahead drew her, with its spill of bright light across the sidewalk under a festive striped canopy. If nothing else, she could check street numbers in comfort, before making one last dash to the bookstore she sought.

A few steps more and she read the store's name: The Next Page. A fat, orange tomcat slumbered under its emblem of a gilded owl.

Travel books offered a sunny escape in the front windows. The bright colors of children's books offered another kind of vacation for tired parents. White walls and blond wood bookcases reflected the light and bright colors, welcoming the casual visitor. The store was quiet now and seemed empty of customers as it awaited the evening rush.

Beth smiled at the sight and walked in. She'd found her diversion.

The doorbell rang softly, announcing her arrival.

Beth quickly fastened her black umbrella, being careful not to shake any water off onto the books. Her eyes studied the store looking for clues to the books she wanted.

The clerk spoke from behind the counter in front and she glanced over at him. Gary, according to his name badge, was thirty-something, slender and very fit with a full head of dark hair above a goatee. His shirt and tie were more formal than she'd have expected, given the neighborhood. But the store advertised old-fashioned service with its modern selection, so perhaps he dressed for the more traditional aspects.

"Good evening, ma'am. Can I help you find anything?" he offered.

"I'm looking for some erotica. Can you help me?" Beth answered bluntly, not willing to waste time.

"Oh, yes, that's right at the back. Any particular kind?" he asked as he headed down the center aisle to show her the way.

"Heterosexual erotica, please," she answered, satisfied with his easy response to what could have been an embarrassing request.

Gary went straight to the back wall and turned right at the row of bookcases leaning against it. "We've got that right here on this shelf. Anything else?"

Beth looked where he indicated. Interesting titles offered themselves from less than half of the shelf. The rest of the bookcase seemed full of titles from other genres, mostly critical studies of literary classics. She sighed.

"Nonfiction sexuality?" she questioned.

"Just to your left, across the aisle."

Beth glanced over and saw some more possibilities.

"Gay erotica, too, please, if you've got it. And perhaps a little lesbian?" she added, hoping for a wider selection.

"Oh, that will be in the bookcases right in front of this one. You'll see the gay erotica first and then the lesbian," he replied casually.

"Thanks," Beth responded as she started looking more closely at the heterosexual titles. They were primarily well-known series from major publishers. She snarled to herself: if she saw one more volume of letters to the editor of a famous magazine, she'd probably scream. She'd come to this eccentric neighborhood to escape the familiar, not to revisit clichés.

She paused, hearing a voice rumble through the wall. The man must be on just the other side, given how easily she heard him.

"No, I'm not interested in their offer, Tim. Business may be slow, but I'm not going to accept an offer of less than half its appraised value. They'll have to do a lot better than that, if they want to beat out the other bidders."

Beth smiled at the controlled growl under the words, sounding as ferocious as a trading floor supervisor. He showed more discipline and force than many of the currency traders she'd worked with in Manhattan. Her fingers stroked a book of couples' erotic fantasies, while she enjoyed the deep music of his voice.

"I'll call Phillips tomorrow and tell him. That everything? . . . Have a good time at the game." A click signaled the call's end.

Beth sighed, unconsciously regretting the lost voice. Her hand lingered on the book for a second longer, before moving along the shelf. She picked up the latest volume of a favorite series and considered its list of contributors.

A door to the back opened, admitting a man. Beth blinked, startled, as she saw a big, blond Viking walk in. He stood well over six feet, more than tall enough to make her five feet, nine inches seem petite. He was built of all bone and muscle, moving with the same unself-conscious ease as a leopard. A jagged white scar etched his right forearm from wrist to elbow, half-hidden under a gloss of bright hair.

The blue flannel shirt above his jeans and work boots emphasized his blue eyes and his strong arms under the rolled up sleeves. He wore a serviceable watch on his right wrist and a narrow black metal bracelet on his left, bearing a single line of text. Perhaps he was selling his truck, given clothes like that.

His hair offered the only counterpoint to the lumberjack image: it was cut high and tight to his skull, leaving a thick golden pelt at the top of his head with white skin on the sides and back. That combination, of dense silky hair with sculptured bone and tendons, promised delicious sensations to the lucky lady who found his head between her legs.

He looked down at her, as he closed the door quietly. From this close, his eyes were the same deep, vivid blue as the Hope diamond. Their eyes met and locked.

He stared at her, his eyes darkening with surprise and interest.

Her gut twisted with lust and her breath caught with a barely audible gasp. Her hand instinctively started to rise, eager for contact.

"Was everything the way you wanted it, Sean?" asked the clerk, coming to meet the newcomer.

Sean froze before he shrugged as he turned to face Gary. "Yes, the apartment's really clean. You and your lady did a great job on that after you moved out. How's business, anyway?"

"Doing good. Slightly better than last year, actually."

The two men grinned at each other, in perfect harmony over a victory, and moved back toward the front of the store.

Dear heavens, Sean looked just as irresistible from behind, broad shoulders rising above a hard, narrow, masculine ass. Old memories stirred, of Scotsmen dancing in their kilts when one of their own came home safe from war in the South Atlantic. Strong bodies sweating and men's eyes gleaming with joy as they held their ladies. Herself at eleven years old, watching quietly from the shadows; neither fish nor fowl with her mixed Scottish and Japanese heritage, but still irresistibly drawn to the big, strong men.

Beth moved to the other side of the aisle. Nonfiction offered a wider selection than heterosexual erotica, plus a better look at Sean.

The two men paused to chat in front of the movies section, with posters gleaming behind them. A young boy with black spectacles and a thunderbolt scar flew out of the sky over Gary's head, an image of scholarly intensity echoed in the living man.

Sean's hand rested on a stark red and black book, its cover shouting *Black Hawk Down*. A warrior's book obviously, next to a man who looked fit to carry a sword in battle.

Beth frowned, shrugging off the temptation to follow him, and returned to browsing. Sean was very interesting, but real life offered more pitfalls than fiction. She'd come into this store to find a fantasy to go to bed with. Surely books were the better choice, their paper-and-ink men far safer than flesh and blood. She could begin the real hunt after returning home, where friends could help her find a good mate.

The front door slammed open, its bell falling into an urgent jangle. Beth glanced up and caught sight of the newcomer in the mirror over the back door.

The girl was too thin, her eyes dark pools in her stretched white face, while her sweatshirt and jeans left trails of water on the carpet. She was shaking as she wrapped her arms around herself, staring around the room. Was the rain why she looked so distressed or was there something else?

Gary and Sean had stopped talking when the door opened. Their eyes met in perfect understanding before Gary went to the girl. Sean considered the store's windows, sweeping every foot of sidewalk beyond with his glance. Then he moved to the other side of the book display, where he was closer to Gary and enjoyed clear passage down the center aisle to the front door.

Was he covering Gary's back?

Beth turned to see more directly, rather than through the mirror and the window's reflections.

"Can I help you, ma'am?" Gary's voice was softer, even more polite than his greeting to Beth. The girl visibly gulped hard before she looked at him.

Beth cursed under her breath as she saw the blood trickling down the newcomer's face. Probably not a bad injury, given the small amount, but it still needed to be attended to. She took a step forward, instinctively planning to help.

A roar of wind and traffic noises announced someone else. A young man burst in, looking like a rabid bulldog with his protruding eyes and clenched jaw. He pushed back his sweatshirt's soaked hood and stabbed the trembling girl with one quick glare.

"Dammit, Shelby, why the hell did you come in here?" A few quick steps brought him to his target. He didn't hesitate when he brushed against a display, sending books tumbling to the floor.

Shelby stammered something that might have been words and shrank toward Gary, who moved up next to her.

The young man cursed and reached for her. "Come on, Shelby! You know better than to run away. Just cut the crap and come with me."

"Perhaps you should ask the young lady what she wants to do." Sean's voice was very calm as he came forward.

The kid jerked around to face the bigger man, breaking his concentration on Shelby. "None of your business. Shelby's my bitch and she knows she can't leave. Just get outta my face and we'll be out of here."

"The young lady," Sean said slowly, with the slightest emphasis on the noun, "may have another idea."

"Doesn't matter if she does. She's coming with me." The kid started to grab Shelby. Sean shifted, blocking the attempt.

"Fuck you!" The kid's hand moved and silver blossomed in his fist. He lunged toward Sean with the knife.

Sean's hands came up as he pivoted smoothly.

The kid yelped, just before metal clattered against a bookcase and dropped to the floor. Sean held him easily, one arm tight against his back. The kid twisted wildly and yelped again before standing still. "Let me go!"

"Not yet. The young lady's wishes have yet to be considered. What do you want me to do with him, Miss Shelby?" Sean's voice was as unhurried as if he discussed dinner plans, instead of an attacker's disposal. Beth's eyes widened at the quiet mastery in his deep voice.

The girl's eyes were enormous as she stared at her rescuer. "I don't want any trouble," she began and stopped. She tried again. "Can you just tell Tony to leave, or something? So I don't have to see him again?"

"Are you sure, ma'am? He might come after you if the police don't lock him up."

"I've got someplace safe to go. And, and, I don't want to talk to the cops. They'd just cause more trouble for me. So would you please get him out of here?" She seemed on the verge of tears.

"Yes, ma'am, if you're quite certain that's what you want."

Shelby nodded jerkily.

Sean frog-marched the kid toward the front. Shelby watched them leave, shaking violently. Just before they reached the door, the jerk halted and tried to turn around. "My knife! Give me back my knife!"

"No. Just be glad you're leaving here with your skin intact."

The kid struggled furiously but his captor quickly brought him under control. Sean spoke again, his steady voice given more emphasis by the boy's anger. "Remember one thing, kid. The deal's off, if you hurt the young lady. You do that and I'm coming after you. Got that?"

Beth shivered at its cold promise. She was hardly surprised to see the kid's face shift from a youthful sneer to terror as he absorbed Sean's threat. He swallowed hard before answering.

"Yeah, I understand," he mumbled, before adding a surprising, "sir."

"Good. Now go."

"Yes, sir."

The kid opened the front door quickly and was running before he reached the next store. Sean watched him go, then turned back into the bookstore, his face relaxed and thoughtful. The orange tomcat in the window rolled and stretched, lifting one paw into the air in an impolite salute.

"How would you like a cup of coffee and some dry clothes?" Gary offered the girl. Shelby eyed him suspiciously.

"It's okay, Shelby. His fiancée owns the clothing store across the street. You can change there and make a phone call, while you drink some coffee."

Shelby visibly relaxed at Sean's explanation. Beth smiled; she understood agreeing to any suggestions couched in a deep purr, especially when uttered by the man who'd just saved you.

"Okay," Shelby decided shakily. "I've got money though, enough to pay for whatever I need."

"Of course you do," Gary agreed soothingly. "Let's go see what Shannon can find. Would you handle the store until I get back, Sean? I'll send one of Shannon's clerks over if I'll be gone long."

"No problem. I'll just do some browsing while I wait."

Gary snorted and fetched an umbrella from behind the counter. He guided Shelby across the street, picking his way through the puddles and sheltering her as solicitously as if she were a queen.

Beth watched Shelby's growing comfort with a smile. A real-life drama had ended happily, unlike many. A strong man had freed a girl, hopefully forever, from another's greedy clutches. Beth wished briefly she'd had that sort of protection from her avaricious fiancé. But she'd ended the engagement herself and paid the price.

She sighed and returned to the books' safety.

She exhausted the nonfiction books in a few minutes and headed for the gay and lesbian fiction. She followed the bookcases' labels, moving deeper into the narrow path between them like an archaeologist following a tunnel into a buried city. Ethnic fiction, Jewish fiction, African-American fiction, all glided past without receiving a second glance. The bookcases jogged to the right and she froze.

The big Viking stood there, calmly reading a book. Beth took a deep breath and considered what to do next. Did he want to strike up an acquaintance? Did she? She quietly took her place in front of the bookcase next to him and waited, hoping he'd act on the interest he'd shown earlier.

Beth quickly realized the gay erotica section was entirely at her disposal, since Sean was standing in front of the lesbian erotica section. The book cover which he held just below the level of her eyes was an elegant but explicit work of art celebrating the joys of women pleasuring each other.

Beth smiled to herself: who was she to complain when she enjoyed artwork emphasizing the male body? And that was a very nice male body only a step away from her, too. Too good to be easily ignored, especially since he wasn't wearing a wedding ring. The lack of a ring was hardly an infallible signal of availability, any more than its presence always meant monogamy. On the other hand, its absence did offer an opening.

"Congratulations on rescuing that girl," she offered quietly, looking up at Sean over a year's-best anthology which featured a cover more remarkable for blandness than titillation.

He blinked and stared at her, clearly startled. "Uh, yeah, Gary did a great job, getting Shelby over to Shannon's place. I'm sure she's already warm and dry by now."

Only years of high-stakes currency trading, where a twinge of emotion could cost millions, kept Beth from dropping her jaw. Didn't Sean realize that she was complimenting him? Or was he just uninterested in talking to her?

"Yes, Gary was very efficient, wasn't he?" she responded and tried to think of something to say that could only be seen as specific to Sean.

Sean smiled and nodded at her commonplace response, coughed briefly, and went back to his book.

Beth frowned then followed his example. Reading seemed a more promising option than conversation. A minute's study convinced her that the anthology was as boring as its cover. She shoved it back into place, easing her frustration.

Then she began to seriously browse the books, enjoying the latest from favorite publishers and authors and discovering new works. She picked out one volume, studied the cover—very nice leather harness on that stud, thank you—before reading the back blurb. The man on the cover looked uncomfortable, as if he'd challenged the photographer to make a good picture.

Of course, Sean would probably look better in that harness than the cover model did, given his advantage in height and broad shoulders. Or maybe scarf bondage would suit him better, offering such a marvelous contrast with his intense masculinity.

A moment later, she was skimming the words inside, looking for images to savor and enjoying the pages' texture as they slid under her fingers. She put the book back, regretting its total lack of plot, and her elbow brushed Sean.

"Oops! Sorry about that." She drew away slightly and he smiled down at her.

"No problem," he said easily.

He didn't stammer when she touched him first. That opened some interesting possibilities.

Beth and Sean slowly worked their way through the shelves, enjoying a companionable silence as they studied covers and turned pages. The scarf caressed Beth's throat like a living being. Her varying positions as they took books from different shelves allowed her to see him from different angles, especially if she took care to never look directly. Her enjoyment of the more blatant artwork was increased by her sidelong glances at him. Images from the books were overlaid by visions of Sean, hot and naked and thrashing. The only sounds were the soft rustle of turning pages and their breathing, with an occasional whisper of clothing.

"Could you please hand me *The Oy of Sex*?" Beth asked, her voice husky in the quiet. "It's on the top shelf, to your right . . ."

Sean handed it to her, just as she reached up to take it from him. Their hands brushed on the book's elegant binding and lingered. Beth slid her hand over his, enjoying his warm strength, and took hold of the book next to his fingers. Her nipples rubbed uncomfortably against the lace restraining them.

Sean stared down at her and smiled slowly. He hummed quietly when he went back to his books. She wondered exactly what he was thinking. He had a splendid bulge behind the zipper of his jeans.

"Excuse me," he murmured.

Beth glanced up, startled out of her fantasies, just as he reached around her to push a teetering book back onto its shelf. Her movement brought her next to him, her shoulder lodged against his chest. She felt his arm encircle her shoulders and she waited, eager for his next move. She tossed her head back to clear a lock from her face and flinched when the movement ended with a jerk.

"Just stand still, ma'am. You've got your hair caught between the bookcases." Sean soothed her. He put his book down on a shelf and gently freed her hair, while his other arm never left her shoulders.

Beth watched him, poised and willing, her mouth half-open as she hoped he would come closer. To her delight, he bent his head to hers very slowly. Her eyes closed in anticipation as she felt his breath on her cheek.

"Sean?" Gary's voice broke the silence just as Sean's lips touched hers.

Sean froze and straightened up. Beth silently rehearsed some unflattering Japanese descriptions of Gary's ancestry.

"Back here, Gary," Sean answered. "It's been quiet since you left." He stepped away from Beth so Gary could see him between the bookcases. She was fiercely glad of his voice's hoarseness.

"Okay," Gary responded. "Thanks."

Sean returned to the erotica section but didn't come close to her again.

Piqued, she considered her options. A quick check of her watch told her that something needed to happen soon, before she had to return to the conference. She turned and headed out of the aisle, back toward the front of the bookstore.

A small smile played her mouth when she heard Sean's sigh at her departure.

"Did you find everything you wanted?" asked Gary as Beth came up to the counter.

"Almost," she said, remembering that big book on the edge of the gay erotica section. "Actually, I was looking for *The Male Nude* by David Leddick. Do you have it?"

"Oh yes, it's at the bottom of the bookcase at the end of the gay erotica. Right next to the lesbian erotica."

Beth thanked him and retraced her steps. Was Sean listening?

Just as she got there, a masculine arm came up from the floor toward her, with a book resting in the big palm.

"Is this what you're looking for, ma'am?" Sean offered.

"Yes, thank you, that's exactly what I was looking for." Her hand glided over his as she took the book. "I could have bought it over the Internet, but I really wanted to touch it first, you know?" she remarked, trying to sound innocent. "Some of these are just so cheap, they're not nice at all to handle. I really prefer something that feels good in your hand, especially when you're going to spend some time with it."

She came to a stop, hoping that he'd hear the hidden meaning. Her focus lifted slowly from his chest to his face. His eyes were heavy-lidded as he looked down at her, and he smiled slowly.

"Is there anything else you'd like to see, ma'am?" He answered her double entendre with one of his own.

"I'd like a look at you," she said honestly, too caught up in the moment's electricity to remember her wariness of relationships.

Sean stared at her and didn't move, clearly uncertain as to what he should do next.

Beth shook her head at him and chuckled softly. Then she looked him over deliberately, lingering on his mouth before surveying the rest of his lean body. He was breathing hard and shaking slightly by the time she finished. But he hadn't tried to leave.

She gripped his elbow and took him to the back, where they found themselves in a narrow hallway. He unlocked an inconspicuous door and held it open for her to go ahead of him.

She found herself in a small room that seemed to be as much storeroom as office. Sean put his books down on the desk, then took up position under the high windows and watched her, his arms folded across his chest. Rain fell from the roofline outside, casting a curtain of sound around the room. She put her books down next to his and turned to face him.

Sean's response was fast and strong. He took command and kissed her like a starving man. His hand tightened on the nape of her neck, holding her head against any effort to move away. Beth responded willingly, startled by his intensity and his skill.

His tongue probed her mouth, twining around her tongue before exploring the various shapes and textures available to him. His cock blazed against her like an iron bar fresh from the furnace, restrained only by his jeans and her suit.

Beth felt his self-control slipping away and tried to think.

Sean's hands slid down her back, pulling her closer to him. His knee pushed but couldn't separate her legs, given her skirt's tightness. He pushed again and Beth gasped, self-preservation starting to reemerge. Thought was difficult, as her year of celibacy demanded relief from this man. Now.

He yanked at her skirt, growling into her mouth. Wool ripped like a gunshot.

Beth jumped and Sean stopped kissing her immediately.

"Back off, mister!" Beth snarled. His hands fell away from her and he stepped back. One step, two steps, before the wall brought him up short. He braced himself against it, like a soldier summoned for discipline, eyes searching her face.

She looked down to see a three-inch tear rising up her skirt's side seam, showing her leg as an evening gown would.

Anger bubbled up in her, followed by silent giggles. He'd ruined her suit but she'd made herself available. She hadn't been this clumsy in an embrace since high school. Two adults, grappling in a storeroom like teenagers. She clamped down hard on the giggles and began to think. A private room, a gorgeous guy who was waiting for her next move. The situation had possibilities.

"I'm sorry, ma'am," he began, looking appalled. "I apologize for ruining your skirt. I'll replace . . ."

"You clumsy jerk. What the hell made you think you could maul me? Is that what I invited you back here for?" Beth growled, coming so close to him that she could see individual eyelashes.

"No, ma'am." Sean shook his head, his face frozen but his eyes narrow, focused. He was definitely standing at attention. Wonderful; he wasn't just an alpha jerk out to maul any woman who happened past. Probably submissive, given how fast he'd backed down when she told him to stop. What fun.

She frowned at him, contemplating what to do next. It was definitely time for her to take control.

He watched her warily. Something in her softened at the caution in his eyes. How long had it been since he'd held a lover, for him to kiss her that hard? Who had rejected him, for him to be that ignorant of a woman's interest?

"Apology accepted, Sean. Now then, this encounter is about what *I* want, not you. We'll deal with your pleasure after you satisfy me. Any problems with that?"

"No, ma'am." He frowned, clearly trying to think what to do next. Beth smiled to herself and pondered how best to surprise him. It was time to play and, hopefully, fan that spark into a flame. She tamped down the voice that said it was too easy to find magic with this stranger.

"Now, you're going to keep your hands to yourself while I study you. Understand?"

"Yes, of course." He was confused. And enticing.

"Do you have any idea how beautiful you are?" she asked.

"What? I'm not . . ."

She stopped his denial with a raised finger. "When I want to hear your voice, I'll tell you. Got that?"

He managed to nod.

"I'm Beth."

He nodded a greeting.

Beth stepped back a pace and brazenly looked him over, feeling the spark between them growing. She had to be gentle with him. Anyone so ignorant of his own attractions couldn't possibly have played power exchange games before.

"I like your taste in clothing. The blue flannel shirt matches your eyes. Step away from the wall, so I can see all of you," she growled. He promptly obeyed with a martial snap, curiosity in his eyes. Beth filed the implications away for later use.

She strolled around him, tracing his shoulders with her fingers. His head swiveled to follow her, but he remained otherwise motionless. When she stepped in front of him again, she put both hands on his chest and gazed into his eyes.

"So soft, too. It rests against you like a lover. A girl could get jealous," she teased and he choked. Good; she'd managed to shock him so much he couldn't find a conventional response.

"You are marvelously sensitive, Sean!" Beth chuckled, watching the color surge in his face. She caressed his cheek and he blushed more. His arousal pushed his jeans against her wool skirt. She bit down on her lust, while still following the electricity between them. She couldn't build a fire, if she lost control now.

"Show me more, Sean. More of you, the flesh and blood man. Not a frozen image, caught in black and white between a book's covers. Show me what that lucky shirt is touching," she purred.

"Beth, please," Sean said slowly, as if trying to feel his way through a minefield.

"Did I say you could speak?" Beth snapped and smiled approval when he shook his head. *Give me a little trust, Sean, and we can work wonders together.* "Now show yourself to me, Sean. You know I can't harm you."

Sean's fingers fumbled, but he managed to unbutton his shirt. He took it off slowly, more because of nerves than art. Beth watched him, pleased at her ability to stay disciplined but scared by the threat he offered. He was so incredibly tempting.

Finally, he managed to drop the blue flannel onto the desk behind him and turned to face her again. He wore no undershirt and his bare chest and back gleamed under the room's single lamp. He was long and lean, beautifully muscled but elegant. He had an animal's economic grace of powerful function, rather than a man-made mass of muscle hiding the body's true potential. He was magnificently furred, in shades of gold. A thick mat of golden hair covered his chest, then darkened as it formed a narrow trail downward. He breathed raggedly but watched her steadily, without any attempt to hide himself. His eyes were vivid blue, as bright as a fire's core.

Beth covered his nipples gently with her palms, enjoying their hard spikes. His hands lifted; she glared at him and they fell back without touching her. His nostrils flared as he drew a shuddering breath.

Beth rested her forehead lightly against him, testing to see if he'd push her again. Sean swallowed hard and trembled, but didn't budge. He smelled of sweat and hunger. He wouldn't move until she gave him permission.

Heat rolled through her body, surging up from where it had simmered deep inside. Her silk panties were suddenly very damp, as her core melted under his blue eyes. She wanted far more from him than the prickle of his hair between her fingers. But caution still sounded in her ears, matched by the need to see his pleasure. Somehow, ensuring that this starving man found joy was more important than any physical satisfaction for herself.

"Unzip your pants," she demanded, her voice harsh with its burden of lust.

He promptly complied, then slowly fanned his fingers to spread his jeans. His engorged cock gleamed hot and red, the color of life, against the white skin of his groin. It was uncut and thick against the dense fur, entirely natural. She doubted her hand could wrap completely around it at the base, just above his foreskin's beautiful ruffled cowl.

She had seen a great many cocks, both aroused and quiescent. She'd played with some and been intimate with a handful. But she'd seen very few like his that made her start thinking of stallions. Big studs, not polite riding horses. A Clydesdale perhaps, or a Percheron.

Her tongue crept out to briefly caress her lips.

Beth swallowed hard and considered his entire body, staring at the magnificent male caught in full living color before her. His appearance was much more exciting than the black-and-white photos of pretty boys in the book on the desk, much more interesting than any other man she'd ever seen. Her body trembled and she jerked it back under her leash. It was the first time she'd felt truly alive since the agonies of September 11th.

Sean's eyes darkened as he watched. His mouth curved in a hard smile as he waited for her next order, barely breathing.

"Touch yourself."

Sean curled a hand around his cock and began to stroke it slowly, watching the way her eyes followed his every move. His thumb traveled over the head in a curling touch before his fingers slowly pulled on his shaft, lengthening it even more.

Beth sighed as the single frozen image of a strong man became a flow of pictures, all colorful, all arousing. She was very hot, her neck dripping with sweat under her scarf.

"Drop your pants and show me your balls."

Sean pushed his jeans down over his hips to his knees and openly displayed all of himself to her. Dear heavens, his balls more than matched his magnificent cock. She put her fist to her mouth to stifle a whimper as she watched him.

His fingers traveled lightly over his balls, outlining them. He stroked them a little more, cupping them in his palm. His eyes caught hers. He wordlessly questioned her approval. Beth's eyes blazed back at him. Couldn't he tell how much she liked watching him?

"Damn you, go on," she hissed.

His smile blazed in startled triumph, that of a man who had set a woman trembling by simply allowing her to see him. He growled, low and deep in his throat like a tiger that scented his mate. Then he began to stroke his cock again, deepening and quickening the contact. His mouth tightened a bit when his rough hand snagged on the delicate skin.

Beth moved abruptly and pulled the scarf from her neck. "Use this."

She tossed the silk at him and he caught it. He ran the scarf through his hand, stretching it out to its full length. It was soft and yet very strong against him, lying over his palm in invitation. It caught slightly on his calluses and yet pressed delicately against the edge of his hand. His breathing deepened.

Sean slid it behind his sac, obviously savoring the feeling as it caressed the sensitive skin. The scarf outlined his arousal and lifted it closer to Beth. He pulled it delicately back and forth, then between his balls to separate them. A few more strokes, and then he swept the scarf around his balls, covering them in a silken fretwork.

Beth purred at the contrast between the scarf's gold and black, his deep red cock, and his groin's white skin.

He slid the scarf up his cock and began to stroke, curving the silk around, moving it back and forth, up and down. Her body throbbed in unison with its dance.

His hand moved faster and faster, until gold seemed to be pouring over his groin. His face contorted in ecstasy at the sensation, still watching her fascination with his movements. A deep bellow tore from his throat as an orgasm seized him and he poured his seed into the gold.

Climax blazed through Beth at the sight, as fierce and unexpected as a shooting star. She bit down hard on her hand to stay silent but staggered trying to stay upright.

Sean blinked slowly, then looked at her.

Beth was shaking after her own release. A thin trickle of blood ran down her hand from where she'd bitten her knuckle. She tried to catch her breath. She'd heard of women climaxing without direct physical stimulation but never thought to experience it for herself.

An electronic ring cut through the silence and Beth jumped. She looked around and grabbed her purse off the desk, fumbling to stop the cell phone.

"Damn, not another one of Holly's so-called emergencies," she cursed, rapidly pressing buttons that seemed all too small at the moment. "Yes," she snapped, bringing the phone up to her ear. The answering voice bewildered her. "Mr. Griffith?"

Beth took a deep breath and tried to think. Why was her office's director, her boss's boss, calling?

"Yes, of course I remember that meeting in September," she assured him. She glanced over to see Sean slowly sliding his jeans back up his hips. She swallowed and yanked her attention back to the voice in her ear.

"Yes, I'd be honored to represent Treasury . . . Tomorrow morning at eight is fine. No, it won't conflict with the conference . . ."

Sean finished fastening his jeans and looked at the wet scarf in his hand. Hot color blazed across his cheekbones. Beth followed his eyes to the scarf and lust pooled again between her legs. Somehow she kept talking, hoping she made sense.

"Can you get me directions to the FBI offices? Thanks . . . Certainly I'll let you know what happens. Good night."

Beth snapped the phone shut. Finally she had an opportunity to get involved in the hunt for terrorists. But all she really wanted to do was put her hands on Sean again.

"I'll have this dry-cleaned for you. When can I give it back to you?" Sean asked.

"There's a reception tonight to kick off the conference. So I can't return until ten or so." Hunger echoed in her words as she ignored the days it would take to see her scarf properly cleaned. What could be more fun than a beautiful, submissive male to play with for an evening? He didn't behave like a dominant, certainly nothing like the way Dennis had when he swept her off her feet—and spanked her—their first evening so long ago. They'd only been lovers for a little while, but she'd always measured male dominants against Dennis's ferocity and self-confidence.

Sean brightened at the promise of another encounter. "Just come back here as soon as you're done. I'll be waiting."

"Are you sure the bookstore will be open? The neighborhood is a little rough."

"I'm the landlord, so it'll be open." Sean smiled at her.

"Okay." Landlord? He looked like a janitor. "If you can't make it, call me at this number." She handed him a business card, which he accepted without taking his eyes from hers. He fumbled in his back pocket and managed to produce a business card, which she took wordlessly.

Beth finished gathering up her books and stepped toward the door before coming to a stop in front of him. She reached up and gently ran her finger across his mouth. He stroked her finger with the tip of his tongue.

"Save the scarf for tonight, huh?" she suggested softly.

He smiled down at her. "Anything you say, ma'am. Anything at all."

Two

Sean sagged back onto the desk an instant after the door closed behind Beth. The bravado that had kept him standing after that incredible rush disappeared with the sound of her departing feet.

Holy shit. Seven years after his wife's death—and no dates—he'd just had the hottest sex of his life. Had it been a dream?

He looked at the card in his hand. Two lines of script showed: Elizabeth Nakamura and a Washington, D.C., phone number. A single rose lay at the bottom, etched in gold and complete with thorns.

He smiled wryly. Fair warning, but he'd risk thorns any day for a rose like her. What games did she want to play when she handed out a card like that? His cock stirred eagerly at the thought.

He'd jacked off as assiduously as any other Ranger during his time in the Army. He'd collected more than his share of memorable jacks along the way from those solitary exercises: the Panama Jack, the Gulf Jack, the Somalia Jack, the C-17 Jack, and more. But none of those compared to jacking off while she observed, then realizing that she'd climaxed from watching him.

Of course, it had been a long time since he'd been with a woman in any fashion. Twelve years since he and Tiffany agreed they shouldn't sleep together, given the discomfort from her second stroke. To tell the truth, staying out of Tiffany's bed hadn't changed much in his life except for killing any hope that she'd come to enjoy sex.

But Beth had blown all the old memories out of his mind. Thankfully, she hadn't been put off by his clumsy behavior. He shook his head, remembering how he'd fumbled the ball in the bookstore. Then he'd heard her voice again, seducing him into the backroom. Not that he needed much encouragement.

He'd backed off immediately, of course, when she said stop. Every real man respected a lady's wishes, no matter when she said no. And after that, hell, it had been so easy to follow her lead, measuring the electricity rising between them by the heat in his cock and the fire in her eyes. And she'd kissed like an angel, too. The lessons he'd learned in high school had sure come in handy.

"Thanks, Adam," he whispered to his friend's ghost. Adam had left his family's real estate business, including this building, to Sean, shrugging off assurances that he'd live for years to come. "I've tried to keep my word to you; guess you just threw in a new twist."

Live for both of us, Adam had demanded on that last evening. *If anything happens to me, you live for both of us.* He'd died the next afternoon, gunned down by a Somalian mob.

"What's his status?" The voice crackled again in Sean's memories. There was a long pause, filled with other desperate voices over the radio, before the answer came.

"KIA." Killed in Action. Silence. All the other Rangers listening in had carefully not looked at Sean, giving him time to regain his composure. Then he'd chivvied them into motion; there was a lot of work to be done to get their remaining brethren home safely. He'd been fiercely glad to go out with the rescue convoy.

Sean looked at the scarf, crumpled up in his hand, before lifting it to his nose. His musk was there but so was a spicy sweetness, evoking womanhood. More woman than he'd ever hoped to encounter. And she'd cared about him and his comfort, enough to give him the clothes off her back. That act alone made Beth totally different from Mrs. Wolcott and her demands on his high-school ignorance.

He closed his eyes and breathed deeply, dragging her scent in and memorizing it.

Beth. Female. Treasury, working with the FBI. Dangerous lady. A skillful, experienced, successful leader, as his cock would gladly attest. Hopefully, he'd see what lay under that proper black suit tonight.

He laughed when his phone rang. At least this interruption had waited until Beth left. A quick flip of his wrist and Caller ID told him who sought him.

"Yeah, Mike," he answered.

"Hi, Dad. Mrs. Hemmings just called to say that she'll be here in twenty minutes to see the furniture."

"I'll be home by then. If she gets there first, just show her the guest room."

"No problem, Dad."

"Mike." He hesitated.

"Yeah, Dad?"

"You got any problem selling your mother's old bedroom furniture?"

"Nah, it just reminds me of how she was so trapped in it at the end. I'd rather remember her in other ways, like how she taught me to cook."

"Okay, Mike, if you're sure." Sean let his voice trail off, inviting his son to say more if he needed to.

"Oh, I'm positive. It's time for us both to clean house and move on. Me to West Point, God willing. And you to, well, something all your own." Mike was very calm, as he usually was on this subject. But he'd always been older than his years.

Sean flinched slightly, not as much as the other times when Mike mentioned the coming changes. Still, he'd rather hunt Scuds in Iraq again than enter the dating game for the first time. Tiffany's pregnancy had yanked him into matrimony before he'd ever seriously looked for a lover.

"Hey, you'll get in," Sean managed to reply, trying to deflect the conversation.

"If not, then I'll enlist." Sean could almost hear Mike's verbal shrug.

"We've talked about this before, Mike," Sean snorted. "College first, then the Army."

"And I've said this before. Army will pay for college, while I'm in. One way or another, I'm in the Army next fall."

"Mike—"

"There're things to be done, Dad. And all I've ever wanted was to be Army."

"Yeah," Sean conceded the last point. Mike was determined to be the fourth generation Ranger in the Lindstrom family. Time to end this subject for the moment. "I'll be home in ten. See ya."

He closed the phone. Was it easier to think about Mike's departure with a woman's silks in his hand?

He pulled his pickup to a stop in back of his small house and ran inside, leaving the scarf on the truck's seat. He could see Mike in the kitchen, talking to Deirdre Hemmings while he stirred a simmering pot. Sean stooped to greet Dudley with an ear rub. Dudley was too old now to jump up in welcome as his golden retriever warmth demanded but he was still delighted when his humans came to him. "Hello, Deirdre. Mike."

"Hi, Dad."

"Hello, Sean," Deirdre responded. She was a good-looking blonde a few years older than Sean, still wearing scrubs from her nursing job. Her daughter Carol, Mike's girlfriend, would look just like her in another twenty years. "Mike makes a spectacular spaghetti sauce. I wish I cooked the way he does."

"It's just the way Mom taught me," Mike shrugged.

"Good thing, too," Sean agreed. "I can manage microwaves and heating MREs; nothing else. Can I get you anything, Deirdre?"

"No, thank you. I just came to see the furniture before Tracy gets home from ballet class."

"Why don't we go up and look at it then?" Sean suggested.

Moments later, they were upstairs in the tiny guest room hidden under the eaves. The white and gilt furniture gleamed in the filtered light from the skylights. He'd had the additional windows installed when an old Army buddy, now a Delta Force operator, came to visit. Rick loved to sleep under the stars and Sean didn't want him to feel confined. At least, no more cramped than that bed made anyone over six feet feel.

Deirdre stopped in the doorway, staring at the bedroom set.

"Wow," she managed, moving forward to finger the lace canopy. "It's gorgeous, Sean. Tracy will love it."

"Good. I can drop the set off at your house on Friday morning, if Dave can help me unload it. It's all solid wood."

"Oh, yes, he'll be there. It's the perfect present for Tracy's tenth birthday. I just can't believe you'd have anything like this in your house. How did you find it?"

"Tiffany bought it while I was in AIT," he answered, referring to his time in Infantry Advanced Individual Training. Fourteen weeks of high summer in Georgia, enduring days with a heat index over one hundred fifteen degrees, while the Army made him into an infantryman. And Tiffany tried to find something she liked about being a military wife. "I refinished it like this after Mike was born so it was just the way she wanted."

"Were the bedspread and canopy hers, too? The pink ruffles and lace canopy are lovely but they don't look like you."

"She picked them out on her last birthday. But the mattress and springs are new since Tiffany's death. It was cheaper to replace them than get them cleaned, after she'd been bedridden for so long. They're seven years old but they've only been lightly used."

Deirdre nodded, still stroking the pink brocade. "Tiffany must have loved this, even when she was sick. A double bed will be huge for Tracy but you must have folded up like a pretzel to fit."

Sean's mouth twisted. Pretzel was a good description for the times he hadn't just hung his feet over the end. Tiffany's petite frame had fit neatly.

He wondered what Beth would look like in this bed and laughed silently at himself. He doubted he'd notice the furniture if Beth was undressed.

"That must be why Mike says he remembers you sleeping on the floor in his room so often, when he was a kid," Deirdre mused.

So Mike remembered that? Well, Sean had done it frequently. The floor had felt like heaven after training or field exercises. It had also been blessedly free of Tiffany's whining.

"Can I have the bedspread and canopy? Tracy's such a frilly girl, unlike Carol, that she'll probably like it."

Sean roused himself, glad to move on. "Sure, we won't use it. I'll get it cleaned and bring it on Friday, too."

"Thanks. We'll be glad to pay for the cleaning."

"Don't worry about it. That's just part of taking the bed."

Sean hesitated for a minute. Carol and her mother were very pragmatic, but Tracy had seemed more fanciful on the few occasions they'd spoken. "Something else, Deirdre."

Deirdre looked back at him, poised to start downstairs.

"Tiffany always wanted a daughter, a little blond princess to giggle and shop with. She'd be glad Tracy has the bed. And tell Tracy that Tiffany didn't die in this bed. The aneurysm broke while she was at the doctor's office, and she died in the hospital."

Deirdre patted him on the arm. "Thanks, Sean. I'm sure she wouldn't have worried about Tiffany's ghost but now, she can just think happy thoughts about this bed."

Sean nodded and stayed silent, glad that somebody had happy thoughts about this bed. He saw Deirdre out and went back into the kitchen, where he grabbed a beer. Tiffany's last traces would be out of the house on Friday, except for a few photos, all but two in Mike's room. "When's dinner?"

"Give you five minutes and then I'll start the noodles, okay?" Mike answered, his husky frame barely fitting into the tiny kitchen.

"Great," Sean answered and headed down the hall. *All busted condoms should produce results like Mike,* he thought, not for the first time.

He automatically shifted his shoulders to avoid brushing the family photos on the wall, which Mike had hung when they moved in. He paused to straighten a favorite, remembering his family's beginning.

He'd been back in that small Dakota town for Christmas, his first leave from West Point. He'd partied hard with Tiffany, both talking about their plans; General for him and movie star for Tiffany.

Later they'd gone to a back bedroom, clumsy with inexperience and alcohol. He could still hear Tiffany's hysteria when the condom broke and his promise to stand by her and the baby, if there was one.

He'd gained a family that night but Tiffany had lost hers. Her father had thrown her out when he learned she was pregnant and had never seen his grandson.

Their wedding picture hung on this wall: Tiffany in black, her pregnancy as blatant as her tear stains, and him in his sergeant's uniform, hours after being released from West Point.

Mike's birth picture held center place, with Tiffany's usual anger and resentment briefly washed away by the miracle of birth. He'd been exhausted and ecstatic when holding his son, after being snatched out of the field during AIT for the birth. It was the happiest time he'd ever known with Tiffany, two weeks before the first stroke hit her and slightly paralyzed her face and right leg.

She had avoided cameras after that.

It had been the first of eight strokes, despite all the people who worked to get her to change her behavior. Sean had tried everything he could think of to get her to stop drinking, stop smoking, eat better, and try to live long enough to see Mike grow up.

But Tiffany had continued to do what she found easiest, while hiding the traces as much as possible. Teaching Mike to cook had helped her eating habits, the only noticeable change she ever made.

There were more pictures of Mike, taken whenever Sean made it home on a birthday or holiday. They were usually outdoors—hiking, camping, fishing, or hunting—with Dudley always panting happily at the camera. It still surprised him that Mike had chosen those memories for this wall, rather than school pictures.

And there was Mike's eleventh birthday, the last picture of the three of them together. It centered on Mike proudly showing off his black belt in karate, grinning from ear to ear. Sean had carefully looked him over, making sure that every pleat was precisely placed in the white cotton and the black silk belt perfectly tied. Then Mike had demanded to inspect his father's turnout, checking every detail against an old manual that he'd managed to squirrel away.

So there was the master sergeant's uniform, three chevrons and three rockers on his left sleeve. Four hash marks on Sean's left cuff, for his twelve years of enlisted service. Black beret with his Ranger battalion badge. The Ranger tab and scroll on his left shoulder, with the scroll again on his right shoulder and its memories of Panama. Silver Star and a Bronze Star with oak leaf, including a V for valor. A Purple Heart, thanks to the Gulf War. Four rows of ribbons in all over his left breast, plus those unit citations above his right pocket.

Combat Infantry badge above his gleaming Master parachutist wings, complete with a Gold Star for that nasty combat jump into Panama. Pathfinder and Expert Marksmanship badges, sitting side by side on the flap of his left pocket.

Sean had stood at attention and kept a poker face while Mike approved the placement of every element with a ruler. Then he'd helped Tiffany into the photographer's armchair and taken her walker beyond the camera's relentless memory.

The picture showed Tiffany in her favorite sky-blue dress, her makeup as much art as anything in the photographer's portfolio. She'd practiced her expression and her posture in front of a mirror, hiding the effects of eleven years of strokes, pain, and careless living on her once fairy-tale prettiness.

The most recent photo showed Mike in his football uniform, poised to throw the ball. It hung between the picture of Sean's grandfather, standing among the prisoners of war he'd helped rescue in the Philippines, and Sean's father, wary and gaunt after a behind-the-lines patrol in Vietnam. Both of them Rangers, as Sean had been.

He touched the realigned picture with a gentle finger.

"I met a lady today, Mom. I'm going to see her again. I think you'd like her," he whispered.

His mother smiled back at him, caught by the camera, three weeks before a drunk driver mowed her down and left Sean alone in the world at age twelve.

He took the stairs two at a time, whistling in anticipation. He quickly stripped beside his big waterbed and got into the hot shower, still whistling. He washed himself automatically, reliving his earlier encounter in Gary's bookstore.

Who'd have thought to find a beauty like that among dusty books? She'd looked both exotic and familiar with those high cheekbones under the enormous dark eyes. Her hair was a hood of living black silk, framing her face and protecting her vulnerable long neck. Her red mouth was the most carnal invitation he'd ever seen, especially when it closed around her fist as she'd watched him come. She'd smelled like some spicy temptation from the Orient, when he'd stood next to her, pretending to look at books. She was tall enough that he wouldn't worry about hurting her if they lay together. Her curves were rich, promising to fill his hands.

And the look on her face when he dropped his pants . . .

He fondled his cock, the shower's mist swirling around him, as he remembered that slow trickle of crimson running down her hand, while her chocolate-brown eyes devoured him.

A moment later he was very hard as he imagined the same lady, now a priestess in scarlet silk with hair pinned up to bare her neck, ordering him to perform for her. Trails of water slid over him, silken as a woman's hair, as he stroked himself, responding to the priestess' detailed instructions. He imagined the lady's mouth wrapped around his cock, drinking him down.

He closed his eyes and fought back the rising pressure in his balls, intent on building his fantasy for as long as possible. He imagined her long fingers cupping his balls, squeezing them slowly as tension built into painful demand. He swore, imagining how her white teeth would delicately scrape his shaft. He gave himself over to his imagination, finally shuddering when the priestess's finger probed his ass and demanded his climax. He groaned as white jets splashed the tiled wall.

Sean opened his eyes and sighed, enjoying a harder-edged satisfaction than he usually took from his hand. Still, fantasies were great but usually remained just that: fantasy, not real life. Maybe she really would come back tonight. If she did, he'd do a lot to make this fantasy live as long as possible.

Mike couldn't know about it, of course. Kids needed to believe in fidelity, not one-night stands.

He got dressed quickly and carried his blue sweater. Months ago, Mike's girlfriend Carol had said that Sean was too hot for women to resist in anything that color. He'd avoided wearing it since, but now he needed all the ammunition he could get. If Beth liked him in blue, he'd wear it.

Mike's eyes widened when he saw the sweater Sean dropped on the table by the door. He glanced at his father's face but quickly went back to serving dinner.

"What's in that box, Mike?" Sean asked as he sat down to dinner.

"Jenny's mom, Mrs. Davison, dropped it off. She made some chocolate truffles and thought we might like some. There's also some of Ms. Anderson's apple pie."

Sean flinched at the mention of the women who kept chasing him. He'd never given them any encouragement.

"I'll take the candy and pie to the women's shelter tomorrow," he decided. The ladies there always liked sweets.

They talked about Mike's science project during the rest of their meal, stopping only when a horn blew from in front. Mike jumped up and started clearing dishes rapidly. Dudley came to his feet carefully, tail wagging as he begged for an opportunity to investigate the visitor in person.

"Go on, Mike. I'll finish that. Try not to stay up too late tonight at Sam's house."

"Sure, Dad. I'll take Dudley with me, too, okay? You know he likes playing with Sam's collie."

Dudley's tail wagged faster at the mention of his name. Sean looked down into the pleading brown eyes and chuckled. "Fine. You two have fun and I'll find something to do on my own."

Mike grabbed his coat and bag, then came back to the table,

reaching into his pocket. A small packet hit the table and he stepped back. "Just in case you need a few extra."

Sean looked down at the table and laughed out loud at the box of condoms lying there. So the young master was helping out the old man. Well, he couldn't remember the last time he'd bought any and hopefully they'd be useful.

He hugged Mike briefly and lightly pushed him out the door. He had dishes to wash and preparations to make.

Sean arrived at the PTSA meeting a few minutes early and took a seat in the front on the aisle. Linda Davison showed up a few minutes late, announced by her usual cloud of stale cigarette smoke. She stood next to Sean and pointed at the chair beside him, ignoring Pete Andrews's opening remarks. He groaned inside but came to his feet, trying not to disturb the people around them any more than necessary.

He returned to his seat but shifted as far toward the aisle as he could, trying not to touch or smell the woman. She was dressed in her favorite outfit, which emphasized three different shades of green. Four shades, if you counted the corrosion on her watchband. The combination reminded Sean of the Florida swamps he'd first met in Ranger School.

Linda pushed her foot against Sean's and a wave of her sour perfume rolled over him. He shifted away but she followed, rubbing her leg against his. He stared straight ahead, looking forward for once to standing up before a civilian crowd.

The meeting was as boring as ever, with the usual speakers rambling on about the usual subjects. Thankfully, Pete introduced him soon and he gave his standard treasurer's account, wincing at Linda's enthusiastic applause. Who did she think she was impressing, clapping for a routine talk about money?

He sat down next to Pete afterward. Unfortunately, Linda stood up a few minutes later to talk about the upcoming school play and found a seat beside Sean when she finished. She leaned over to whisper to him as soon as the next speaker began. Mercifully, Deirdre hissed at Linda from the row behind to be silent.

He made two more reports, talking about the annual ski trip and repairing the school's ornate façade, glad he'd written the reports in advance. The time spent addressing the meeting was unusually welcome, as it gave him time to breathe some clean air away from Linda. Finally he returned to his seat, ready for the meeting's open forum portion.

Sean's mind slid to his approaching encounter with Beth and he began to review his preparations, barely listening to the long-winded talk about fund-raising. Nobody mentioned anything that he needed to answer as treasurer. He wondered what Beth would want to do tonight; his body promptly, and enthusiastically, responded. He shifted slightly in his chair to ease the tightness of his pants.

Linda Davison glanced at him and he went very still to avoid further notice. He shifted the financial report on his lap, hoping to hide the swelling behind his fly. He tried to focus on something messy, like cleaning up the school's usual burden of graffiti, to soften his arousal but failed.

His pants kept getting tighter, as he thought about the coming rendezvous, until his zipper pressed into him. He bit down hard on the inside of his lip. He forced himself to relive that Florida swamp, remembering every detail of its mud and Water Moccasins and dammit stumps. He reviewed every type of poisonous snake found in that Florida swamp, all the details he'd memorized as a Ranger instructor. But even thoughts of those dangerous snakes or the tree stumps, waiting below the water for an exhausted hiker, couldn't calm his unruly body.

Heat stayed coiled in his gut, even as the pain built in his cock.

His arousal finally disappeared when Mrs. Davison leaned over to whisper a question about the school's sewers. One whiff of her hair almost erased the memory of Beth's perfume.

Even so, it seemed forever until the meeting ended. Linda Davison immediately started talking to him, and he concentrated warily on her words.

"Did you have a good meal tonight, Sean?" she cooed. Sean managed not to cringe at her breath's reek.

"Yes, thank you. Mike made spaghetti. His mother's recipe, which we both enjoy." He smiled to himself, when her eyes flashed at the mention of another woman, and kept talking. "Thanks for the candy. I'll take it to the women's shelter tomorrow, as a treat for those ladies."

Linda's mouth opened and shut. Unfortunately, she found an alternate tack. "Perhaps you'd like to come over to my house now?" she cooed.

Sean's eyes narrowed slightly at her tone.

"I've got some more chocolate that you could taste, just to make sure those poor ladies would enjoy it. We could have some wine, too, and tell each other all about the good times and the bad."

Sean stiffened and began running excuses through his head. Linda kept talking, oblivious to his withdrawal.

"I've just had the most dreadful weekend. The toilet in my bathroom keeps running all the time," she whined. "I'm sure you could help me with it. And, afterward, we could get to know each other better." She walked her fingers up his arm. He reshuffled his papers, forcing her hand to drop.

"Have you called a plumber?" He refused to think of how many times she'd mentioned her toilets to him.

"Well, no, I haven't. I wasn't sure what to say." Her voice trailed off, inviting Sean to step in.

"Just tell him what you said to me, Linda."

Her eyes narrowed and she started to say something else, clearly determined to gain his assistance. Mercifully, Deirdre Hemmings cut in then, her eyes laughing at him over Linda's head. "Linda, aren't you one of the chaperones for Thursday's Drama Club field trip?"

Linda stuttered, caught by the reference to her and her daughter's obsession, then turned to Deirdre, losing contact with him. "Why, yes, I am, Deirdre. Did you have any questions?"

Sean escaped swiftly, grateful to Deirdre for covering his retreat, and fled the school without making even the slightest promise to Linda of future contact.

He parked his pickup behind the bookstore and ran upstairs to Gary's old apartment, a furnished one-bedroom directly over the store. A few minutes' work and he had the scene set for seduction: dim lights, candles, wine. A quick check showed a variety of coffees, in case the lady wanted something nonalcoholic.

Then he scattered some of his favorite books of erotica around the living room and bedroom: *Exit to Eden, Venus in Furs,* the *Beauty* trilogy, and others. Hopefully, the same things would turn Beth on and she'd take the hint.

Mrs. Wolcott wouldn't have given a damn about the books. She swore she only did what felt right, whether it was a demand for oral sex or to lay a belt on her husband's ass. He'd caught them at it from time to time when he was a hired hand, seen Mr. Wolcott iron-hard under his wife's punishing hand just before he exploded into a climax.

She'd told Sean the same thing on the Saturday night she spent with him as a graduation present. He'd enjoyed his hours with Mrs. Wolcott but he'd known there'd only be that one time. He'd departed that small town for West Point the next day, finished with high school and intent on his future.

He'd never talked about it. But sometimes he allowed himself to remember. How alive he had felt, more intensely than at any time except in combat—and with Beth this afternoon.

Beth was so different from Mrs. Wolcott that she seemed a fantasy come to life. He'd dreamed so many times of having a woman watch him, while he jacked off. She'd cared about his comfort, too. He trusted her, at least enough to suggest going further. That rich voice of hers had led him on so smoothly that he hoped she knew more, especially of things mentioned in his books and videos.

His books looked unfamiliar when seen in the open air, not engulfed in his hand or locked in a cabinet, hidden from Tiffany's shouted prejudices or Mike's youthful curiosity.

Old fears rose to haunt him but he fiercely set them aside. He'd do whatever felt good, as long as everyone was pleased and not harmed. And Mike didn't find out, of course.

A glance at the clock showed that there was still time left before Beth's arrival. Sean sat down in the bedroom to refresh his dreams. Seconds later, he lost himself in his favorite scene from *The Claiming of Sleeping Beauty*. His cock strengthened under the intimate words but he refused to touch it, simply enjoying the ache as he waited for his flesh-and-blood lady.

He lifted his head when the wind blew a gust of rain hard against the roof. The clock caught his eye and he cursed at the time shown there. He dropped the book on the bed and ran outside to wait for her.

Three

Beth kept a polite mask on her face and continued chatting about forecast price fluctuations for Singapore dollars and Malaysian ringgits, as she covertly watched Akira Ono observe her. Another ten minutes and she'd leave for the bookstore, to hunt for more of the excitement Sean brought. An adrenaline rush that only the living could feel. It was in marked contrast to the past weeks, so full of funerals and grieving friends that any change, any excitement, was a blessing.

Pressured as these meetings were, they were still only low-level discussions to prepare for when the true decision-makers would come to an agreement. Beth had been abruptly assigned to help arrange this conference after the new administration decided to pay more attention, albeit "informally" and "privately," to concerns over the Japanese banks' debt portfolios and their possible impact on the Japanese economy. In other words, they'd finally realized that an overburdened Japanese banking system could damage the U.S. economy, and sent the Treasury to help.

It was still disconcerting to see the most senior Japanese banker present hover where he could snatch a few words with her. She'd dodged him earlier, letting Ed Johnson spout the necessary formalities. Akira had obviously waited until only a few people remained at the opening reception. Most of the attendees had left for smaller, more informal gatherings, to renew old connections before starting the in-depth talks tomorrow.

Who was he looking at? The Treasury bureaucrat, with colleagues that could help or hinder his bank, or the Western female, too ugly to be welcome in his family? His sister-in-law, the *hakushaku fujun*—or countess—had described Beth as too tall, too fat, mouth too wide, and a voice too deep for a woman. Beth's grandmother, the *koushaku fujin*—or marquise—had judged Beth "not enticing enough" in a voice colder than an Antarctic ice flow during that last confrontation with Catriona Nakamura, Beth's mother.

Beth snapped her mind away from past humiliation. Both families had been right about one thing: she was far too Western to settle into a Japanese marriage to a Japanese man, and enacted according to Japanese customs.

But why was Akira so eager to see her? For her connections now, or because of their clans' history? She could think of multiple reasons why he would want to talk to the woman who'd been his nephew's fiancé. He wouldn't create a scene, not here. But things could still get very nasty.

Professor Hiroki Nakamura could probably make some guesses about Akira Ono's intentions. But Beth hadn't spoken more than formalities to her father since that dreadful day in Tokyo. He'd been mute while her grandmother and mother dueled over the broken engagement. Her mother had shot torrents of scalding vehemence in Beth's defense, while her grandmother had parried and finally thrust with icy words that cut as deep as a glacier's crevasses.

Both women's words had hurt, but not as much as her beloved father's silence. She'd been a very sickly baby and her father had stayed home to look after her and write, while her mother worked. That experience had carried through the rest of her life, an unspoken ease with each other unusual between a father and daughter. Now, her Japanese blood understood the need not to attack the family head in public, no matter how disastrously Nakamura Obasama had been proven wrong about her pet alliance with the Ono clan. But Beth's Scots blood hungered for warmth and reassurance from her favorite parent. She still couldn't forget that her father hadn't wrapped his support around her in front of his mother.

Beth eased out of the conversation and watched the two bankers depart for the hotel's bar to further dissect currency, a safe conversational topic before tomorrow's talk of debt restructuring. Akira approached her and she greeted him formally, her words soft and her spine stiff as she bowed the smallest amount consonant with propriety. She addressed him in English, behaving as a Treasury bureaucrat. "Good evening, Mr. Ono. It is an honor to see you here."

"Greetings, Miss Nakamura." His answering bow was lower than required. "I am delighted to be here and have this opportunity to speak to you in person."

She nodded politely and waited.

"It is a pleasure seeing old acquaintances, is it not, in unfamiliar places? But then, travel can take anyone to enlivening experiences."

What on earth was he leading up to? "Indeed, the contrast of old and new can be fascinating to see," Beth responded courteously.

"Exactly." Akira smiled in genuine relief, which baffled her. "A good parent should ensure that his child has the broadest education possible, which travel helps provide. My brother, for example, has just sent his son Genichi to Algeria."

Genichi? The pampered youngest son in an Islamic region of Africa? Beth blinked, trying to imagine how her ex-fiancé would amuse himself far from Tokyo's nightlife. "An ancient country with connections to both East and West."

"Precisely." Akira beamed at her but controlled himself quickly. "Your grandmother recommended the broadening effects of travel and my brother thought Algeria offered the greatest potential for learning. Indeed, he insisted that Genichi spend all his time there except when he is at home in Japan."

Beth nodded and bit down on the inside of her lip, trying not to snicker. Where on earth would Genichi find in Algeria the lavish lifestyle he demanded? What would he do for nightclubs? Shopping? Or gossip? Who would pay compliments on his wardrobe? And Algeria had been engaged in a civil war, although there hadn't been much talk of that recently.

"The *hakushaku* and *koushaku fujin* are famous for their wisdom. I'm sure Algeria has much to offer the studious mind," Beth answered piously, invoking the aristocratic pasts of Akira's family, the Counts of Ono, and her own, the Marquises of Nakamura, to use the English versions of their titles.

"Quite so," Akira agreed heartily. "My son Daisuke plans to study at Berkeley, under your esteemed father, next year. It is our hope that his sojourn will result in many blessings, including warmer ties between our kin."

Beth's eyes widened briefly. The two families had feuded for generations, exacerbated when her father had ignored the unspoken assumption that he would marry an Ono daughter, and chose instead Catriona McKenna, daughter of a British naval officer and granddaughter of an Orkney fisherman. Nakamurakou (more formally, the Marquise Nakamura, and Beth's grandmother, or *Nakamura Obasama* in Japanese) was a very formidable lady who'd singlehandedly rebuilt the family fortunes in the chemical industry, after her naval hero husband's death in World War II. Her youngest son's marriage to a penniless Scotswoman had infuriated her and she refused to speak to him, or his family, for years. The breach was healed shortly before Beth's birth and Nakamura Obasama had helped her son obtain the prestigious teaching position in California. Beth—and no doubt her parents, too, were cynically aware that the rapprochement had occurred just after oil was discovered in the North Sea. It had been very advantageous for Nakamura Chemicals to have family connections so close at hand, in the Shetland Islands, to so many suddenly wealthy buyers.

But the old feud still lingered, with the insult to Ono family honor unassuaged. As balance, Beth's grandmother had strongly encouraged the engagement to Genichi Ono and been furious when Beth ended it, no matter how great Genichi's insult to the Nakamura clan. For Daisuke Ono to become Professor Nakamura's protégé meant that both clans seriously wanted to end the dispute.

"I will pray for many such blessings for both our families," Beth answered in all sincerity. She roused herself from contemplating the implications of this news and offered an olive branch of her own. "Have you spoken much to Mr. Johnson yet? He is an ardent fancier of antique roses and might be interested in your gardens."

"I had the honor of meeting him but we didn't discuss roses." Akira brightened, pleased at the personal information about the most senior American bureaucrat present. Such touches were the essence of Japanese relationships, where business negotiations depended on the link between the individuals involved.

"He had some spectacular red roses in his office last week; you might have heard of them."

"Gallica roses, perhaps?" Akira eagerly half-turned toward Ed Johnson but recovered quickly.

Beth smiled at him.

"Let me take you over to him. I'm sure he'd be delighted to talk roses with you." She rested her hand on Akira's arm and headed for the group by the fireplace. Ed quizzed her silently and she nodded fractionally. He finished talking to Eli Rosenbluth and smiled at Akira and Beth. "Ed, did you know that Mr. Ono raises some of the most famous roses in Japan? My grandmother says he grows many of Empress Josephine's roses."

"Really? Which ones?"

Beth smiled and removed herself from their company, glad that the two gentlemen were doing well with each other but personally disinterested in flower gardens at the moment. She glanced at the mantel clock, a stunning example of Art Deco in the restored hotel. It was past time to leave and she reviewed her options, strolling down the hall toward the lobby and the stairs up to her suite.

Should she spend time with Sean? Risky in many ways because she didn't know him and none of her friends in the scene had recommended him, as they had every partner since Dennis. She wished once again that she'd listened to her friends about Genichi, instead of her Tokyo relatives who'd extolled the advantages of a suitable marriage, with its bonus of ending the old antagonisms.

What would Dennis have said about Sean? Dennis had been friend and teacher, as well as one-time lover and sometime master. He'd had an excellent eye for men, as befitted a bisexual male dominant. But his wisdom had been silenced forever on September 11th.

She swallowed to erase the tastes of grief and fear in her mouth, only to find the familiar nerves over a new encounter. Could she and Sean gratify each other, especially if he truly enjoyed submitting? If he was a switch—but that was too much to be hoped for. Besides, he'd been so perfectly submissive in the bookstore's back room, with no trace of dominance except for that first kiss. Best to see him as simply a beautiful male sub.

It was always unpredictable, trying to guess exactly what and how best to please a new partner. And what if she wanted more of him than one night? That was a more frightening thought than pondering tonight's events.

Beth pulled Sean's business card out of her purse, for one last consideration. See him again or not?

She turned the little bit of pasteboard over in her fingers, considering what it said about him. Sean E. Lindstrom, President. Hepburn & Sons, Inc. Black letters below gave an address and phone numbers. The card was as clean and direct as the man himself. Did it smell of him? A draft snatched it out of her fingers and sent it fluttering to the floor.

"Here, let me get that," a man's voice rumbled.

"Thank you, Dave."

Dave Hemmings plucked the card up neatly, matching the tidiness of everything else about the Secret Service agent. He'd been brought in after September to handle security for this meeting and rapidly calmed everyone's fears. His average height and ordinary features could readily disappear into a crowd, his presence marked only by his physical fitness and grace.

"Thinking of buying some real estate here in Seattle?" he asked.

"No, not at all. I met Mr. Lindstrom in a bookstore this afternoon," Beth answered.

"The Next Page? Gary's bookstore?"

"Yes. How did you know?" Beth accepted the card back.

"Master Sergeant—then Sergeant First Class—Sean Lindstrom was one of my instructors in Ranger School. He served with Gary in the Mog—Somalia," he explained at Beth's unspoken query.

"I saw that fight on CNN!" Beth exclaimed. *Dear God, the blood and the deaths. Sean had been through that sun-scorched hellhole?*

Beth stepped sideways against the wall, to allow latecomers access to the elevator. Dave moved with her so that they were in a small nook, under an ornately gilded sconce. She kept her attention on him, willing him to keep talking.

"I didn't serve with him because I was never assigned to the Regiment. But people talked about him, called him a legend." Dave paused, looking back in time. "Silver Star from Panama, Bronze Star with V for valor from the Gulf."

Dave nodded confirmation at Beth's surprise over the awards.

"There were a lot of stories about him but he'd never tell them. Especially jokes about how he could sleep anywhere, no matter what was going on." Dave's mouth twitched in remembrance. His radio hummed briefly and he came alert, then relaxed at the routine conversation. He started talking again, more briskly this time. "Sean spent his entire career as a Ranger, except for some time in the Old Guard just before he got out. That was after the Mog, where his best friend died." He crossed himself at the memory.

Panic's edge retreated from Beth, as she absorbed Dave's admiration of Sean. "Married?" she asked cautiously, shifting to a subject of immediate concern to her.

"Widower." Dave didn't add anything to the bald declaration, seemingly lost in memories. Beth remembered Sean's ignorance of his attractions and managed not to curse a dead woman.

"I'm meeting him tonight. Do you have any recommendations?" She kept the question open-ended, allowing Dave to discuss the subjects he felt important. Being Dave, he caught the implications.

"You can trust him, Beth. My daughter's dating his son and I'm not worried about her. Well, not too worried," he amended. "But Sean is the man I'd ask to look after my wife and family, if I thought my time had come."

"Thank you." She relaxed, a little surprised at the intensity of her relief.

"Just one other thing."

Beth cocked her head at Dave's hesitation.

"My wife, Deirdre, said Sean's girlfriend would be the luckiest woman in Seattle."

Beth blinked and blushed at Dave's grin. "Thank you, Dave, for your confidence. I'd better be going now, if I'm going to get there on time."

She ran upstairs to grab her coat, free to enjoy the night's potential. Playing with Sean had advantages, because she could easily walk away afterward without worrying about any commitment. She wanted to feel the overwhelming rush of physical pleasure, nothing more, as her body relearned its most basic purpose in a man's arms. She knew they could both enjoy themselves, given communication and trust. Tomorrow and its fears would have to look after themselves.

Beth relived their previous encounter as she drove toward the bookstore, remembering every word said and every movement either of them had made, as she looked for clues on how to proceed tonight. Sean had followed her instructions promptly, emphasizing her control of the situation.

She sighed softly, relishing the memory of how powerful she'd felt. Tonight's brief encounter could be a pleasant release from both the stresses of her job and the memories of her conservative behavior during her engagement.

Beth had always followed Genichi's smallest suggestions during their courtship and engagement, as befitted a proper Japanese woman being courted by a desirable Japanese man. She had felt the need to avoid any hint of aggressive Western femininity, given her half-Scots ancestry. Nevertheless, even behavior that her Japanese grandmother would have praised hadn't prevented Genichi from publicly humiliating her.

She'd been in an important meeting at the American embassy in Tokyo that morning, planning to accompany Genichi to meet her parents and grandmother for lunch. When the formal meeting ended early, she took some of the participants back to her office for informal discussions. They'd walked in to find Genichi in flagrante delicto with the department secretary on Beth's desk.

Beth could still hear the secretary's hysteria, when she climaxed at the same time she saw the audience. Beth could still see the Japanese bankers' faces as they avoided looking directly at Genichi, with his bony ass pumping below his French silk shirt. She'd dropped her engagement ring on the floor and walked out, to face her family's upheaval and the world's gossip. She'd gone willingly back to Washington after that, glad to find fewer whispers.

She pulled herself away from the old memory and found herself facing another agonizing one. Dennis's voice in that last phone call from his burning office at the World Trade Center on September 11th. *Live for both of us,* he'd demanded. *Make the most of being alive, for both of us. Find that one man who'll suit you and build a future with him.*

She'd promised Dennis that she would, while the tears ran silently down her face. Her office had been a silent refuge against the upheaval in the hallways beyond, as her coworkers first tried to absorb the news from New York and the Pentagon, then left in a tumbling rush when the evacuation order came. She'd been too calm on the Metro that day, as she plotted how to get involved in the hunt for Dennis's killers.

The first time she'd felt blazingly alive since then was when Sean had displayed himself in the room behind that quiet bookstore and the intensity of a scene had snapped into place between them. There were so many more joys she could find with him. A big, blond Westerner, gifted with a knack for submission, to play with for a few hours. Dennis would surely have approved.

The rain was coming down hard when Beth reached the corner across from the bookstore, driven by a strong wind that blew sheets of water into her face. Her hair was plastered to her skin by the time she reached Sean, but her shoes were only slightly damp, thanks to some careful puddle dodging. He immediately caught her by the elbow and whipped her into the bookstore, where water fell off her coat, landing with soft plops onto the floor.

Beth smiled ruefully up at him, conscious of the mascara blurred and running down her face. This was not how she had planned to meet a potential lover.

"You look wet to the skin, Beth. Why don't you come someplace where you can get warm and dry?" he offered.

"Thank you, Sean. That sounds lovely."

Beth found herself moments later in the small apartment above the bookstore, tidy and clean with candles casting a soft light and a gas fireplace burning brightly. "Do you live here?"

"No, it's a rental property. Vacant at the moment."

Beth nodded and looked around more closely. An old-fashioned cuckoo clock hung above the mantel and a store's neon light pulsed against the curtains, its red glow emphasizing a couple of books laid out on the small table. She started to remember the books' plots, but quickly turned her full attention back to Sean when he spoke.

"There's a bedroom and bathroom through there where you can freshen up. Would you care for some coffee or maybe something stronger?" He took her coat.

"Thank you, I'd like some coffee. Decaf if you have it." Beth accepted and turned down the hallway. She caught his reflection in a framed poster's glass, as he avidly watched her departing back. Strength slid into her hunger for him. She kept her eyes straight ahead, not showing that she'd caught the revealing look.

She closed the bedroom door and easily found the bathroom. A brief search revealed a hair dryer and she set to work repairing the weather's attacks on her person. Unfortunately, her hair and makeup had taken the worst of it. Still, a few minutes saw her hair acceptable again. And her purse provided the ingredients needed to rebuild her appearance, with a quick gloss of mascara and lipstick. A simpler look than she normally wore to play with a man but, hopefully, still effective.

An open book on the bed caught her eye, as she left the bathroom. She picked it up curiously and her eyebrows went up as she read how the Queen spanked Prince Alexi.

A moment's reflection brought the realization that the books in the living room were also stories of men being dominated by women. Further thought convinced her that the books must be Sean's and their presence planned. He was cruising for a lover, telling her what he hoped for. No pressure on her, just an open door for her to walk through, if she chose to.

Beth began to consider possible responses to Sean's strong hints.

Chastity? Hardly. They both knew this evening would end in the bedroom.

A vanilla evening, with pleasure for both, while ignoring the books' suggestions? The safest course, but lacking the heart-pounding rapture of a well-played scene.

Sean had trusted her enough to risk humiliation by exposing his inner wishes. He couldn't be an experienced player, given his clumsiness at the bookstore. He could probably taste his nerves right now.

Years of practice knit themselves in Beth's backbone as Sean's fantasies hummed in her blood. She could show him a good time, taking the responsibility for their joint pleasure by dominating him. He wouldn't have to worry about a thing, which was possibly best for his inexperience.

Oh, the delights of introducing him to sexual play during a power exchange. Beth's eyes slitted as she purred at the possibilities, enjoying the throb of arousal beating in her throat.

The riskiest course but she'd take it. After all, if it didn't work with Sean, then she hadn't lost a relationship that mattered. She'd never dominated a stranger before, only men that she already knew were comfortable at submitting to a woman. Dominating a man was tricky, especially given the intense connection necessary to read his unspoken responses quickly and accurately. Rigorous safe sex practices, of course; they'd protect her health and his, as was customary in the scene. Besides, the discipline necessary to do so would also help leash him.

She took a deep breath and focused her energies on feeling confident and strong and sensual. Her little black dress, fresh from the runways of Milan, and her pearl earrings were the epitome of classic feminine power, especially when combined with high heels and black stockings. Her figure was emphasized by the sleek style, although only a small amount of décolletage showed.

Beth opened the door into the living room. Sean's head came up, and he watched her from his post by the window.

"How do you want your coffee, Beth?" His voice came out in a clumsy rasp.

"Coffee can wait." Beth waved a dismissive hand. "Care to have some fun first, handsome?"

"Of course." His blue eyes widened and he swallowed hard.

She strolled across the room to him, enjoying how his eyes followed every movement. She looked him over slowly, taking in every detail of his appearance from the golden hair crowning his head to the leather boots on his big feet. Her eyes lingered longest on the growing bulge behind his fly, and Sean's breathing faltered. Her eyes traveled slowly back up to his face, and she smiled slowly, lasciviously at the open lust on his face.

She walked her fingers delicately up his right hand, enjoying the contrast between their hands. Hers were beautifully manicured, with nails only lightly frosted, while his bore signs of recent hard work. She caught his hand up and traced the lifeline in his palm. The gentle, repetitive caress eased his breathing into a rhythmic pattern.

Next she glided her fingers up his arm to his shoulder, feeling the long lines of muscle under his brilliantly colored ski sweater. A cashmere or alpaca sweater would have been handy, either soft enough to let her feel more of the muscle and bone underneath the wool than this sweater did. His eyelids grew heavy as he watched her face.

Beth stepped in closer to him and traced his jaw with a single fingertip. Such a strong face, with eyes set under level brows, a straight blade of a nose, a slash of a mouth. The upper lip was tightly controlled above the more sensual lower lip, ready for laughter before cynicism.

"Were you in the military?" she asked. Only this moment mattered, not what anyone else said.

"I was a Ranger for eleven years."

"Did you wear a helmet?" She traced his temple back to his ear, finding the faint prickle of freshly shaved skin.

"Yes, ma'am." His heavy eyes watched her, questions kept back.

"How far down did the helmet come on your forehead?"

He marked the line with the edge of his hand.

"On the sides of your face?"

He showed her with both hands. She caught his wrists, keeping the frame around his eyes and mouth.

"Viking," she breathed, recognizing him from pictures in museums and old textbooks. From childhood dreams. He blinked in surprise but had the sense to stay still, letting the chemistry build between them.

"Viking," Beth said again and kissed him. She traced his lips with her tongue, exploring their shape and strength, until his mouth opened under her gentle urging.

"Viking warrior," she breathed into his mouth, just before hers took possession of him. They kissed slowly, learning each other's tastes and textures, until she pulled back. His hand dropped from her waist while she continued to caress his cheek.

Sean took a deep breath and let his eyes close. She fondled his neck, enjoying the difference between his masculine strength and its innate vulnerability, laid bare by his severe haircut.

Beth gradually remembered her self-discipline. "Have you ever wanted to worship a woman, Sean?" she queried huskily.

"Yes. Hell, yes," he groaned.

"Care to try it here and now, with me?"

He nodded, a pulse pounding in his jaw. He was still frozen, outlined by the rippling firelight.

"Of course, as the goddess present, I get to say what I want and you get to do it. Can you manage that?"

"I can do whatever you say, Beth," he vowed, his eyes blazing blue fire.

"Good lad," she sighed. "I'd rather like to be worshipped tonight. Come over here and rub my feet."

Sean immediately obeyed, dropping to one knee and reverently lifting off first one shoe, then the other. He set the shoes aside carefully, neatly aligned by the end table, and cupped her left foot in his hand. He slowly ran his thumb from her big toe up to her ankle, stretching and relaxing her aching bones. Her feet ached badly tonight, thanks to the combination of the old diving injury and cold, wet weather. His big, warm hands were the perfect antidote.

Beth purred happily as he carefully rubbed her left foot and then her right. It was surprising that he followed her order so easily. This must truly have been his fantasy, although obeying orders of any type might be easier for a military man. But his enthusiasm relaxed her, and she felt more and more like an irresistible woman.

"Enough, Sean," she directed, when both feet were relaxed and eager to face new adventures.

Sean sat back on his heels slowly and looked up at her, his eyes slightly glazed. His chest rose and fell raggedly, above the fat ridge in his trousers.

"Now take off your sweater and shirt. Fold them and set them aside, so I can see your bare chest."

Her tone allowed for no argument, and he showed no hesitation. He pulled his sweater over his head, then quickly stripped off his shirt, settling them as neatly as she'd demanded. He looked up at her again, waiting for her next instruction.

Beth studied Sean where he knelt, displaying the upper half of his body for her. The bright hair on his head formed a thick pelt, snatched back from curling by the short cut. Its gold was echoed by the dense mat of hair on his strong chest, hiding the small male nipples there, and the line of darker gold that led down to his waistband. Veins showed clearly, under the milk white skin, and emphasized hard muscles. Beth doubted she could get both hands around one of his upper arms. And those beautiful forearms of his, with the elegant tracery of blue veins under the gilding of hair, were tempting beyond belief.

She walked slowly around him, studying every detail of his exposed torso. His back was burnished by a light sprinkling of hair, just enough to lend shading to the lines of muscle. He trembled when she ran a finger down his spine, cherishing the silky skin and delicate hairs found there.

Beth swallowed hard, fighting the temptation to simply grab him, and moved to the sofa, dropping her purse on the floor next to her seat. A few details needed to be discussed, before yielding to mutual hunger.

"I'll take that decaf now, Sean." She managed to keep lust out of her voice. "Black, please. Have some yourself, if you like. We need to talk about a few things before going further."

Sean gulped and stood up. He fixed drinks for both of them and brought them out. Beth accepted the mug and sipped it slowly, watching him.

"Did you bring the scarf?" Beth asked.

Sean nodded and fetched the black and gold trifle from his coat pocket. Beth ran it slowly over her hand, feeling the changed texture where his semen had soaked in. She rubbed her thumb over one particularly sticky spot, lifted it to her nose, and sniffed it, enjoying the scent of masculine musk.

Sean's breath stopped in a faint gasp.

Then she set the scarf down in her lap and took another sip of coffee. Beth indicated the seat next to her and he sat there, holding on to his mug as if it were the one familiar thing in a changing world.

"Do you have a significant other?" she asked quietly, unwilling to mention Dave Hemmings's words. "I was engaged a year ago but broke it off."

"No, I'm a single parent; my wife died seven years ago." Sean hesitated a moment before going on. "I've got an eighteen-year-old son and I haven't had time to get involved with anyone since then."

It was a solid reason for his clumsiness. She did wonder what Seattle women were thinking, to let him stay celibate.

"I don't have any diseases that I know of," Beth said quietly, steeling herself for her first discussion of this touchy subject since Genichi. "However, I broke off my engagement because I caught my fiancé with another woman. I've been tested regularly since then, for diseases that he might have given me, always with negative results."

She blinked at the violent look crossing Sean's face, following very quickly after his first relief. It had seemed as if he could commit murder when he heard of Genichi's infidelity.

"I don't want you to have any reminders of Genichi, okay? So let's say the rule is not to exchange any fluids, just to keep things on the safe side. Agreed?" Beth watched Sean absorb the implications and smiled when he nodded hard.

Beth's tension faded in his confidence's bright light and she let herself take another taste of his willingness. She ran her fingertip lightly over the back of his hand, feeling the prickle of hair. She began to lightly trace patterns, exploring the hard calluses and small scars. Her fingers glided slowly up his right arm over the old scar.

"Purple Heart?" she asked softly.

"Training accident," he dismissed.

Something that big hadn't earned a medal?

"Do you have a Purple Heart?" she whispered, sliding the black metal bracelet around his wrist. Her eyes prickled at its remembrance of a friend named Adam and she quickly looked farther to the living flesh underneath. She admired the branching vein, gleaming blue as it twisted over the muscle.

"Yeah. A bullet wound here, on my thigh." He showed her the spot with his free hand. She touched it carefully, recognizing its

DIANE WHITESIDE

closeness to his hip and the vital organs there. His hand dropped back to his side, opening and closing slowly like his other hand.

"Hospital time for it?"

"Couple of months," he shrugged, rejecting the opportunity to brag.

"Brave samurai," she murmured in Japanese. His eyes flickered but he didn't speak, as she continued her delicate exploration onto his chest.

Her finger traced a pectoral muscle to its crowning aureole and his eyes closed slowly. Beth caressed his nipples and chest, savoring the varying textures. Her hand spread flat, fingers sliding into his fur as her palm absorbed his heat. He shuddered and his breathing stopped, then slowly recovered as her hand stayed still.

"What form of service to a woman are you best at, Sean?"

Sean blinked and then looked at her. His eyes were very blue and very dazed. There was a long pause before he answered. "Going down on a woman, ma'am."

Beth swallowed hard at the thought, feeling her belly clench with lust. Time to shift things into a higher gear.

"Stand up and take your boots and socks off. Place them with the others, socks folded."

Sean obeyed quickly, eagerness blazing from every jerky movement.

"Now get rid of your pants." Sean dropped his trousers and set them aside neatly. His cock was visibly throbbing.

"Give me your wrists." Sean immediately held out his hands to her. A few quick loops saw the scarf wrapped around his wrists. He could have freed himself in an instant, but he didn't try. He simply stood still, his hands turning slowly as he watched the silk grip him.

Beth retrieved a small shopping bag from her purse and dumped its contents onto the table next to her. Thank heavens for the stores in this eclectic neighborhood.

Sean's stunned eyes focused on a variety of condoms and dams, their diverse functions and sizes hopefully recognizable to him. He shook his head once, as if clearing his thoughts, and looked at her face. His enthusiasm still shone, strengthened now by trust in her judgment.

"Begin serving me, Viking," Beth said hoarsely, her own craving increasing to match Sean's blatant hunger.

Sean dropped to his knees before her. His slow caresses of her legs were followed by gentle laving as his mouth explored her. Beth slid her hands into his hair and savored every sensation. Her knees fell open and he murmured wordlessly as he explored higher, sliding her skirt away. He followed muscle to the vulnerable hollow behind her knee. He licked and sucked first one hidden pulse point, then the other knee. Trails of fire ran up to her core from every touch. The scarf echoed his movements with delicate silken caresses against her legs.

Beth laid her head back, moaning encouragement, and slid her hips forward on the sofa. He worked higher, growling with pleasure when his tongue slid under the edge of her silk stockings. She groaned when he nipped her bare skin lightly, then licked it sweetly to ease the small pain. He sighed in a tone so deep it almost rumbled when he finally slid aside her briefs' black silk and found her melting center, every fold already gleaming with dew for him.

"Sean."

He snarled but stopped before his mouth reached her there.

"What did you forget?"

He blinked at her, confused.

She had no safety net, no friends to call if he lost control and pounced on her. Nothing except slowing him down and making him obey, making him be careful. "What did we agree to do, to protect each other?"

Comprehension flashed over his face. He cursed softly and turned to retrieve a dam from the heap on the table, then hesitated at the wide selection.

She relaxed slightly and decided to tease him a bit. "Think now, Sean. What color do you think would be best? Remember they're flavored, if that makes a difference."

"Flavored?"

"Oh, yes, darling. Vanilla or perhaps a fruit scent, to add an accent to my taste."

He grabbed for one as the last syllable glided into the room. And he fumbled when he opened the packet, releasing the scent of vanilla and cinnamon.

"Good lad," Beth cooed and leaned back for him, her eyes dancing as she watched his clumsy placement of the dam over her nether lips. About the size of a piece of paper but actually very thin, very flexible latex, lightly powdered and scented. Originally designed for use during oral surgery and refined for oral sex, they were far more exotic and blatantly sensual than the commonly used Saran Wrap. "Careful now. They're very thin so you can feel everything. Everything, do you understand, darling?"

She stretched and purred when his tongue found her again. It slid leisurely along her folds, learning her outlines and developing a rhythm that pleased her. Backward and forward his tongue traveled, to a regular beat that built a matching tattoo in her veins. Her body tightened and flowed wet for him, like a mountain spring under the warmth of a May sky.

Then he turned his attention to her clit, circling and lapping until it rose proud and strong for him. Beth gasped when he hummed his enjoyment, making her flesh vibrate in delight. Sean was incredibly good at this, his lips soft and flexible while his tongue was capable of surprising strength.

Beth clasped his head, eager for more contact, her voice husky as she sighed her pleasure. She caressed him, enjoying the primal connection to his muscle and bone. Letting her hands tell him when to repeat or move on, when to go lighter or harder, where to go next. She eased into her orgasm slowly, savoring every ripple of pleasure that rolled through her body.

When Sean tried to pull away afterward, her hands tightened on his neck pulling him back into her.

"More," she demanded simply.

He obeyed, just as simply. Her stockings were discarded at some point and later her briefs. Beth paid little heed to those details, being far more interested in how he used first one finger, then others deep within her. Only the moment's rapture mattered now as she rode the long, deep waves. Her hands and legs stayed in touch with Sean and his tension.

He varied his strokes, using a pattern that drove her wild until she realized he was writing her name with his tongue. Then he changed his rhythm until she could no longer guess when he would touch her next. She dissolved into another climax, her breath sobbing in a plea to him for more.

Sanity stirred. Time to finish now, while she still had enough stamina to attend to him. "Enough."

The word hung in the quiet room. Sean hesitated for a moment, then stopped. Her magnificent male lion had obeyed her.

Beth dragged herself back from near unconsciousness and watched him as he sat up slowly, his face wet from the many orgasms he'd given her. She lay quietly against the sofa, too weak to move as she savored the aftershocks. She could have stayed there forever, enjoying the efforts of his hands and mouth between her legs, the feel of his hair.

She saw Sean step away and closed her eyes.

Then a washcloth began to clean her up. She swallowed hard as emotion caught her unawares. No man had ever cherished her like that, pleasuring her and easing her down afterward, unless she'd given him a direct order. Amazing that Sean did so, especially when he'd had no satisfaction himself.

A small door shot open and the cuckoo popped out to begin whistling midnight.

Four

Sean knelt on the floor in front of Beth, fighting himself for control of his arousal. He needed to grab her and pull her down on the floor under him. Fantasies crowded into him, frantic to come to life with a willing woman. Tasting her and driving her into rapture had been great. He had felt so alive and powerful when her body moved in response to his urging.

But long years of military discipline, learned in the harshest surroundings, restrained him now and kept him obedient to her leader's voice. So far the rewards of obedience had been better than any fantasy: the smell and taste of her, the shock waves rippling through her under his mouth and hands. Heedless of such niceties, his body now demanded completion for itself. Just when he thought he had to reach for her, her voice broke the silence.

"Stand up and take two steps back." He rose immediately, still facing her, his hands held together in front of him by her scarf. He had retied it when he washed up and it clung to him now, still wet from when he pleasured her.

His fully erect cock throbbed with life and leaped when he saw her eyes on it. Her voice caught him again, before conscious thought could return.

"Turn around slowly." Sean rotated, intensely aware of every change in her breathing as she studied him. His skin seemed to burn under her gaze. He growled softly, as he grew even more aroused.

Beth stood up and walked over to him. He shuddered when she touched his back, but began to moan as she lightly caressed him. Her hand traveled up over his shoulder and then down his chest, as she circled him to finish in front. Both hands began to play with his pectoral muscles, then his nipples, evoking groans from him. Her mouth enjoyed one nipple, nipping and licking, lingering over the taste and texture. His hands clenched in the scarf. Where had she learned exactly how to drive him mad?

Just when he thought he couldn't stand it any longer, she shifted to the other nipple. He closed his eyes, totally lost in sensation as she worked first one nipple, then the other, harder and harder. Her hands drifted lower but never stroked him where he was hardest.

"Spread your legs. Wider. Yes, that's good."

Beth broke off suddenly and walked away to the table, where she studied the scattered safe-sex supplies.

"Extra sensation? Yes, you'd probably like those little ribs rubbing you when I start licking," she mused. "Extra large, of course. Colored? No, I don't think so. I'd like to see your natural skin tones."

His mind struggled back to life, fighting to process the implications.

Beth's eyes danced at his expression. "Flavored, perhaps?" she offered.

He choked but turned it into a strangled cough.

"Like the sound of that? Okay, flavored it is. We'll go with the classic: mint."

He'd shopped for sex accessories and toys before; considered the merits of cock rings, tit clamps, vibrators, butt plugs, and more. He'd bought and played with them in private, locked the ones he liked best in the cabinet under his bed, and discreetly disposed of the others. He'd considered himself an experienced shopper. But he'd never shopped for condoms, never studied their advantages and disadvantages, since he'd left Tiffany's bed and the need for protection behind him.

His jaw fell open when Beth came back and dropped to her knees in front of him. She studied him closely for a long time and his lungs forgot to fill.

She leaned forward and blew a single, soft warm breath that rippled the clear liquid dripping slowly down his cock. His knees buckled but he locked them fiercely. He would remain standing, somehow, while a woman's mouth touched him intimately for the first time in a long while.

Her hands were quick and deft as she sheathed him, then leaned back to study her work. He couldn't think, couldn't move, couldn't breathe. She was so unbearably skillful with that condom.

She kissed his groin, where it gleamed white behind his deep red cock. Her hands cupped his balls, his blond curls wrapping her elegant fingers as she studied him.

"Beautiful," she murmured and puffed on them gently. His hips quivered as her mouth and hands danced with him. Her scarlet mouth closed around him, looking just like his fantasy.

Then she went to work, humming with pleasure against his inflamed skin. She explored every fold in his foreskin, teasing out every nerve ending until he begged for mercy. Then her tongue dealt long strokes that glided up and over, then down his aching cock. Delicate flicks against the sensitive point under his glans, rich swirls around his tight balls. She cherished each of his balls in her mouth until he was sobbing, overwhelmed by an electricity that he couldn't resist.

Beth cupped his ass, guiding his response until his hips thrust in rhythm with her expert touch. Her black hair tangled with his blond thatch, intimate and startling. His world narrowed to the feel of her mouth, driving his need to completion, until he was more desperate than he'd ever been in his life.

She straightened up and shook her hair free, allowing him a clear view of her movements. Her tongue delicately outlined the slit at the uppermost tip of his cock, then began to swirl around and around, lower and lower. Her breathing shifted as her tongue swept over him, devouring him like hard candy. Her mouth prowled down his cock and took him entirely into her. It was a more astonishing sight than the first time he'd seen a man point a gun at him, intending to kill him.

He gasped, his pulse pounding deep within his balls. Words broke free from deep within. "Beth! Dammit, Beth, please. I beg you, you've got to . . ."

His breath broke as her throat gripped him. "Fuck," he groaned. "Oh, fuck."

Her finger circled his asshole and then pressed hard.

"Yes!" he shouted. "Fuck, yes!" he shouted again as his orgasm burst, every wave thundering through him from the base of his spine, through his entire body, tearing out of his balls and bursting through his cock. She worked him greedily, her hands and throat muscles combining to drain every drop out of him into the condom.

Sean collapsed on the sofa as his legs gave out on him. His eyes closed, unable to accept any further stimulation.

A few moments later, a hot, wet washcloth tenderly covered his genitals. He whispered his gratitude, as she gently took care of him.

Beth sat down beside him and wrapped her arms around him, stroking his hair and crooning softly. He buried his face against her shoulder and held on to her, still shaken by the intensity of his climax. She'd even cleaned up the used condom, as he'd tidied up the dams.

"Let's go lie down, darling. Come on." She urged him to his feet and into the bedroom. He collapsed on the bed, still dazed, and she tucked him up under the covers. His hand shot out and caught her wrist.

"Stay. Please stay just a little while longer," Sean pleaded, not caring how he sounded. He needed every minute he could get with her.

Beth hesitated then nodded. "Let me get out of my dress."

"You can put on my shirt, if you'd like," Sean offered. She patted his shoulder gently, and he closed his eyes.

A few minutes later, the bed gave under her weight as she got in on the far side. He immediately turned to her and pulled her into his arms, delighted at her nudity. He cradled her, breathing in her scent, while trying to rebuild his sanity.

Minutes passed while his breathing returned to normal, echoing the steady rhythm of her heart as her breasts rose and fell against him. She traced an idle circle on his back, as her satin-smooth leg rested between his.

Sean tried to stay awake, even as his sated body relaxed against her soft skin, so he'd have more to remember later. She was so close to him that he felt the breath moving through her body and into his, until their chests rose and fell in unison.

"Do you dream about being spanked by a woman, Sean?" Her voice was a soothing thread in the sheltering dark.

"Yes," he answered cautiously, trying to find words. Beth rubbed his back, silently urging him on. "After my mother was killed, I lived with foster families until I went to West Point. One lady spanked me. I don't even remember why; could have been any number of things. But I do remember how hard I was, while she did it, and how good it felt when I jacked myself off afterward."

The words came easier now; Beth hadn't shrieked curses at him for perverted thoughts.

"I was a pretty wild kid until Coach straightened me out, reminded me of my mother's and grandfather's teachings. He wanted me to stay on the wrestling team and go to college. My last year in high school, he got me a job at the Wolcott place, the biggest ranch in town. Mr. Wolcott was quite a man. He had a world championship buckle for bull riding, and a Bronze Star as a Marine in Vietnam."

Sean fell silent, remembering that spread in the Dakota Badlands and the big man who dominated it and the small town nearby. Beth leaned her head against his arm and watched him quietly, her brown eyes soft and curious. "What happened then?"

"One afternoon early on, I was cleaning out an old toolshed by the house when I saw Mrs. Wolcott and Mr. Wolcott . . ." Sean stopped, startled by the surge of lust that welled up at the memory.

Beth rubbed his nipple, then flicked it. He blushed at the reminder, that she liked his stories and his arousal.

"Uh, Mrs. Wolcott was applying a leather belt to Mr. Wolcott's butt. Lots of blows, lots of force. His ass was red as flame, and his cock was rigid enough to dig a well with. Then she made him lie down on the kitchen floor, and she rode him like he was a wild bronc."

"Go on," Beth murmured and began to delicately lick his nipple, keeping it erect but not urgent.

"I'd been with girls before but not much. I'd certainly never seen anything like that. Christ, I damn near came in my pants just from watching. After that, I started spying on them. I can still see her taking his quirt to his back, or her fancy high-heeled shoes, if he didn't lick her just the way she liked. They played games like that a lot."

Beth dragged her teeth lightly over him and he croaked the next words. "He enjoyed it as much or more than she did, judging by the look of his cock."

Beth's tongue circled him, as she eased off just a bit.

"I studied and memorized what they did, so I could remember it later. Matters went like that all of my senior year and through graduation. They enjoyed themselves while I spied on them, then played it back in my dreams."

"Then what?"

Sean pulled his few remaining brains back from the feeling of her suckling slowly and happily on him.

"Finally came the Saturday night before I left for West Point. My friends gave me a good-bye party but I didn't stay very late. I went back to the Wolcott ranch to look around for the last time. That's when Mrs. Wolcott spoke to me."

"What did she say, Sean? Please tell me the rest," Beth urged softly. She watched him from luminous, eager eyes, while still caressing him with one hand. Still interested, still sexual, still unoffended.

Sean shrugged and went on, biting back fear. He'd said this much, so he might as well finish. Maybe she wouldn't turn away afterward or scream curses at him, as Tiffany had.

"She knew I'd been watching and she wanted to give me a special good-bye present: spend the rest of the night with me, playing the same games she did with her husband. I tried to say no but she countered every argument I had. Her husband was in Fargo and wouldn't be back until Monday. Hell, he'd even told her to do it!"

Sean shook his head, still unable to really believe that a man would tell his wife to fool around with somebody else.

"None of the hands ever came near the main house for chores, so nobody would know. And I agreed.

"We played games that night until my ass was so sore I couldn't sit down comfortably for days. It made riding the bus out of town into pure hell and I didn't care. She taught me a lot, about how to pleasure a woman with my hands and mouth, punishing me hard when I didn't do things just right. It was every dream I'd had, and more. And I loved it, and I don't regret any damn bit."

He looked into Beth's eyes fiercely, willing her to believe the next part. "I didn't come once, though. At least, not inside her cunt. That would have been adultery."

"I believe you, Sean, and I'm glad that you had such a good time. Plus . . . you're so sexy when you think about past pleasures," Beth purred, sliding a little closer somehow. "Did you ever see her again?"

"No, the last time I went back was the following Christmas, and the Wolcotts always wintered in Arizona. Tiffany and I, we partied together some and the condom broke. She got pregnant, her family threw her out. We never returned after we married."

Sean brooded over the past, seeing Mrs. Wolcott's serviceable white bra above her tight jeans, that wide leather belt gliding through her hands. Beth traced his jaw with a finger and the old memory vanished.

"I had a lover, too, that I'll always remember," Beth offered. He looked down at her, startled and curious to hear what she wanted to reveal.

"I went to Harvard for my MBA, a long way from home and any of my former boyfriends. I attended an alumni reception one Saturday night, just to meet people. I saw Dennis there, talking to a professor who intimidated me to death. But that professor was trying hard to impress Dennis! I was fascinated and kept watching. When Dennis left, he asked me to come with him and I said yes. I was in his bed within an hour."

"Did you like him?" Sean tried not to let too much jealousy into his voice.

"Dennis? Yes, very much. We had a wild affair for the next year before things cooled down, to mostly friendship. Then he started really teaching me, although he'd taught me a lot before. First, he taught me how to submit, which was sweet. And then he taught me how to dominate a man, which I loved." She held her breath, waiting for his reaction.

"So he's the one who taught you how to lead, like you did today?" Sean supposed he should be thankful to this unknown man.

"He taught me most of what I know. He introduced me to other doms and subs who could also teach me. I've been involved in the BDSM scene for eight years now." Her voice died away.

"Do you still see him?"

Beth looked him straight in the eyes. "He died on September 11th. His office was at the World Trade Center above where the plane hit. He called me to say good-bye, when he knew he wouldn't make it out."

"Oh, damn, I'm sorry, baby! I shouldn't have made you think of that. Please forgive me."

"It's okay, Sean. I've got to learn how to talk about him."

Still, she buried her face against him, her shoulders shaking slightly. Sean caressed her head, letting the silky strands fall through his fingers. He hated bringing grief into anyone else's life. Slowly the silence became more comfortable.

"Fantasies, Sean? Care to talk about fantasies?"

"Yes, if you want to." He tried to think of one that might interest her. "In the Army, I used to dream about being a soldier in a fantasy world, full of swords and dragons. Captured by Amazons." He went on more strongly when she smiled up at him. "And then tested to see if I was good enough to serve the Goddess's priestesses." His voice trailed away, as he tried to phrase another story to make it acceptable to a strong woman like her.

Beth broke the silence after a few minutes. "I've got fantasies, too, Sean. I think a lot about spending a weekend with a man who'll do anything and everything I want. I can imagine so many things to do with such a man."

Sean's arms tightened around her. "Oh, hell yes!" he breathed against her hair. His cock twitched slightly against her hip and subsided slowly. He cuddled her closer and remembered the fool who'd humiliated her. It would be a privilege to show her what cherishing really met.

"I've fantasized about being a Frenchwoman, interrogated by a Resistance leader for collaborating with the Germans. Questioned fiercely. And sensually." She sighed at the vision, then went on. Sean shivered at the thought of her, tied up but still spitting defiance.

"And sometimes I dream about being overpowered by a barbarian, just slamming into me. Forcing me . . . and yet always knowing that he wouldn't really harm me."

Her voice was very soft as she made the last confession. He kissed the top of her head.

"It'd be an honor to carry out a fantasy of yours, Beth. Maybe take some time and do it up right," Sean murmured.

Beth licked his chest in response. "Time? Perhaps a weekend's worth of fantasy, Sean?"

"Oh, yeah," he rumbled, his body warming to the possibility. A few days' adventures with Beth? "Yeah, I could spend a weekend with you easily."

He kissed her cheek, before finding his way to her mouth and a long, sweet kiss. Finally, he lifted his head. "Think about it, sweetheart," he suggested. "Two of us, alone for a couple of days, making some memories to take back to the real world? I'm game, if you are."

Beth caressed his cheek, her smile a quiet glow in the dark room. "I'll think about it, Sean."

She relaxed silently back into his arms, and he settled her more closely against him, relishing how easily she snuggled. The only sound was the clock in the other room, its regular beat marking each minute. He fell asleep, thinking about barbarians and Amazons, Beth's soft hair teasing his throat.

"Wake up, Sean. I've got to leave in a few minutes but we need to talk first."

Beth held a coffee mug under Sean's nose. His eyes opened and he was immediately alert, hearing the cuckoo whistle from the front room. How the hell had he slept through her rising? He'd always been a very light sleeper, even before he joined the Army. Then every detail of the previous night ran through his mind, and coalesced into the realization she was still here with him. A glance at the bedside clock told him how little time she had left, before that meeting with the FBI.

He relaxed and sat up, instinctively pulling the sheet up over his lap to cover his hard-on. Beth put the mug into his hand and sat down next to him. Fully dressed, dammit. The rain whispered against the windows, quieter than the beat of his heart.

"Yes, I'd like to take you up on your offer of a weekend. As you knew I would," she teased gently. A small grin tried to form on his mouth, but he kept his eyes fixed on her. "So, next weekend? From Friday night until Sunday night."

It wasn't really a question but Sean nodded slowly anyway. Mike would be spending that time with the Hemming relatives in Portland. Dudley had an invitation, too, earned by his shameless fondness for Mike's girlfriend.

"Do you have any limits on what you will or will not do, Sean?"

"No, ma'am. I'll do anything you want." Being with her was unpredictable but ecstatic. He knew a weekend with her was the best offer he'd ever had from a woman or would ever get, no matter what she intended.

"The excitement for you will be what I want."

"Oh yes, ma'am, that's exactly right." His cock throbbed at the thought of her pleasure.

"Physical limitations," Beth considered. "I broke my foot during an international dive meet, but it's healed now. Still, I don't like to stand for long in very high heels. Do you have any limits?"

Sean shook his head immediately. "No, ma'am. I've got no problems at all, since the doc said my back was healed. I still work out as I did in the Army so I'm up to whatever you want."

Beth's eyes sparkled at his eagerness. "I do yoga every day, Sean, plus swim and hike regularly. So don't worry about me." She paused for a moment before going on. "Don't agree so easily. You have to do some other things before Friday."

Sean's gaze flashed up, caught by her tone.

"I want you to write down at least one of your most submissive fantasies and one of your most dominant fantasies. You have to give me the complete story, everything that happens and how much you're turned on. Step by step."

Sean gulped at the thought. Write down every detail?

Beth chuckled wickedly. "Just leave the packet for me at my hotel before Thursday night. I've written the address down in the kitchen." She kissed his shoulder, then nipped him lightly. "And fair is fair. I'll do the same and send it to your office. Double-wrapped envelope, to protect your privacy."

Sean blinked at the idea of seeing her fantasies on paper, something outside any of his previous sexual experiences or imaginings.

"Now, you're a generous lover but we both need a little more reality than just saying whatever you want, plus writing a couple of fantasies. So, have you ever heard of a list of things that you can say yes, no, or maybe to? Things like oral sex, bondage, spanking, whatever."

Sean thought hard, considering some of the nonfiction books locked in his bedroom. "Are you talking about a negotiation checklist? I've seen something like that in several of my books and I've read them on-line, too."

"Excellent. Fill one out, including every activity that you can think of. Also be sure to write down all your needs and desires, what you must have and what you hope to occur, if you're going to be sexually satisfied this weekend. No guarantees of exactly what will happen, of course, since I choose what goes on."

"Okay," Sean answered slowly. She wanted him to write up that sort of thing? Just so she could be sure he'd be happy? But how could he talk about something he'd always kept so private?

"I also left a jazz club's name in the kitchen. Meet me there on Friday night, ten PM. You'll be back there forty-eight hours later, on Sunday night. Park your car where it'll be safe for the entire weekend. Bring only the clothes you stand up in and the scarf, which must be clean. Got that?"

"Yes, ma'am," he agreed promptly, fascinated by her operations plan.

"Preparations," she mused, before snapping out her remaining requirements. "No alcohol or other mind-altering drugs for at least twenty-four hours before Friday night. In addition, and this is not negotiable, no orgasms for any reason whatsoever, for twenty-four hours in advance."

Sean's jaw dropped open.

"Do you agree?" she demanded.

"Yes, ma'am." He shut his mouth.

Beth searched his eyes for a minute and then nodded. She went on briskly. "You'll also need a manicure, pedicure, and facial. The facial must occur no later than Thursday. No hair removal except a maintenance haircut."

Seán nodded, storing away the instructions. A facial? Why did she want him to do that? Men don't need fancy skin treatments, surely. Or maybe they do in her world. Full comprehension would come later, especially after his cock stopped doing the thinking. It stood at full attention right now, more than ready to charge into any battle she commanded.

"Repeat what you're supposed to do."

"Report on Friday night, at twenty-two hundred hours in a sober condition, to the address given. Bring the scarf provided, but no other clothing except the street clothes being worn. Complete a manicure, pedicure, and facial no later than Thursday, plus routine haircut."

"Very good." A small smile curved her mouth. "What are your clothes and shoe sizes?"

Sean rattled them off.

"Any questions?"

"No, ma'am," he replied promptly.

"Good. I'll see you Friday night then, Sean."

Beth leaned forward and kissed him on the mouth. Sean quickly put his coffee cup on the nightstand and kissed her back. They both gave themselves up to the embrace, until Beth finally stopped it and sat up. Sean watched her, enjoying the sight of her swollen mouth and heavy-lidded eyes.

"Now be sure to show my friend a good time," she whispered in his ear, and squeezed his cock hard and fast. Sean choked and jumped, only to chuckle reluctantly at her grin.

Sean leaned back with a sigh as the front door closed, sliding the sheet back to fondle himself. The events of the previous evening had astonished him, but plans for the coming weekend surprised him even more. He had considered a weekend rendezvous before, especially after Mike started going away on trips with his friends, but this was very different. He didn't have to plan anything, unlike the offers other ladies had hinted at. He would be free to enjoy himself and her.

He looked down at his cock, rearing red-hot and urgent against his belly. She'd welcomed it as her friend. He shook his head at how comfortable she was with his privates.

A good time? He remembered one of his most familiar fantasies.

The guardsmen were at their usual afternoon's sword practice, their intensity only slightly increased by knowledge that the queen was in residence and possibly watching them from the tower above. She was a hard mistress, who demanded the utmost from them, and they worked hard to satisfy her. Her implacable standards had been confirmed by battlefield victories, time and time again. Now men came from miles around to serve her, but only the best survived to serve in her personal guard.

Today was a different day from most. Every man on the terrace knew that the queen had tossed her latest page out of her quarters before dawn, complaining he was a boy who knew nothing of how to please a woman. No matter that the lad was four and twenty and a prince of the neighboring country.

The guardsmen had seen more than one man stagger from the queen's rooms. They also knew that, in this mood, she'd hunt the castle for a man to satiate her, and they all wanted to be that lucky fellow.

Sean fought hard against the other two guardsmen, practicing the strokes and counters needed to face a pair of attackers. A final flurry saw them on their knees, offering their swords in surrender. He waved them away and leaned on his sword, as he caught his breath. Sweat pooled under his padded leather vest and breeches. There was still time for one more bout before sundown.

"Captain!" shouted the chamberlain. Sean bowed in response and waited.

"The Queen commands your presence. Come with me." The chamberlain pivoted and strutted off, his rich silk robes swaying. Sean tossed his practice sword to his second-in-command and followed, his boot heels very loud in the sudden silence. The other guardsmen made way, their faces changing from sudden comprehension to envy.

The chamberlain led him down a long corridor inside the palace. Sean kept his face controlled, trying not to show the wild hope that built in him with every step. Two eunuchs sprang to open the heavy doors at the end. Sean's leather breeches were suddenly too tight as he passed through the doors into the famous rooms beyond. He had heard whispers of these quarters but never thought to see them.

"Well, Captain? Do you have any objections to what follows? You do realize what is about to occur." The chamberlain's shoe tapped impatiently. "Her Majesty demands nothing less than absolute willingness."

"No, sir. That is, yes, sir, I am entirely willing to serve my queen in this manner, as in any other." Sean's throat was tight but he got the words out. He tried not to watch the queen's chief eunuch, waiting just beyond the self-important chamberlain. Tonio had served her since she came to the throne as a girl and knew more of her secrets than anyone else still living.

"Quite right. Tonio, please forgive my haste in fetching the captain here. I'm afraid there wasn't time to wash him."

"Of course, sir. We'll make sure he is very thoroughly cleansed before he goes upstairs. We cannot let anything else upset our mistress."

Merciful goddess, he was truly going to see the queen. Would he be permitted to view her naked body?

"Get undressed, Captain, and put everything in that chest. We've a great deal to accomplish before sundown."

Sean stripped to the skin, stored his belongings as instructed, and followed the stout little eunuch into the next room. It was tiled in crisp patterns of black and white, highlighting the line of spigots along one wall and the ceiling above. An enormous tub held pride of place in the center. His sweaty, stained body felt clumsy and out of place in a washroom designed to show any speck of dirt. Two enormous, ebony-black eunuchs awaited, dressed only in black leather aprons.

"Scrub him well, boys," Tonio snapped, his embroidered silk sleeve falling back as he shook a finger in emphasis. "A triple dose, rather than the single dose we gave yesterday's pretty boy."

The eunuchs saw him through two cold showers and a hot bath, until he would have sworn that no dirt dared linger under their suspicious eyes. Then they made him crouch over a curved pole that held his ass in the air for all to see. They filled his backside three times with warm water from a greased hose, never allowing him to fight the intrusion before they drained it out. In fact, Tonio lectured him at great length on the importance of being clean throughout his body, given the queen's fondness for riding men's asses.

Sean considered Tonio's lecture rather superfluous, given the hardness of his cock during the process. Like every other man in the guardhouse, he'd heard stories of the queen's delight in utilizing every portion of a man's anatomy. Like most, he'd trained his ass in hopes of one day experiencing those likings, and his arousal reflected his anticipation.

They oiled his entire body and shaved every hair not present when he left his mother's womb. When he was as clean and smooth as a new sword, they showered and bathed him again. Finally, they covered him again with the same scented oil, until he gleamed like a marble statue. The oil was probably an aphrodisiac, given their care in handling it.

Tonio led him into the last room, where mirrors caught his reflection from every wall and soft carpets hid any sound. His eyes widened when he saw the golden jewelry Tonio brought out for him. The cock ring was a gilded leather strip, adorned with sparkling diamonds. There was a golden phallus to match, its jeweled handle cunningly carved to permit passage of a leather strap. He needed several minutes of slow, deep breaths before he could shelter the immense phallus inside his ass. Its pressure sent a surge of blood through his pelvis and beyond, making the cock ring bite harshly into him.

"Excellent," Tonio praised. "Smaller than her usual choice but still large enough to prepare you."

Sean shivered at the possibilities.

Then they harnessed him in gilded leather, straps running between his legs to hold the cock ring and phallus steady by anchoring them to the wide belt around his waist. More leather crossed his shoulders and chest, accenting his muscles and leaving his nipples available. They promptly responded by tightening and Tonio clucked approvingly. Jeweled collar, cuffs, armbands, and soft boots completed the set. A sprinkling of gold dust on his shoulders, chest, cock, and balls accentuated his straining excitement. The entire outfit was an eroticized version of a smith's attire when working the forge.

Tonio wrapped a crimson velvet cloak around him and took him upstairs through a secret passage. His cock felt huge against the restraining leather, as the velvet caressed it with every step. They emerged in the queen's bedroom and Sean looked around eagerly.

"He's ready," Tonio announced as his eyes swept the room.

"Not now, you dolt!" the chamberlain snapped at Sean. "There's no time to gawk. Get on the bed at once!"

Sean's mouth dried when he saw the huge bed. It was stoutly built of the kingdom's finest iron and had four pillars, one arising at each corner. A torch burned from each pillar, lighting the bed like a stage for one of the queen's favorite pageants. Crimson velvet spilled to the floor on all sides in a blazing sweep of color, almost distracting him from the golden straps falling from every side and pillar.

Tonio snatched the cloak off Sean, who climbed up on the bed then spread his arms and legs as directed. The chamberlain and Tonio quickly strapped his wrists, ankles, neck, and waist to the bed, leaving him virtually immobile. They departed silently and hastily, leaving him alone to face his mistress.

Sean looked up and saw a stranger in the gilded mirror cunningly mounted on the ceiling. Body opened wide for any touch, eyes and mouth heavy with passion, cock begging for use. He was caught in a gilded spider web, awaiting his queen.

She came in silently and he saw her first in the mirror. She wore a long, white robe that gave away few of her secrets. Her black hair spilled over her shoulders and she studied him for a long time from hooded eyes. Then her gaze lifted and she scorched him with a single glance of lust.

"Your Majesty," he croaked, all poise gone. She smiled at him and his blood ran cold. Or was it hot under so much hunger?

"Have you waited very long, Captain? You seem eager."

"Years," he growled. Her laughter rang through the room.

"Such a long time, Captain!" she mocked. "Still, I think we can find a use for such patience." She ran her hand down the closest pillar and up the strap to his wrist, checking the tension. He trembled but managed not to jerk against the bonds.

"Well placed; tight enough to hold you fast and enough slack that you can last for hours. I shall have to compliment Tonio."

Hours like this? He prayed for the strength to satisfy her.

She checked every strap that held him. Then she explored every outstretched limb until he was quivering.

"Please, Your Majesty," he began, too aroused and frustrated to maintain his usual silence. "I beg of you . . ."

"So you have a voice! Splendid. I was beginning to wonder if you could utter sounds that entice as much as your body."

Sean tried to make sense of her words. She wanted him to talk?

"Sing again for me, my stallion. Your voice belongs to me as much as your arousal." *Her hands slid up the inside of his thigh until they cupped his balls.*

"Please!" *he choked, jerking against the bonds.*

Her thumbs circled his balls, lifting and separating the fragile orbs in their pouch.

"Oh, please, fuck me, please . . ." *The words poured out of him.*

"Excellent," *she purred. She left his balls and he cursed loudly. Her hands came back to him in a sweep from his shoulders to his waist before returning to his chest. She played with his nipples until he bucked violently, promising anything if she'd only do something soon.*

She disappeared and he looked for her wildly. He couldn't find her in the darkness beyond the torches, and he prayed loudly to all the gods for her return. Then her hands covered his eyes and he thanked the same gods for her.

She kissed his mouth, sweet and long. Their tongues coupled together, as he silently promised her a greater coupling with his loins.

She took her hands away and he saw her climb onto the bed above him. She knelt over his head and smiled wickedly, when his body strained toward her.

"Curb yourself, my stallion. Show me what your tongue can do for my nether lips. A woman likes to be well pleasured before she rides a mount like you."

"Gladly!" he vowed. Thought fled when she lowered herself, and his face slid into her folds like a ship entering port. She rubbed herself restlessly over him, and his mouth and tongue went eagerly to work. He licked, sucked, and nipped at any part of her that came within reach. But he enjoyed it just as much when she used his features, especially his nose and chin, exactly as she pleased.

He exulted the first time she came, her thighs tightening around his head as the sweet ripples rocked her. He snarled in triumph, when she rose over him again and sought more attention from his greedy mouth.

Still, he lay shaking with his eyes shut when she finally rose from him. "Your Majesty, I beg of you," he pleaded.

His cock was only slightly less willing than it had been. His blood burned in his veins and his seed clamored in his loins, fighting to escape the leather bonds. He didn't know and didn't much care, whether it was because of her or the aphrodisiacs they'd soaked him in. He simply knew he needed her now, as he'd never needed another woman. And that he would need her just as much for hours yet to come, if not the rest of his life.

"Sing for me again, my stallion. Let me hear the sweet sounds of your hunger."

She squeezed his cock hard and he jerked, nearly breaking one of the straps that held his belt. "Please fuck me now, dammit!"

She leaned over him and pressed her hand down his belly from navel to his cock.

"I beg of you, fuck me! Oh merciful goddess, fuck, oh, fuck . . ."

She took him slowly, agonizingly slowly, into her womb. His voice died away at the feel of her hot channel around him and how the pressure of her body pushed him more firmly down on the great phallus.

"You are too quiet, my stallion. Sing for me again."

"Fuck, please fuck me, fuck, fuck, fuck . . ." He chanted his hunger, slowly at first then faster and faster as she rode him, matching the speed of his words to her tempo, the phallus pounding his backside emphasizing her every move. His voice grew louder and louder, when she squeezed him as she rode. Everything he was or had ever been centered on the woman above him.

"Sean! Come with me!"

He exploded into his orgasm at the sound of his name, his seed fountaining into her until it overflowed back down his shaft and over his groin. Her matching orgasm throbbed around him, and he screamed himself hoarse.

It seemed a long time before she stirred on his chest, although his body still shuddered. He watched the warm female body mantling him shift as she turned her head to look into his eyes. Chocolate brown eyes met blue eyes confidently.

"I think that I have finally found a splendid stallion, Captain. One good for more than a few hours. Days at least, but perhaps weeks or months. Even years if the goddess so grants. Do you agree, Captain?"

"Hell, yes, Your Majesty," he growled. Then his head fell back to the bed as she began to explore the pulse under his jaw. Somehow, he was still semi-hard above the cock ring.

Sean took a handful of sheet and began to wipe his chest dry.

Friday night seemed like a very long time away.

Five

Beth entered her suite with a sigh of relief at escaping the conference's pressures, if only for a few minutes. Refereeing a conversation about how much to discount a quarter-billion dollars worth of real estate loans had made her long for either chocolate or a really good stud.

Her phone's message light was flashing, of course. Still, the modern re-creation of Roaring Twenties' opulence embraced her warmly. Twentieth-century luxury and twenty-first century security, as Dave Hemmings always reminded everyone on the planning committee. They'd been lucky to reserve this hotel after September changed everyone's ideas of risk.

She picked up the phone and started checking her messages, stretching her back as she did so. The hotel staff notified her that a courier had delivered an envelope for her at noon; they'd deliver it to her room immediately, of course.

Beth drew the envelope closer to her as she deleted the voice message. A local doctor's office? A minute later, a doctor's note dropped into her hand, politely informing "whomever this may concern" of Sean Lindstrom's excellent health and cleanliness, in regards to all private social matters. She smiled fondly at Sean's thoroughness and checked again for any other correspondence. He had delayed recording his internal needs in a fantasy, while rushing to provide a doctor's blessing for his exterior.

She pulled out her PDA and scribbled a note to ask her doctor to send a similar seal of approval to Sean. She quickly changed some items on her checklist from "maybe" to "yes," given Sean's attention to detail and his partner's well-being. She'd look over the checklist again after tonight's banquet, when she finished writing her fantasies. A few more clicks locked her PDA against prying eyes.

She kicked off her conservative gray shoes, which went so well with her suit, and checked messages on her cell phone. High-heeled shoes, but not so tall as to appear that sex was the only thing on her mind. Beautifully tailored, charcoal gray pinstripes, but not so tight as to look as if getting back into Sean's bed was her first priority.

The first message, of course, was from Holly, better known as the Wicked Witch of D.C. to her subordinates' families. Five minutes later, and three replays, Beth decided Holly had at least one more thankless chore lined up for Beth's return to Washington. She hadn't said which project, so there was probably a mountain of useless tasks, all designed to make Holly shine before her superiors and frustrate

Beth. At least she'd agreed Beth could take some time off, before returning to the office after the conference.

The second message was from Mr. Griffith, asking Beth to call him at his home that evening. She scribbled down the number and dialed it immediately. "Mr. Griffith? . . . Yes, this is Beth Nakamura."

His deep voice boomed in her ear, evoking an image of the man himself. A decade on Wall Street and twenty years of government service had polished, but not erased, the All-American linebacker from Alabama. It was her first chance to talk to him alone, and Beth reveled in the opportunity to stretch her mind with currency movements, the game she knew best, and tracking down terrorists' money.

Finally, the conversation started winding down, and Beth double-checked the clock. She still had some time to write before changing her clothes.

"Are you interested in becoming more involved in this effort, Beth?"

Beth's heart skipped a beat but she kept her voice steady. "Very much so, sir. It's important work, both for the country and me personally. I gave the task force my contact information and I've already answered several additional currency smuggling questions for them."

"Hoped you'd feel that way. It always helps when there's something useful to do, after seeing your friends pass over."

Beth murmured an agreement, eager to start on something beyond grieving. Her body felt intensely alive, and yet her mind was crystal clear, rapidly sorting through that morning's meeting for clues to Griffith's purpose.

"Well, just keep doing what you can out there. Maybe I can shake something loose on this end for you."

"Glad to, sir." The phone went silent as Griffith hung up.

The Switch

Beth put her phone down very carefully and quietly. Then she pumped her fist in the air, hissing "Yes!" in triumph. Finally, she was getting the chance to do something. Another sliver of the cold that had gripped her since September 11th cracked and fell away. She paced the room for a few minutes, her mind whirling in excitement, then quickly stripped down to her silk underthings, and ran through a handful of yoga exercises. Relaxed and focused afterward, she sat down to write, eager to let loose some of the energy boiling up inside.

What was Sean doing now: writing perhaps? Or pleasuring himself? Hell, just thinking about that man pleasured her. Then she picked up the pen and began to write, letting her instincts drive the submissive fantasy she had promised him.

Beth waited for her knight on the steps to the great tower, beside but slightly behind his lady mother, with her eyes downcast as was proper. Excitement bubbled up inside her until she could hardly wait to be alone with him.

He rode in at the head of his guard, their horses' hooves stirring up the dust, and sent the assembled crowd into a fury of welcome. His great white warhorse sidled, but quickly steadied under his firm hand. A groom ran to its head and he swung down easily.

He came up the steps, sword swinging at his side and armor clanking, and she felt his eyes find her, while he stripped his gauntlets off. She gave him a small smile and waited modestly, while he greeted his mother. Then he came to her at last. She began to bow, but he caught her face in his hands, halting her public homage.

"Little dove," Sean murmured and kissed her on the mouth. Sweeter than honey, but not for nearly long enough. His hands gripped her

shoulders hard, just short of bruising her. She leaned closer, yearning for more. But he lifted his head finally and smiled down at her, a cruel satisfaction curling his hard mouth.

"I destroyed the scum who insulted you. The monks chant prayers for his soul now, and his brother vowed to build a chapel to Saint Elizabeth, your patron."

She smiled, too pleased to hide her savage delight. It was not Christian to hate an enemy or be so glad at his death. Still, she had not been a Christian until her knight married her, and old habits died hard. If her knight had been injured while dealing with that creature, she would have ruined the foul beast herself.

He kissed her again, hard and fast, heedless of their watchers. She yielded quickly, embarrassed at enticing him. She should have remembered he liked occasional ferocity in his lover.

"Soon, little dove," he promised. She blushed, at making her eagerness so apparent, and cast her eyes down again. He lifted her chin with a finger.

"Is my bath awaiting us?" he questioned softly.

She glanced up, startled, and met his eyes. Color flooded her cheeks again at the look there, and she nodded. "Everything is ready, my lord. You need only bring yourself."

"Very soon, little dove," he vowed in a deep rumble. "Let me deal with a few matters first and then I shall come to you."

Those few matters took longer than she would have liked, but less time than she expected. She changed into a silk robe from her own country and wrapped a silk obi around her waist. He loved seeing her with only a single layer of silk covering her skin, unlike the two or more layers of kimono that would have been appropriate in her homeland.

Finally, she heard his booted feet and spurs on the stairs to her solar, the glorious, sunny room his mother had given them. She shrugged when he brought his squire in. Much as she wanted him alone, she knew that she wasn't strong enough to disarm him herself.

She bowed a greeting and offered him a goblet of his favorite spiced wine. He sipped it, while the young man worked silently to remove his armor. Beth waited and helped as she could, her eyes hungry for every glimpse of him. He never spoke of his injuries, and she scanned the padded undergarments for any hints of damage. But everything was as it should be.

Beth took a deep whiff of his scent from the padded vest: leather and horse and the sharp tang of the oil used to keep his armor moving freely. It was so intensely masculine that it sent a bolt of lust through her body. She fought for breath and caught the smell of his sweat, mixed with a hint of his musk. Fresh musk, as if his body stirred now in anticipation.

She glanced over to his lap and saw his wool breeches tented by his cock's pressure. He cleared his throat in a harsh rasp and her eyes flew to his face. She blushed again, at the naked hunger there, but didn't look away.

"Thank you, lad. Get yourself gone; it'll be tomorrow before I have need of you again," he ordered, his eyes never leaving hers. She veiled her expression at the reminder of their audience and waited until the door closed behind his squire. She rather thought the young man would be quickly seeking a maid to ease his lust, judging by the evidence in his breeches.

Sean stood up and unlaced his breeches. She sighed at finally seeing his beloved cock again, rising in red-hot splendor against his beautiful body. Her hand itched to touch it but she could not, without his per-mission. He pushed the breeches off and dropped them casually on the floor before walking over to the tub. He settled into it, with barely a ripple, until the water rose past his waist, and sipped his wine again. Rose petals circled and lapped softly against him.

Beth allowed no hint of her disappointment to show. It was not for her to choose the time or place when they would couple again. She envied the innocent petals for touching him.

She quietly tidied up the solar, placing his clothes where the maids would find them. She stole glances at him from under her eyelashes and trembled when she saw one big, scarred hand idly circling a nipple. He knew her fondness for the taste of him there, how much she loved the strong muscles of his chest leading to those little nubs, how much she adored urging them into jewels that echoed the strength of his great cock rearing up below. She whimpered, the merest hint of sound, when his fingers plucked and released. Her body quivered like a tightly-drawn bowstring, above the wetness between her legs.

"What is your name, little dove?"

"My lord?" She spun to face him, bewildered at the question. Was this the start of a new game? "It is Elizabeth, as you honored me by remembering the blessed saint. Or Beth sometimes, as it suits you."

"No, little dove. What is the one that you carried first? The name they gave you in that far off country where you were born."

"Keiko, my lord." She slid her hands into her sleeves and gave him a deep bow. It evoked the customs of that distant land, with its snow-covered volcanoes standing fast against the raging ocean.

"Keiko," he drawled, pronouncing it correctly. He had learned how to say it years ago, in the Holy Land where he captured her from those he called Infidels. Her eyes closed at the sound of the harsh voice lingering over her name.

"Keiko," he said again, his voice deepening. "Did they teach you to remain so far from your master?"

"Of course not, my lord!" She came to his side quickly, hunger lancing her veins like wildfire.

"You still keep yourself at a distance, Keiko," Sean drawled, hot blue eyes measuring every one of the few inches between them before sweeping over her body. Answering heat crowded her body and her nipples lifted in salute to him. She hesitated, looking at the hot water surrounding him.

A big arm caught her and swept her over into the tub. She squeaked and caught his shoulders for balance. Then he slowly allowed her body to slide down over his, his knees coming up to support them both. Her silk robe floated up around them in the water. Her hands fluttered against him, uncertain whether to hold onto him or deal with the robe.

He laughed and her eyes flew to him. Then she giggled, a silvery sound like the sunbeams dancing overhead. He hugged her close and they laughed together.

"It is good to be home with my Keiko," he told her, his fingers stroking her high cheekbones. Her eyes slanted shut, almost purring at the caress. Surely he wouldn't deny himself much longer. "Do you have skin to pleasure me, underneath the cloth, Keiko?"

She giggled again at the question. Enough water had entered the silk that it was nearly transparent everywhere on her body. "I believe so, my lord. Should we look to see?"

"Indeed, little dove."

Her fingers fumbled a bit but she managed to remove the obi and toss it onto the bench nearby. She'd carefully placed the bench there earlier, just in case her knight wanted to play in his bath. Not everything recovered gracefully from a soaking.

Her kimono still clung to her chest and she paused for a moment, enjoying the flush of arousal on his cheeks. Then she slowly slid one panel aside, baring a single breast.

Sean growled and pulled her close, his head diving down to seize her. She groaned at the heat of his mouth, and her head fell back help-lessly. He suckled her strongly, and she arched against the intense pleas-ure, gasping and sobbing at the echoing tremors in her womb. His hand skillfully played her other breast, and she twisted on his lap, frantic for completion. "Sean, please! Oh, master, I beg of you, finish me! Please, please . . ."

His free hand swept down her back and over her ass where she nes-tled against his hip. Beth rubbed against it eagerly, willing him to finally give her his cock. She could feel it like an iron bar direct from the fur-nace, cradled between her buttocks.

"Please fuck me," she groaned and lifted her hips to try to capture him. He gave her his hand instead, tracing her folds like a map he wished to learn. She wiggled against him, her fingers digging into his shoulder. He took one breast into his hot, wet mouth, sucking her deep as if to take her entire body into him. Her hips tensed again and again, thrusting against his all too skillful fingers.

"Onegaishimasu," she implored him.

His eyes blazed in triumph at the heathen words, spoken in the lan-guage she'd avoided since becoming a Christian. He rubbed her clit roughly, in the stroke she loved, and she fell into orgasm.

While she was still spasming, he lifted her half out of the water and brought her down onto his cock. She cried out in surprise and satisfac-tion, at the fullness she finally felt deep within. Another orgasm claimed her, while his cock sank smoothly into her.

He lifted her and dropped her again, using his arms' great strength to pound himself into her. She gasped and sobbed, as her orgasm's pulses refused to fade and instead built stronger into her spine. She couldn't breathe, when he circled his hips a little, just enough to send tremors through another portion of her channel. Water splashed in every direction and rose petals clung to their skin well above the tub's walls.

He grunted, the sound barely recognizable as words. "Fuck, fuck, fuck . . ."

She tightened her muscles around him, desperate to claim everything possible from his impending climax. He swelled further inside her and pulsed, then went over the edge, howling like a lion as his body poured everything it could into her.

She shrieked again as his hot flood propelled her into a final climax, this one thundering through her body in rhythm with his cock's ecstatic throb.

Beth collapsed against him, her lungs heaving as she struggled for breath. At least she'd had the wit to place towels where they could catch the worst of the tub's overflow. She'd tell him about the coming child later, when she could think more clearly.

Beth laid down the pen carefully, savoring the last ripples of orgasm floating through her body. She'd definitely have to wash up before dressing for dinner. She also needed to erase the last sentence. She had never shared that fantasy with a man and a casual affair was no place to start.

Beth was calmer when she saw her room again, late that night. The banquet had gone more smoothly than she'd expected, given that most of the real negotiations occurred then, under cover of fine wine and seemingly idle questions. She'd had to concentrate fiercely, an effort that left her both drained and exhilarated. They really were on track, an astonishing feat considering the number of major banks represented and the amount of money to be repaid.

She blinked at the flashing red light; it was too late for a call from the East Coast. The phone yielded a message from her brother Jason.

"Beth? Jason here. Hey, Dad gets home from Japan on Monday morning. The whole family's meeting him and Mom at the airport. Since you're out here on the Left Coast anyway, care to join us? Call me back when you get in, no matter when. Hugs."

Jason's message was entirely too casual. The hair prickled on the nape of Beth's neck. What did he really want?

A family gathering? She hadn't been home to Berkeley since last Christmas. Then, all the grandchildren's antics had shielded her from too much conversation with anyone. Her parents hadn't pressed her to talk. Of course, Father had never needed to coax Beth to speak to him. And Mother? Well, Mother always had so much to say, she rarely waited for Beth to speak.

Beth stirred, driven to honesty with herself. She was the youngest of four children, and her three brothers had a different relationship with their mother. They frequently spoke fiercely but respectfully with her, never hesitating to argue with her or each other.

She was quieter, preferring to think and act, rather than cast a cloud of words over a topic. She and her father had always understood each other, with only a few words exchanged. But Mother and her brothers needed to blather a great deal.

Beth was very comfortable with Jason, the brother closest to her in age, and at ease with her other brothers. But she had always flinched away from Mother's dramatics until finally she removed herself from her mother's orbit. In kindergarten, they had gossiped together, at least as much as a mother and daughter could. The level of communication had faded to a warm courtesy by the time Beth graduated from Harvard.

The Switch

Last Christmas, Beth had still cringed at any reminder of her mother and grandmother's argument in Tokyo. Any sound of her mother's brisk voice, honed to a commanding bark by years as an obstetrical surgeon, had sent Beth flashing back to that dreadful day. Instinctively, Beth had retreated into her shell and shut the recurring pain out, by not talking to her mother unless absolutely necessary.

Of course, everyone else had probably noticed the relationship was even worse than before. So Jason's message must mean that he wanted to patch things up, a typically clumsy attempt at subtlety.

Need stirred in her harshly, to be part of a family again, no matter how imperfect. Sudden death had claimed Dennis and too many others. She needed to be part of a circle again, safe and protected by past memories and future hopes. She fought to think logically.

Jason was her favorite brother. His new wife was carrying their first child, due to be born after New Year's. It would be good to see Father again, hopefully as friends. Maybe it wouldn't be too bad to spend a little time around Mother.

Beth picked up the phone and dialed Jason's number from memory. Holly had given her a week's leave, to be taken after the conference. She could spend as much of that as she chose, in Berkeley.

Wednesday's negotiations were rougher than Tuesday's. Twitching with the need for a diversion, Beth used an unscheduled break to send her fantasies and checklist to Sean. A quick phone call sent her doctor's note to him as well. The best news at day's end was the message that her friend Jennifer had checked into one of the upstairs suites.

Beth brightened and called immediately. Five minutes later, the two women were hugging and laughing. They looked almost like sisters: the same height, the same slanted brown eyes in an oval face, very similar black hair. But Jenn came from a mixture of Vietnamese and African-American, rather than Beth's combination of Japanese and Scottish.

Finally, Jenn stepped back. "Come on now, turn around and let me see you. Gotta make sure none of your measurements have changed since we last met."

Beth obediently stepped away and posed, pivoting a quarter turn every time Jenn flapped her hand.

"Girlfriend, I swear you just keep looking better and better. You're going to put all us old married women to shame. You been working out more?"

"Same old, same old as I did at Harvard. You remember." Beth shrugged. Jenn raised a skeptical eyebrow and went to the wet bar for a drink.

"Okay, I'm teaching yoga twice a week now," Beth yielded a more detailed explanation. "I still volunteer Saturdays at the hospice, giving massages. No big deal."

"And I'll bet you're still working out with weights, just to maintain your back for the next time you set a whip dancing." Jenn fixed a stern stare on Beth, who spread her hands wide.

"So what if I do? It's good for my health, too."

"Yeah, right! And there's the daily yoga practice, and the three times a week swimming, and the hiking. You train for dominance as hard as you used to train for those international diving championships." Jenn snorted, handing Beth a glass of iced tea. "Relax. It's my own herbal tea, brewed just for you."

"Thanks." Beth sniffed appreciatively and drank, letting the golden liquid flow down her throat. "How're Jarred and the boys?"

"How much time we got?"

"Two hours before the really big dinner."

"So we've got two hours to talk, while you look over what I've found."

"I'll need to dress for that dinner," Beth pointed out.

"Got that covered."

Beth raised an eyebrow.

"Beth, you told me that there's a man in your life you wanted to look good for."

Beth choked on her tea. "That's not what I said!"

"Near enough as makes no difference," Jenn corrected her sternly. "What does he look like?"

Beth opened her mouth and closed it again. They'd been best friends since their first day at Harvard School of Business. If Jenn had reached that conclusion . . .

Beth took another swallow of tea. Still, the affair with Sean was only for a week, making it excellent practice for a different relationship. Hopefully something permanent, back in Washington. But she could talk to Jenn about that option later. Jenn knew everyone and loved playing matchmaker.

"Good girl," Jenn approved her relaxation. "Now, tell me about this stud."

Beth frowned at Jenn but complied. Once Jenn had made up her mind, you might as well try to topple the Sphinx. "Remember the British TV show you liked, the one about Spain during Napoleon's time? And the British officer who'd been a sergeant?"

"In that tight green uniform? Beth, that boy was fine!" Jenn whistled appreciatively. "Are you telling me you've found yourself a hot one like that?"

"Oh, yes," Beth nodded, taking a deep swallow of tea and trying to avoid saying more.

"Well, if you think a few nights with a man like that is going to be enough, you've got more willpower than I do!" Jenn laughed, but sobered when Beth said nothing further.

"Beth, honey, just let me pass on some advice my grandmother gave me. There are just not that many good men out there. If you find one, then you'd better snatch him up quick before someone else does."

"He's interesting, Jenn, not perfect."

"Girlfriend, if you're waiting for perfect . . ." The words trailed off and she gave Beth a quick hug. "That's enough from me. You know I'll be there for you, no matter what happens. Now then, I've got a lot of clothes for you to try on while we catch up. There's a couple of numbers that would do for a fancy dinner."

"You do like being a stylist." Beth fell upon the new topic with enthusiasm, glad to be free of discussing her intentions toward Sean. Odd feeling, since she'd told always told Jenn everything about her boyfriends.

"Oh, yeah, best thing I could have done with that fancy Harvard degree. Lots of fun to be had, shopping with other folks' money. Now get out of those clothes, down to your thong, and let's start looking at what I brought."

"Okay, but you have to tell me about Jarred and the boys now." Beth kicked off her shoes and started peeling off layers.

"Jarred's doing fine. Likes being a prosecutor, which surprised me. I thought he loved the police so much he'd hate changing."

"Well, he had to do desk work after the shooting, didn't he? So isn't prosecution better than pushing paper as a cop?"

"I wasn't sure he'd think so. Maybe he'd love the police so much that he had to hang around, even if it was behind a desk. But he's happy as can be now. His leg has almost returned to normal, but he plans to stay where he is, even talking about becoming a judge one day."

"A judge? Well, maybe that's not surprising. Remember how he lectured us when we first met?" Beth shimmied into a black dress. Matte silk jersey soothed her as it clung to every line of her body.

"Do I! Lord, you'd have thought the man only believed in the missionary position, the way he carried on." Jenn rolled her eyes and tossed a pair of black sandals to Beth. Beth raised an eyebrow at the stiletto heels but obediently sat down to put them on.

"Not surprising, since he had just arrested us at a fetish club," Beth pointed out. She looked at the one shoe she'd managed to don and shook her head at Jenn. Her friend tossed another pair over without missing a beat.

"Then the man turns out to be one of the best submissive males you're ever going to find," Jenn laughed, watching the second pair go on.

"Closeted, of course." Beth stood up and checked her balance in the high heels. They were taller than anything she'd worn recently, but better than the stilettos that Jenn favored. She'd still be shorter than Sean.

"Of course! A tiger to the world but a pussycat in the bedroom, until I say he can roar. He said to tell you thanks for the Vegas trip. Yup, he'll join me out there on Friday, after I'm done setting up for your big weekend," she answered Beth's unspoken question. She studied Beth's appearance critically, waving her hand until Beth finished turning. "You like?"

"You know it's perfect for dining out. What next?"

"Your goddess outfit for the big scene in Vegas. Brought you several choices for that one."

"Okay." Beth pulled the dress over her head and took off the shoes at Jenn's nod. "How're the boys?"

"Growing like weeds, when they're not driving their daddy and me crazy. Your godson's the worst."

"Really?" Beth's voice was muffled by black lace, as she twisted the dress into place.

"Oh, yes. Did the oatmeal in the VCR business, three times already this week."

"I thought you only had two VCRs." Beth tugged the zipper into place and turned to face the mirror. Black lace, high necked and cap sleeves before it swept down her body to her knees, ending in just enough of a flared skirt to permit walking. Sheer black illusion silk backed it from her breasts down in a nod to propriety. She looked like a cross between an Oriental goddess and a Venetian courtesan. "Nice dress but not for that scene. I'll keep it though."

Jenn came up behind her to look. "Had to replace the VCR in the family room twice in the same week." She frowned at Beth's reflection. "Of course, you'll keep it; don't I always know what suits you?"

"That's just because we've gone shopping together so often. I taught you everything you know."

"Yeah, right! But thanks for taking me on those overseas trips. I'd never have learned so much or made all those connections without you."

"Don't mention it; you've done as much for me." The two women hugged before Jenn pushed a handful of red silk at Beth.

"I've never tried this one on. My figure's just not as firm as yours. But if you're in half as good shape as you look, this should make your man's eyes pop out of his head."

"He's not my man."

"Still missing Dennis?" Jenn asked softly. Their eyes met in the mirror.

"Yes, but I'm not in love with Dennis. I'm not sure I ever was!"

Jenn waited, letting Beth talk it out.

"I loved him but I don't think I was ever *in love* with him for more than five minutes, every year or so. Every time I started to fall, I'd get reminded that he was bisexual and he liked having more than one lover in his life. He loved them, and cared for them all, but I couldn't fit in that circle." She flinched, remembering how deep the gulf had been between their needs, no matter how much they cared for each other. "He used to tease me about being too monogamous for my own best interests."

"That's not true!"

"He was right, Jenn. I want a lot and I want it all in the same man. If I was willing to have more than one guy in my life, I'd have an easier time." Beth fastened the gold button holding up one shoulder.

"What about Bob then, that great sub you've been seeing off and on? You know he'd lay down and die for you."

"Bob's a great guy but he's always submissive. Okay, so he's only submissive in the bedroom, but still! And he's not really much into sensation." Beth shook the finely pleated silk into position. "I want more."

"Like what?" Jenn's tone was carefully neutral.

"I've had a lot of time to think, Jenn, so I can answer that now. I want a sensation slut, somebody who'll enjoy stretching his body's limits for sensory play."

"Of course you want heavy sensation; anyone who's seen you play would know that."

"And someone who is good at role playing," Beth continued, nodding agreement with Jenn's comment. "Rougher stuff, like soldier and Amazon, not schoolboy and nursemaid."

"Fair enough. That all?"

"You know it isn't. I want a switch, somebody who can make me want to submit to him, too."

"You're asking a lot, girlfriend. Heaven knows there's hordes of submissive men and it was still hard to find my Jarred." Jenn's tone softened. "But you're asking for a man who can take you, just as fiercely as you take him. And you want marriage, too, not just frequent play dates."

"I know. One in a million, especially after you add in all the standard relationship stuff like honorable, kind, good with children, funny . . ."

Jenn frowned and tweaked folds into place, achieving the appearance of an Old World goddess for Beth. "There's a fellow out there for you, I know it."

"I hope so and I plan to start hunting as soon as I get back to Washington in two weeks. Will you help me?"

"Of course!" Jenn hugged her. It was a few minutes before they looked at the red dress.

"Oh, yes. In fact, hell yes!" Beth struck poses reminiscent of classical Greece.

"You'll really get this guy's attention," Jenn said softly and handed her a pair of shoes.

Beth glanced at her friend in the mirror and decided to change the subject. "Dennis made me his heir, did you know?"

"I'd wondered about that. Here, try on this leather number, just for me."

"He left a lot to charity, plus quite a few items to various people. But the bulk came to me." Beth paused significantly. "Including his dungeon and almost all of its contents."

The effect was everything she could have wished.

"Everything? Good God, girlfriend, he had more toys than anyone else in New York! Even if he usually did stick to a handful of favorites."

"Lots and lots of toys," Beth agreed, trying to zip up the strapless dress.

"Whips and floggers and paddles and canes." Jenn tried to make a list. "Nipple clamps and butt plugs and dildos and cock rings and . . ."

"Keep going. You haven't even mentioned the equipment like the rack or the slings."

"The collection of whips alone, honey! He had some beauties, stuff that's not made anymore. That set of Jay Marston whips, that beautiful, ruby red Norman whip . . ."

"He did leave one of the Jay Marston whips to Steve." Beth stretched the leather smooth so she could finish zipping. "And that fabulous Mad Dog blacksnake went to Toby."

"Dennis sure knew his whips." Jenn sighed, stepping up to help fasten the dress. "Lovely things to go thud or sting against a man's behind, get him all hot and bothered and ready for love . . ."

"Lovely things," Beth agreed, tucking the zipper pull into place. She considered herself in the mirror.

Jenn knelt so Beth could step into the matching shoes. "He showed you how to use them all, didn't he?"

"Yes, he taught me very carefully, until he was sure that I understood them and would handle them well. We always met at least twice a year, just to play with flogging." The leather dress hugged Beth like a lover, covering everything but hiding nothing. She looked both powerful and irresistible at once.

She lifted her arm experimentally, moving into position to bring a flogger down on a lover. The dress stayed with her, still concealing her nipples. "Perfect but not for this weekend."

"Maybe you should push him a bit, flash him some leather. Got a nice deerskin flogger with me you could borrow. It's soft enough for a rookie."

"No, I don't think so. He's ex-Army, a Ranger."

"Wowee, girlfriend, sounds like you got a tiger lined up for you!"

"You've heard of the Rangers?"

"Jarred's brother, the Green Beret? He was a Ranger first. Won't talk about what he does now, but he'll tell you stuff about those Rangers."

"Really?" Beth felt a bit hemmed in by testimonials for Sean.

"You might want to think about leather," Jenn encouraged.

"No, he hasn't demanded it, and I want to do something that he doesn't expect. I figure he'd know how to deal with pain and humiliation, thanks to the Army. So I'm going in a different direction."

Jenn laughed. "You could have a point about that Army training. Do you really think it'll work?"

Beth smiled, the cream-licking smirk of a well-fed cat.

"You should have seen him blush when I admired his flannel shirt."

"Wicked. You are just totally wicked."

The two women looked at each other, trying to keep their faces straight. Then laughter burst through and they fell together, shrieking.

Beth returned to the hotel just before midnight, thankful the dinner was finally over. She wore one of Jenn's finds, a gold brocade dress reminiscent of Audrey Hepburn. It had a high waist, deep neckline and little cap sleeves above a straight skirt that hugged her curves. A slit in the back made it possible to walk and a matching stole kept it suitable for winter wear.

Dave Hemmings waved at her from his post by the fireplace and she smiled at him. Then her eyes widened, as she recognized his companion. Sean was here in the hotel.

She came over quickly, her eyes alight with welcome. "Hello, Dave. Sean."

"Hello, Beth," Sean drawled, his hand coming up to stroke her arm briefly. She shivered at the touch. "I was just dropping off that packet for you, when I ran into Dave here."

"Really?" Only a more interminable dinner than usual, or an overwhelming attraction to this man, could account for such an inane reply.

"Good to see you made it back safe, Beth," Dave broke in. "I see Tyler is back now and I'd better go talk to him. Night."

"Good night," Sean and Beth echoed. They stayed still after Dave left, until more people came back into the lobby, shaking Beth into awareness of where they were.

"Would you like coffee or something, Sean? It's a nasty wind out there."

"Sure, that'd be good." He fell into place beside her.

She hesitated when she saw the number of people in the hotel bar. "Would you like to come up to my room? It's a suite and I can make coffee there."

"Whatever you want."

Beth turned to face him, considering the implications of her offer and his response. A day and a half since she'd last seen him, but her body was as hungry as if it had been months. "Actually, I've been thinking about something strong and hot and masculine. I can make coffee if you'd prefer, but I'd rather start with the other."

His blue eyes gleamed. "As I said, ma'am. Whatever you want will be fine with me."

He was silent in the elevator, avoiding contact with the other passengers by moving to the back. Beth sidled closer, until she was leaning against him. His arm came around her waist, low enough that the others wouldn't see. She purred very quietly at his heat surrounding her, rising from the strength of his body and his breath in her hair.

He nuzzled her neck while she tried to open the door to her room. She thought about mentioning the security cameras overhead, then decided to focus on the door. She wanted to be filled by that big cock of his, as they hadn't done before. And she really preferred Sean naked in the bed for that, rather than a quickie in the hall.

Finally the door opened and they stumbled inside, only to kiss passionately. "Oh, yes," she murmured, dropping her purse so she could lock her arms around his neck. "Oh, yes, Sean."

She abandoned herself to the kiss, enjoying the lips and tongue that worked her mouth so thoroughly. His hands stroked her ass, in perfect rhythm with his mouth. She wrapped a leg around him, opening herself.

He shuddered at the increased intimacy and squeezed her. She moaned encouragement and pressed even closer.

"Beth, honey. Beth."

She opened her eyes at the hoarse croak and tried to think. "I've got condoms in the nightstand," she offered.

"It's not that." His hand rubbed the underside of her lifted leg, then let it down slowly as she pulled herself together.

"If you're not saying no . . . And I don't think you are, given this," she wriggled her hips against him, enjoying the hard ridge behind his zipper. "Then what is it?"

"I want to make love to you. But I'd like to take my time at it. Get to know you and what you like."

Beth cocked her head, caught by his tone of voice. "Have you ever done that before? Explored a woman the way you want to?"

Color rose, bright and hot in his cheeks, but his eyes stayed locked with hers. "No, Beth, I haven't."

She could be his first, the one who allowed him to evoke the pleasures of a woman's body. It was the sexiest thing anyone had ever said to her. Her body coalesced into a surge of longing. "Yes," she croaked, then tried again. "Yes, of course, you can, honey. Where do you want me?"

He considered the options, surveying the dining table, the sofa, and the bedroom beyond. She thought wryly that his night vision must be excellent, since the only light came from a small lamp in the distant bathroom. Any light from the outside was blocked by the heavy curtains, closed by the night-time maid service.

"On the bed will be good. I'll turn the lights on, too, if I may."

"Certainly." She dropped her stole on the table and took up position by the bed. He turned on the lamps and the overhead light, leaving the sitting room in darkness. Anyone on the bed would be fully exposed, yet isolated from the world beyond.

Beth had seen games staged at great expense for SM parties that left her far less excited than his simple arrangements. Moisture gathered under the gold brocade gown, leaving her both powerful and yielding at the same time.

He shrugged out of his heavy jacket, her eyes hungrily following every movement. He emptied his pockets carefully, setting the contents on the dresser.

He caught her watching him in the mirror and shrugged. "I don't want to lose anything and mess up your bed."

"That's all right." Why did such little gestures echo through her blood to her bones until she couldn't talk?

"Do you want to take your clothes off?"

"Sean." His name was a hoarse cough. She tried again. "This time is for you. Tell me what you want and I'll do it."

He stared at her, startled. Understanding lit his eyes, followed by a bright blaze of delight. The thread of a successful scene, of his dominance and her submission, snapped into place between them. When he spoke, it wasn't what she expected. "Are those diamonds in your ears?"

"Yes, and around my wrists."

"I've always wanted a woman wearing nothing but diamonds."

Hot color swept over her breasts. They tightened and ached against the lace bra. His lips curved to show a hint of white teeth. She trembled slightly but waited.

"Take the dress off."

She slid first one shoulder, then the other free, moving as slowly as she could. She arched her back to reach the zipper and heard him hiss. His face was impassive when she looked at him, but she still exulted in her effect on him. Finally, the dress fell to the floor, and she stepped free of it.

"The bra next."

The black lace of her pushup bra lent itself to even more delay. But, eventually, it too reached the floor.

"Thong now."

She shimmied out of it, timing her moves to the harsh sounds of his breathing. Now she wore only stockings and heels, plus the diamonds.

"Sit down on the bed."

He hooked a chair and sat down before her. "Lean back, honey. On your elbows so you can watch, too. And give me your foot."

She lifted one foot to his knee. He studied the handmade Italian shoe closely then took it off, moving at a speed that made her efforts seem like a Grand Prix race. He rubbed her foot and she purred, eyes slitting as she enjoyed his touch. She also confirmed that he had a foot fetish.

When he had reduced that foot and its attached limb to something resembling a warm puddle, he spoke again. "Other foot, honey."

She opened one eye to look at him when he stopped. Both of her legs were relaxed now and totally sensitized to his touch. They lolled open, allowing him clear sight of her folds and the dew covering them. She was hot and wet and bothered, more than willing, and ready for his next move.

"Now, watch me take off the stockings."

She obeyed, enjoying how his thumb found the sensitive point behind her knee. She liked feeling his rough hand there, without the silk to hide even the slightest contact. Her eyes tried to close, so she could focus more on his fingers, but she managed to keep them open. He had ordered her to do so, after all.

He stroked the inside of her thighs, unerringly returning to the same spots that he'd mapped once before with his mouth. "Lie down, honey, and show me your breasts."

She blinked at him, then obeyed reluctantly. Her hands slowly circled her breasts, then followed the delicate veins to her aureoles. She cupped and lifted her breasts out to him, rubbing her thumbs over her nipples and trying desperately to entice him closer.

He sat quite still and watched her.

Beth bit her lip and started again. This time, she half-closed her eyes and acted simply to please herself. The movements came more easily and her breasts responded eagerly, swelling and rising into her touch. She moaned and closed her eyes, arching her back to let her nipples push against her palms. She twisted and tugged one fat pink bud, gasping at the hot surge that flooded her body.

Suddenly Sean leaned forward and covered her breasts with his big hands, stopping her movements. Her eyes flashed open to stare at him.

"Take your hands away," he growled. She obeyed, running her tongue over her lower lip in anticipation.

He stayed still, simply encasing her with the rough warmth of his touch. Beth took a deep breath and tried to make her chest move against those tormenting hands. His mouth twitched but he didn't shift a muscle. She rocked her torso back and forth, trying to get the sensations she craved.

"Freeze," he snapped and she did so, startled by his tone of voice.

"Please, Sean," she begged, feeling the wetness gliding down her thighs. "Please!"

"Are you hungry, pretty lady?" he asked, his voice deepening. "Do you want me to handle your tits?"

"Yes!"

"Maybe," he drawled. Beth whimpered but waited for him.

"Pretty lady," he said again. Then he finally handled her. He traced veins and muscles, mapped nerves until she wriggled, desperate for release.

"Please, Sean! Please, I need more!" she gasped as he finally took her into his mouth. Her head fell back and she clutched him closer, until his body half-covered hers.

He grunted something but never broke contact with his mouth. Something in her bones noted that he was a fast learner, as his early awkwardness soon fell to a focused certainty. Maybe he was just a good observer.

"Sean!" she yelped at the first nip. He stopped immediately. "Damn you, Sean, more!" She yanked at his head and he chuckled, only to start using lips and tongue and teeth to drive her wild. She writhed under him, pleading for more. He gave it to her with his hand, shoving three fingers inside. The sudden fullness, combined with the forceful thrust, vaulted her into climax.

She started to come down from the peak, gasping for breath. But his hand never stopped. He kept thrusting into her, riding her without mercy, until she begged again for more. Then he moved to the other breast and repeated the process, until she shattered again. "*Iku!*" she gasped, reverting to Japanese.

She sucked in a deep breath when his hand covered her navel. His head lifted and he watched intently as she shivered under his light touch. "Here, too?"

"Oh, yes, Sean. It's . . . not . . . called . . . my center—eee—for nothing." She tried to breathe, as her body fluttered and tightened under his explorations. His finger circled, then probed into her navel.

What would happen when his mouth found her navel? Two more orgasms, the second when his big fingers found a new spot deep inside her. Stars burst behind her eyes and she arched off the bed, when he repeated his attack on her G-spot.

She would have stretched like a well-fed cat, if she'd had any remaining energy, when he finally lifted his head. He didn't touch her and she tried to open her eyes. "Sean?"

"Roll over now."

Beth's eyes widened at the command in his voice. She wouldn't be able to guide him with her hands then, only respond to whatever he chose to do. She would have to totally yield and he knew it. But he demanded her consent first.

Hunger that she'd thought more than satisfied rushed back into her.

Six

Sean looked down at the woman sprawled below him, her chest heaving and her brown eyes wide as she considered his order. Then she gathered herself together with a visible effort and rolled onto her stomach, exposing her beautiful backside to him. She turned her head toward him and hummed at the look on his face.

Damn, but she was the most gorgeous creature he'd ever seen. Strong shoulders and back, narrow waist leading to the flared hips, long legs above those elegant feet. His mouth went dry for the rich globes of her buttocks. Diamonds gleamed at her ears and wrists, against the ivory silk of her skin.

His dangerous lady, laying herself down for his pleasure.

He started at her neck, leaning over to touch her as delicately as possible. She shivered at the contact, telling him wordlessly that she liked this. He grew bolder, exploring points his readings had mentioned and following the clues of her body's response. She moaned and writhed, her eyes closing in primal anticipation.

He nipped her shoulder, remembering she had enjoyed roughness elsewhere. She jerked and sighed, relapsing into shudders, as he eased the mark with his tongue.

"You are so damn good at this," she gasped, her voice barely recognizable. He growled his success and nipped her again. Soon she was trembling under him, as much as she ever had for caresses to her breasts.

He worked his way down her back and over her sweet ass. He hesitated there: would she permit this lust of his? If she refused, he'd honor that, of course. Still, he slipped his hand between her legs and encouraged her craving, without permitting release.

When she was almost incoherent under him, he spread her buttocks to see what was hidden in the cleft. Hell, her asshole was small and sweetly puckered. What would it be like to ride it? Better not try that any time soon.

Still, he snatched a dam from the pile he'd dropped on the nightstand and covered her asshole. Then he kissed down from her spine, waiting for any objection.

"Sean! How did you know I like this?" Her hips bucked back at him and twitched restlessly under his hands' pressure. He snarled in triumph and went to work in earnest, using his fingertip to tantalize her clit, while his mouth thoroughly enjoyed all the sensitive points around her asshole.

She came under his encouragement, sobbing something in Japanese as her pelvis tried to grind itself onto his hand.

He rolled her onto her back afterward, shivering slightly at how boneless she felt. She yawned and stretched languidly, then looked up at him. Her chocolate brown eyes blinked like a Siamese cat waking up on a sunny day, pleased with life now but willing to find more fun.

He had taken Beth to this level of sexual fulfillment, but she was still ready to go further. This time was for him, she'd said, but she looked as if she'd enjoy it just as much as he did.

Even Mrs. Wolcott had never hunted for this much excitement.

"What next, darling?"

He smiled tightly at the lust shining in her voice. His cock couldn't wait for many more options. Maybe she was ready now to take him inside her. At least she wasn't afraid of his cock's size. "I want to come inside you, honey."

Her eyes leaped. To his shock, she gushed wet against his hand where it rested between her legs. "You better believe that's what I want," she agreed hoarsely.

"We'll go slow, honey."

She chuckled and shook her head at him. "You don't have to, on my account. You've made me more than ready for that big cock of yours."

"Damn, honey," he breathed. His fingers circled and pressed against her. She wriggled against him, opening herself up to him, as he stroked and played. Two fingers, then three glided into her. She moaned happily, as her hips rocked against his hand.

Four fingers fit into her, stretching her wide. Beth groaned, blatantly enjoying being fucked by his hand.

Sean stood up and stripped with more urgency than art. Beth watched him, her fingers twitching on her thighs.

"Play with yourself, honey. Keep that fire burning for me, while I get dressed for you."

He cursed under his breath when she obeyed. Years of watching videos couldn't compare to seeing a woman fondle herself at his request. He managed to grab a condom from the new stash in his wallet, and fumbled it over his cock. He needed to practice looking good at this, but she didn't seem to mind. Finally, he knelt between her legs. He leaned forward to kiss her, so she wouldn't be too frightened.

She touched his shoulder before he came close. "Do you want to watch, Sean?"

He blinked.

"See yourself enter me? Fucking me?"

"Hell, yes," he rumbled, breath catching in his throat.

She spread her legs wide. He didn't need a second invitation, before he took his cock in his hand and guided it carefully into her. She took him sweetly, her breathing deepening as her body flexed around him. "*Kakko ii,*" she muttered approvingly.

Sean choked, recognizing the compliment from Mike's collection of anime, then kept pushing in.

"More, darling," she sighed, watching their joining as avidly as he did.

"Fuck," he growled at the sight. "Oh, fuck," he growled again as still more of him disappeared into her. Then only the last inch was left in sight.

"Give me everything, darling," she said clearly.

He stared at her, startled.

"All of you, Sean. I can take you." She shifted under him, lifting her hips and wriggling slightly. His cock disappeared into her, until their hair kissed, and she smiled like the Mona Lisa. She stretched, settling herself more firmly around him. Her eyes half-closed, and her muscles squeezed his cock in welcome.

He made a sound his primate ancestors would have understood. She was the first woman to take the full length of his cock.

"Fuck me hard, darling."

He snarled again and his control broke. His body lunged into action, hammering her. She would be bruised in the morning, maybe unable to walk, yet he couldn't stop. He needed this woman now, needed this ride, with an intensity he'd never felt before.

And Beth responded to his urgency, throwing her hips up at him and grabbing his cock deep inside her. He grunted and growled, snarling sounds without words or tone, as lust boiled up within him. He rubbed her clit hard, snarling at her to hurry.

He drove their bodies up to the pinnacle as if it was a fortress to be stormed, then hurled himself into his climax like a victory. His entire body shook with the effects, leaving him half-blind and shuddering in the aftermath.

He managed a single half-coherent thought: had she finished? Then he felt her orgasm's echoes dying away through her body. He barely had time to dispose of the condom before he fell asleep, still on top of her.

Sean yawned as he watched the coffeepot brewing the caffeine he needed. Beth's phone had rung far too early in the morning for his body. Maybe he was just getting old; he'd lasted longer without sleep during Ranger School. Still, he sure as hell hadn't this kind of fun then.

They'd said quick good-byes after she ended the call. Now he only had to wait until tomorrow night to see her again. And get the ridiculous facial, manicure, and pedicure over with before then. She'd reminded him of that step, although he hadn't forgotten and would have carried out that requirement. Orders were orders, no matter how silly they felt.

Sean stopped at Crissy's spa that morning to see if she could help him. They'd met in the Army, where she'd been a helicopter crew chief, and he'd helped her start up this business. Now, she ran one of the most successful day spas in the Pacific Northwest, at this remodeled bungalow overlooking Lake Washington.

"Good to see you, Sean! What can I do for you?"

"I, ah, wanted to get some work done and hoped you could tell me where to go."

"Sure. If I've got an answer, I'll give it. Shoot."

"I need to get a facial, manicure, and pedicure and I have to do it today." He looked straight at her, daring her to make a comment about his request.

Crissy blinked briefly then became all business. He remembered her briskness from the Gulf, where she'd been a five-foot bundle of energy that terrified most of the men she met. "You'll do that here, Sean. Think I'll let you go anyplace else?"

He was grateful she didn't fuss over him but worried about being an imposition. "I don't want to bother you or take away from your regular customers . . ."

"Don't worry about that. We've had a couple of cancellations so there're slots to spare."

"Okay." He took a deep breath now that he was committed to this craziness.

"How much time do you have?"

"I've got the day open. Some meetings cancelled for me, too. So whenever you can fit me in."

"Then you'll spend the whole day here and we'll get you out in time for dinner. Relax; we provide lunch."

"What? How the hell can a guy spend the entire day here?" The listening receptionist gave a strangled laugh, which she quickly turned into a cough.

"The gentleman's day package has hydrotherapy—including an underwater massage—a full body polish, sports massage, cleansing facial, pedicure and manicure, scalp treatment, and a haircut. We can substitute a deep tissue massage for the sports massage, if you'd prefer. My hair stylist is ex-Army, so he knows high and tight, like your cut. All on the house, of course."

"Crissy!"

"We made the deal when I first started out, remember? All those hours that you personally spent remodeling this place, I'd repay you in kind. So you're just letting me work off that debt. Any objections?"

"Uh, no, that'll be fine." He recognized the futility of arguing with her. And the more time he spent here, the happier she'd be squaring the old debt. "The gentleman's day package it is."

An hour later, Sean knew that he'd been suckered in by the starting hydrotherapy. He'd had a lot of massages before, while recovering from that back injury, including hydrotherapy. He'd even felt right stripping down to the buff, given the impersonal atmosphere here that reminded him of the hospital's physical therapists. Seawater had been a different touch, but the basics had still felt familiar. He'd simply relaxed into the big tank, enjoying the jets of water pounding the muscle tension out of him.

It had left him so mellow, in fact, that he hadn't blinked when Joe produced the strange goop to rub on him. But he'd smelled enough to wonder what was going on. He sniffed suspiciously. What was this stuff? It felt like honey but couldn't be.

"What are you using for the massage?" Was this the *body polish* step Crissy had mentioned? What the hell was a body polish? He tried to keep his voice casual.

"Dead Sea salts, sir, mixed with aromatherapy oils," Joe answered quietly, his slender fingers kneading the stuff into Sean's shoulders.

"Sea salt?" Didn't Mike use that for cooking?

"A very special kind of sea salt, sir, imported from Israel just for this purpose. Folks have been swearing by this for thousands of years." He continued to work it into Sean's back.

Sean tried to figure out what was really going on. Joe was rubbing salt, mixed with smelly oils, into his entire body. What was the purpose? What kind of man spent money for smooth skin?

"Please relax, sir," Joe asked, sounding as if he made this request every day.

Sean swore under his breath. Craziness, but he couldn't walk out now. He began the breathing exercises he'd learned in the hospital, until he was loose enough that Joe could go back to work.

Joe finally finished and left the room, while the stuff worked on Sean's skin. Sean closed his eyes and tried to sleep. Maybe this would be over sooner if he didn't think about what was going on, thought about his favorite fantasy instead.

Sean let himself quietly into the big old house, glad to finally be home. He'd been away on deployment for weeks, unable to see his lady. Thank-

fully, nobody'd gotten seriously injured, and now he could finally relax. He dropped his duffel by the stairs and went hunting.

He spotted her from the kitchen windows, sunbathing facedown in the backyard, her ivory skin gleaming in the dappled sunlight. She liked to soak up rays, covered only by her favorite rich lotion when it was this hot, protected from prying eyes by the old oak tree. Her back rose and fell slowly as she slept, her raven hair pulled away from her neck and one arm brushing the grass.

He was on her in seconds, his big body covering hers on the lounger and his hips snug against her sweet ass. He rubbed himself against her, tasting the outer approach to her hot crack, which he'd soon invade.

"Damn, honey, you are so hot," he growled against her hair.

"Sean! You'll ruin your uniform! Get off me!" She bucked under him, trying to twist away from him.

He captured her hands and yanked them over her head, cuffing them in one of his big paws and leaving the other free to find her breast. "You're mine, mine for fucking, mine for anything I damn well please."

Her skin was slick and greasy, making it difficult to hold her. He felt the oil soaking through his sleeve where it pinned her arm.

"Sean, the cleaners won't be able to save your uniform!" She writhed harder, fighting to get free. His uniform's buttons rippled across her back as she slid away from him, nearly getting out from under him.

He snarled something anatomically impossible about the cleaners and dropped his entire body onto hers, controlling her by his weight. She still squirmed and argued, but he smelled a new muskiness in her scent.

"Give it up, darling! Time for a good ride." He nipped her neck, in the age-old greeting of a male to his mate, then explored the resulting marks with long, slow swipes of his tongue. She gasped and bucked again. But this time, her hips lingered against his, then wriggled.

"You're my bitch and don't you forget it," he growled. He nipped her again, drawing a drop of blood for the first time. She moaned and her hips circled under his.

He nipped and licked her again and again, unerringly returning to her most sensitive points. He kept her hands trapped while he rubbed himself over every inch of her back, setting his mark on her with the passage of cloth and metal over her soft skin.

"Please, you . . . you always know what I want," she sighed, her voice fading away.

"You're so sexy. Feel my cock fucking your back." He settled his bulging fly against the crack in her ass and rocked against her, letting the steady movements separate her and nestle him between her cheeks.

"Damn, my hand needs some of your action, too." He slipped a finger between them and rubbed her clit, rumbling in triumph at the answering surge of cream from her core. She quivered, driven beyond words, as her body answered him with its own rhythm.

"Yeah, wiggle for me," he murmured as his free hand quickly opened his uniform, so his cock could find her.

"Feel how damn big you've made me." He slipped into her hot center slowly, luxuriating in her little whimpers and moans, when he insisted on keeping to his pace, not her urgency. "So damn tight when your hot pussy grabs me. And those big beautiful tits of yours . . ."

He fed his hand under her and pulled her even closer to his chest, lifting her just a little so he could squeeze and roll her nipples. She sobbed in frustration, her inner muscles trying to pull him deeper.

"That's right, honey, that's right. Now, honey, now!" He settled fully into her at last and she climaxed, keening her release, when his zipper's base first rubbed her.

He continued moving, keeping her hot and eager so she couldn't ease too far down, savoring the waves rolling through her.

"Oh, yeah, honey, you're so fine," he praised her, relishing the pulses gripping his cock and destroying any brains he had left. "Hot damn, honey! Gotta . . . gotta pump you." He adjusted his angle slightly, needing more from her. She gasped and shifted in response, tilting her hips, and he groaned.

"Hell, yes!" His cock settled into that perfect fit, where her hot depths enveloped every inch of him, and he drilled her pleasure point at every stroke.

"Oh, goddamn fucking yes!" He grunted as he rode her hard, his mare to be enjoyed as he chose. Need built deep in him and he fought it, straining to make this final climb last as long as possible. She orgasmed again, her shock waves ripping through him as if they truly were one body.

His head snapped back, and he shouted as he pumped her full of his cream, then collapsed onto her back.

After a long, sweaty moment, her head turned and Beth's chocolate-brown eyes smiled up at him.

"Missed you, darling," she sighed.

He'd sacrifice a uniform to this, any day.

Sean opened his eyes slowly and stared at the wall. It was the first time he'd seen the fantasy woman's eyes or heard her voice. Maybe pleasing Beth was reason enough to pull a stunt like this.

He faced Crissy warily at day's end, acutely conscious of how different his body felt under his usual work clothes. His skin was so soft now, he felt his jeans' crotch seam rubbing his ass. He felt good, too, energized somehow, probably just from all the attention that folks had given him. Still, there were cheaper ways to get the same buzz.

"You look good, Sean. But are you pleased?" she asked shrewdly.

He shrugged. "I'm okay."

Crissy's mouth twitched. "Doing it for a lady? Don't worry; she'll like the effect. And you may change your mind about how much you enjoy it."

Sean didn't quite shrug, not wanting to disagree with Crissy.

"Besides, what's the harm in doing something just to feel good? If you've got the money, then go for it. A lot of my male clients come for themselves, not because their girlfriends tell them to."

Sean raised an eyebrow in disbelief. "Whatever floats their boat. But I don't think you'll ever catch me in a place like this again, just to suit myself. Thanks for everything though. I'm sure Beth will be pleased."

"Good luck, Sean." Crissy hugged him suddenly. Surprised, he put his arms around her and returned the embrace. "Just be sure to have a good time with Beth."

"Thanks."

Later that afternoon, Sean and Mike worked quietly to load the furniture into Sean's old pickup, while Dudley ran alongside, barking whenever they left him in the house. To his embarrassment, Sean found himself using gloves to protect his hands. It seemed a pity to ruin all the effort that Crissy's staff had put into making them look good.

They finished the job by tying down a heavy tarp over the top, to keep the furniture and mattress dry until it could be delivered on Friday. Sean tossed a rope over the top to Mike, who caught it easily. "Good catch!"

"No problem, Dad. Just the two Lindstrom men working together, right?"

"Of course, right," Sean laughed at the twist on their old saying. He'd first charged Mike with being a Lindstrom man at the age of five, asking him to look after his mother. They'd promised to always stand together, after he'd gotten Mike out of juvenile hall, and sworn they'd always be united, despite all odds, at the beginning of the custody fight. They'd kept their word, sticking together through thick and thin ever since.

"Bill Owens said his uncle's selling his old Range Rover. It's pretty worn out, so he's not asking much," Mike said, as he helped put the last rope on.

"I thought Bill was going to buy it."

"No, it's in such bad shape that he can't afford the parts. But you might be interested."

"Yeah, I'll think about it. Maybe give him a call next week." He'd wanted a Range Rover ever since he'd seen the SAS driving them during the Gulf War but their cost had always put them into the category of look but don't touch. Maybe Bill's uncle knew somebody who could rebuild it for him.

"Do you want leftover spaghetti for dinner, Dad?"

"How about Chinese instead? That might be fun and easier than cooking." They usually ate out on Sean's nights for dinner duty. But Thursday wasn't his night to provide a meal.

"Sure, I can go for that." Thankfully, Mike didn't ask why the unusual restaurant meal. Or why Sean was wearing gloves for this chore. He just whistled as he tossed a stuffed dinosaur for Dudley to fetch.

Sean wore gloves again when he helped Dave Hemmings rearrange Tracy's bedroom. First, they cleaned out the existing furniture, an odd mixture of bunk beds inherited from her brother and thrift store bargains that Deirdre had found.

"Sometimes the woman is a genius," Dave grunted, as they carried a remarkably ugly chest of drawers into the garage. "And sometimes, she just hasn't got a clue. Maybe I'll be lucky and somebody will buy this at her next garage sale."

Sean laughed, understanding the sentiment. His house was also furnished with bargains that he'd picked up over the years. He'd bought and fixed up what he could, and sold what he couldn't, until all his furniture was at least comfortable. What would Beth think of the result? He turned from the thought that she'd probably never see his home.

"Do you want to put the bed in the same place as the old one?" he asked, returning to Dave's concerns.

"Yeah, that's the only place it'll fit."

Finally, the men stood back and considered the results. The white and gold furniture glowed in the sunlight. New curtains hung at the windows, perfectly matching the bed's lace and pink ruffles. It looked like an enchanted grotto for a fairy princess, a young, pretty fairy princess.

"I hope Tracy likes this," Sean said, thinking of the effervescent little girl.

"She'll love it," Dave said positively. "She drew a picture of what she wanted and this is it."

"Great."

"You want some coffee or maybe a beer?"

"Coffee would be good."

They were both cradling mugs, watching yet another storm blow in from Puget Sound, when Dave spoke again. "Beth Nakamura is quite a lady. I've enjoyed working with her but it's been a challenge. Not much, if anything, gets by her."

Sean took a careful sip of coffee. "Yes, I've been very impressed by her."

"Yeah." Dave drank some more from his mug. "She's apparently a rising star at Treasury. Very few opportunities for somebody like her in Seattle."

"I can imagine. I'm sure she'll go a long way."

Sean's eyes met Dave's. Better set this straight now, if only to pour reality over his dreams. "We're both adults, just having a little fun together. I know it'll end when she goes back to Washington. I'm okay with that."

"Fine. Just thought I'd mention what I've observed." Dave didn't sound entirely convinced but he didn't press.

The silence turned companionable in the kitchen's warmth, while the sky darkened outside.

At least Sean could look forward to forty-eight hours with her this weekend, revel in the freedom to try anything he wanted. No worries anymore about losing Mike this time, should a court hear how he liked to be enjoyed by women.

Seven

Beth sat in the limousine and watched the clock slowly count the time. She had seen Sean walk in five minutes ago, but she would wait until exactly ten PM before following. A Mozart violin concerto played softly in the background, chosen by the chauffeur. Jason Birch was a slender, young, African-American male, who moved with the unconscious grace of a dancer or martial arts veteran, and made easy small talk about the current opera season. Once upon a time, Jenn would have found his black eyes and café au lait skin irresistible.

She considered the implications of this weekend as she sipped her champagne. Jenn had made her opinion very clear, that this man meant more than a brief fling. Terror touched her again at the chance her best friend might be right. Surely she couldn't fall for a chance-met stranger from a bookstore.

What other opinion did she care about?

What would her father think of her spending a weekend with Sean, a man she knew little about except for their sexual chemistry? But Father would probably understand. He always beamed quietly when his wife told the story of their first meeting, how she'd asked the tall Japanese student for a dance at the Chemistry department mixer in London. He still blushed when his wife concluded the story by saying that she'd spent that night with him and every night since.

Well, perhaps love at first sight had worked for her parents but she'd never sought it. Formal introductions followed by a gradual building of trust and intimacy were more reliable. But a weekend flurry would be a delightful way to unwind and renew herself, before seeking a more permanent arrangement.

She took a deep drink of the champagne, enjoying the bubbles fizzing against her palate. It would be fun to watch Sean's face, while she played oral games with that stunning cock of his. An ice cube perhaps, or menthol to slow his response, maybe a fizzy drink. And, oh, the delight of slowly removing honey from him.

Time had passed too slowly since Wednesday's rendezvous with Sean. Even the intense financial negotiations, as the conference ended, hadn't distracted her from thinking about him. She'd thrown herself into shopping, as she sought the toys needed for the coming weekend. Jenn was a great help with clothing, but Beth preferred to select her own playthings, especially since Sean's checklist had contained some surprises. He'd wanted some heavy sensation, which definitely changed her choice of toys.

She'd always enjoyed planning the games to be played with responsive partners. It was amazing how well she meshed with Sean, how easily they moved with each other to create sensual magic, how intense the satisfaction was. After all, they were still almost strangers, even if they did dance together well.

He'd written some fantasies, which definitely interested her. Hopefully, hers would have the same effect on him, although she did wonder about his reaction to her dominance fantasy. It was so very different from the others, especially her World War II submissive fantasy.

She'd first written the space opera years ago, pulling elements from both Japan and Scotland, even her grandfather's naval stories. But it hadn't taken flight until she rewrote it with Sean as the legendary pirate Lindstrom. All that golden magnificence hers to play with and hold for a lifetime . . .

"Golden Dragon and her consorts have entered the system, Captain. Two minutes until they have weapons lock."

Alarms went off and were ignored, as much expected as the pirates' arrival. Captain Elizabeth Nakamura nodded, watching the holotank intently. The convoy commander bleated orders and the fat, slow supply ships began to scatter. Keeping her disguise as a refrigerator ship, Tsushima turned also. Out here in the Vladivostok Sector, where refugees from long-dead countries mixed uneasily with outlaws, rapacious miners, and pirates, everyone traveled with company.

"Careful, Chief," Elizabeth ordered her helmsman, glancing down at him. "Try not to look so military."

"Aye, skipper." An unusually flat tone of voice, not his usual crisp arrogance.

She gave him more details, knowing he'd forgive her under these circumstances. "Yaw a bit, Chief. Delay making the turn. Overcorrect when you do turn. Remember you're just a frightened civilian, facing the notorious Captain Lindstrom."

He chuckled a bit, as she'd hoped, and obeyed. Tsushima *wavered, then settled on a course, almost straight at the* Golden Dragon. *The pirate ships increased speed, arrogantly certain of their superiority over fifty cargo ships and only two visible destroyers. Elizabeth could almost see* Golden Dragon's *captain, his big body suited in combat armor, his famous blue eyes hidden by his helmet as he snapped final orders to his men. His dossier and picture stood in her night cabin, supposedly so she could understand him better. In actuality, they only triggered dreams of him, in which all that magnificent golden masculinity was put to its best use—in her bed.*

"One minute until Golden Dragon *has weapons lock, sir. Can we open our gun ports now, sir?" Number One's voice was icily controlled, just the way the Imperial Academy demanded, from the station next to Elizabeth.*

"Negative, Number One." *The hardest part of commanding a ship like this was waiting while the enemy approached, until she could open her ship's gun ports and blast the pirates with everything she had. Underneath its guise of a refrigerator ship carrying expensive climate-controlled goods such as medicines,* Tsushima *was actually an Imperial pocket cruiser; strong enough to wipe out a squadron of Romanov battleships, carrying enough Imperial Marines to empty a squadron of pirate ships. But her military weapons and armor slowed her in comparison to* Golden Dragon, *a modified passenger liner, although she was faster than most naval ships. So Elizabeth had to sit still and wait for the right moment, like one of her currency-trading ancestors, holding her breath until the pirate came too close to escape. Which was a very small distance indeed.*

"Thirty seconds, sir."

"Engage main targeting computer," Elizabeth responded. The Office of Naval Intelligence swore Golden Dragon couldn't possibly have sensors as good as an Imperial dreadnought. She saw no reason to take chances and preferred to wait until the last possible minute to trigger the computer and its telltale signature. Just as she'd done in fleet maneuvers last year when she won the trophy, and a week's leave for her crew in Kaneohe. Sean Lindstrom was certainly as dangerous an opponent as those senior captains had been. She had no doubt he'd claim her as his personal prize, if he caught her, and put her to use in his famous harem.

Like hell.

"Twenty seconds, sir. Engine room reports power plant at 125 percent."

"Full speed ahead, Chief." Tsushima shot forward, leaving the convoy behind and hopefully out of the worst danger during the coming fight. The two destroyers, previously darting distractedly around, closed in behind her, ready to follow her into battle.

"Targets acquired, sir. Ten seconds until Golden Dragon has weapons lock."

Elizabeth calmly closed and locked her helmet's face plate, as did everyone else on the bridge, preparing for the chance of decompression. She had too much respect for Lindstrom's Golden Dragon not to believe it could seriously damage her Tsushima.

Suit pressurized and ready, *whispered her internal computer.*

"Golden Dragon has recognized us, sir, and is turning to engage."

Good; he'd realized he couldn't escape into hyperspace before Tsushima could damage him.

"*Execute Togo Turn. Open gun ports,*" Elizabeth snapped. "*Fire all batteries.*"

The pocket cruiser deliberately, briefly, exposed herself to the pirate's fire. A single volley sang into her, thanks to Lindstrom's excellent gunners. Tsushima *shivered slightly, then finished her turn—and saw every pirate ship vulnerable to her great guns. Her first barrage blasted across space and into the* Golden Dragon *as it charged forward. The other pirate ships maneuvered clumsily, caught off-balance by the unexpected Imperial attack. A few wild shots left trails of light in the holotank, but no sullen glows marking injured merchant ships.*

More lights flashed green on Number One's weapons panel, as Tsushima *rearmed.*

"*Fire all batteries.*"

"Golden Dragon *has fired her port batteries, sir.*"

Too little, too late, Lindstrom. *Elizabeth smiled, well aware her expression was savage.*

Golden Dragon's *barrage howled into* Tsushima *just after the Imperial Marines' first wave departed. Sirens wailed, damage reports flooded in.* Tsushima *fired again. But her first salvo had won the battle by knocking out half of* Golden Dragon's *batteries. Everything after that, however bloody, was just mopping up, even launching the boarding parties and picking up the few survivors from the dying pirate ships.* Tsushima *and Elizabeth's gambler's nerves had wiped out* Golden Dragon *and his pirate fleet as a threat to shipping.*

Her only question now was, would she capture Lindstrom alive?

Elizabeth strode into the holding pen, still seething over the politicians' idiocy. Deliver her prisoners—hers, dammit!—to the local authorities.

And then an invitation from those fat dirt grubbers to the hanging, where they'd make an example of Lindstrom and his men. Bloody assholes, she was the one who'd had the brains and nerve to trick Lindstrom. Her people had paid in blood for those pirates and she'd not deny them the customary pleasures of victory. Thankfully, the Admiralty had seen the light and allowed her three days to follow naval traditions before handing over the captives.

She reached the center of the raised dais and spun to face the assembled prisoners, Number One at her elbow. Her escort of armed Imperial Marines flanked her, anonymous behind their helmets with weapons armed and ready. She was wearing her personal armor, a hideously expensive suit that stopped most energy weapons cold—and looked remarkably like black leather from Old Earth. The room was ringed by her people, those whose performance had earned them the right to be rewarded first.

The pirates faced her warily. All men and all unmarried; Lindstrom's flagship was crewed solely by bachelors, supposedly to encourage recklessness. Six hours had seen the worst of Tsushima's damage—and theirs—healed. Nicks, bruises, a few scrapes and scratches showed but nothing serious. Certainly no broken bones. Tsushima's medics would have been insulted if captives' wounds were treated worse than her crew's.

Standing in the center at the front was the famous Sean Lindstrom, his blue eyes blazing defiance and more magnificent than the vids had shown. He'd led her Marines an exciting dance, before a dozen of them managed to capture him alive, thank the gods. Like the rest, he was manacled and cuffed. The grid in the holding pen's floor was active now, trapping the men's feet until they could only move a few inches and pulling the cuffs toward the floor.

He was completely naked, of course; no one wore a stitch under battle armor, which was itself long gone. Tall, broad-shouldered, a warrior's strong face. Mental and physical augmentation well-hidden, as befitted a refugee Norse aristocrat. Those heavy muscles and that thick, long cock made her mouth water . . .

Elizabeth's throat tightened. A tingle of awareness tightened her breasts and slipped down her spine. He was too magnificent to die. That big, strong back was made to dance under her whip, as she worked him into a sexual ecstasy. She wanted him in her quarters now, his beautiful mouth focused solely on her pleasure and his superb cock at her service. Damn those politicians and their hunger for unearned glory. Losing somebody like him to the gallows was sheer foolish greed.

She gritted her teeth and reminded herself of duty, of the honor gained by following orders. Then she realized the Admiralty had not forbidden certain, rather old-fashioned, fruits of victory. A wisp of a plan stole into her mind.

Elizabeth deliberately surveyed the pirates before she spoke. "Welcome to the Tsushima, men. You are now my captives."

"Greetings, Captain Nakamura," Lindstrom returned. Good; he'd recognized her. "So kind of you to join us." His blue eyes ranged insultingly over her body, lingering on her breasts and hips before traveling down her legs, finishing at her high boots. His cock began to swell, until it lay fat and rich with blood against his thigh. He snarled softly but his cock stayed full.

Perfect; he wanted to be angry but couldn't help lusting after her. Her plan strengthened.

"Bills of attainder have been sworn out against you and all of your men, Lindstrom," Elizabeth answered, watching him closely. "The Commonwealth of New Hebrides has claimed the right to try you."

Manacles clanked with incautious movement. Someone choked. One of her crew growled but quickly stopped.

Lindstrom's mouth tightened. Then he wiped his expression clean, turning it to one of bored attention. "Still angry about losing that brewery we stole, are they? Fools."

She was inordinately proud of his stoic response to his death sentence. Time to put her plan into action. "However, until then, Tsushima's crew will celebrate naval custom and enjoy the pleasures of your bodies as we see fit."

The pirates barely stirred at this undoubtedly expected announcement. Some deliberately yawned in a pretense of disinterest. But Lindstrom's eyes flashed with hunger and something more. Hope, perhaps? Surely not of escape; he knew the cuffs around his wrists would explode if he went more than a kilometer away from Tsushima.

Elizabeth raised her voice slightly and stared at her crew, silently demanding that they follow her. Work with me on this, good people. We've come too far together to see jackals filch our lawful prey. *"In honor of the five hundredth anniversary of the Imperial Navy, we shall also observe the custom of* uchtaigh. *If any one of Tsushima's crew chooses to claim a prisoner, then they shall be deemed to have fostered him forever. The prisoner will be freed into his* tuismitheoir's *custody for the rest of his life. All previous crimes shall be forgotten for so long as he wears his* tuismitheoir's *golden lariat."*

Shock rolled through the crowd. Uchtaigh was an ancient custom, often practiced by pirate crews who wished to build up their numbers with trustworthy men. In it, the altrama—or fosterling—*became the legal shadow of the* tuismitheoir *and could only be legally punished by filing suit against their* tuismitheoir. *However, naval crews rarely followed* uchtaigh, *because* altramas *could only be entered on the ship's* roster as lifetime sexual slaves to their tuismitheoir. *It was an intense commitment on both sides, since only fools would give the golden lariat to an unwilling recipient.*

One of Tsushima's *crew chuckled, then another and another, as their eyes lit in anticipation. The pirates glanced at each other. Lindstrom's eyes widened briefly before he sneered. "And risk the chance of death at our* tuismitheoir's *hands, for some fancied slight? Little pleasure in that."*

Elizabeth stared down her nose at him. It was true that few courts would interfere between a tuismitheoir *and* altrama, *even if the altrama was killed. However, there were other dangers. "And a* tuismitheoir *will be executed, should his* altrama *return to evildoing."*

Lindstrom stiffened at the reminder, his beautiful mouth tightening.

"But a wise altrama *will temper his behavior," Elizabeth went on as required by naval custom, "since he can stand surety for anyone he personally knows, with his* tuismitheoir's *permission."*

Hope flashed across Lindstrom's face at that. It meant anyone not lassoed could still be fostered, if claimed by an altrama *as a personal friend. If just one of* Golden Dragon's *crew was claimed for* uchtaigh, *then all of them might be saved from the gallows. A risky move, but Lindstrom was too good a leader not to welcome any chance to keep his men alive.*

"And now, my people, it is time to begin choosing our diversions. Your comps will announce your number. If you wish to celebrate without a captive, simply inform your comp. Then relieve one of your mates still standing watch so they can enjoy themselves."

A third of her crew left the room quietly. The captives stiffened and waited. Lindstrom was watching her intently, his eyes lingering on her face, her mouth. His cock was still swollen but not fully erect. Good; she preferred a male who enjoyed danger but was not driven by it.

"As captain of Tsushima, it is my right to choose first." She pointed at Lindstrom. His eyes flared with pure lust and his cock abruptly jolted into full arousal. Oh my darling pirate, your hunger for me will become your downfall—and your salvation.

The door to her private quarters opened with a soft hiss, just as Elizabeth, Lindstrom, and her Imperial Marine escort reached it. Its mirror-bright surface perfectly reflected the marines' weapons and Lindstrom's physical beauty. Elizabeth shut it as soon as possible; she hated having this man's nakedness displayed to any passing crew member. Odd, that need for privacy with him; she'd never been noticeably possessive about a concubine before.

Thankfully, Tsushima's designers hadn't skimped on the captain's quarters when they camouflaged a pocket cruiser as a merchant ship. The harem suite had three separate bedchambers, plus a large central chamber that connected to her night cabin. It was lavishly furnished with antiques from her grandmother's collection, resulting in a space that would have made a fabled Arabian sheik jealous.

She had no concubines on this voyage, whether contracted for money or friendship, so the only sound here was the fountain's melodic gurgle—and the soft whoosh of the great black web dropping from the ceiling. A regularly-spaced black mesh, like an old-fashioned rope net, stretching from floor to ceiling and half of the room's width. Arachne's Web ready as requested, *her comp reported.*

No visible reaction from Lindstrom to the web, only a swift all-encompassing glance around the room. He probably thought it was one of the crowd control meshes used in large drunk tanks, good for slowing down unenhanced humans but tissue paper to someone with his augmentations. Poor darling, you'll be so surprised when you learn what it can really do.

Elizabeth smiled and heat shimmered deep inside her, purring at the possibilities. She flexed her fingers slightly, feeling the emptiness of Arachne's Web. "Place him next to it and release the leash."

The Marines silently obeyed her and stepped back quickly, well beyond the web's reach. Lindstrom shuddered as the web swayed closer but didn't run. It brushed his shoulders and ass, clung, settled. His warmth echoed in the palms of her hands, repeated by her comp's link with Arachne's Web.

Black tendrils grew from its vertices, wrapped around his arms, legs, torso. It stretched, pulled his arms and legs wide. He grunted, cursed Elizabeth's ancestry—and adapted. The web adjusted its thickness and dimensions until it was once again a regular black mesh. With a beautiful golden man held firmly in its grasp, every inch available to satisfy Elizabeth's whims. She stretched her arms and hands, absorbing the feedback from Arachne's Web into her own nervous system.

"Remove the cuffs and manacles, then leave," she ordered absently, as she considered where to begin. Lindstrom was slightly taller than she was, even with her boots on, and definitely broader. She began to stroll around him, studying every beautiful inch, while Arachne's Web rearranged itself to allow her free passage. Heat deepened in her core, tightened her breasts. The door closed, cutting off the sound of the Marines' retreating footsteps.

"You are, of course, planning to divert my attention and break free of the web," Elizabeth commented. His ass was superb—high, firm, muscled. Built with the strength and stamina for a long night of fuck-

ing. She set her hand on his hip, splaying her fingers over one buttock, contrasting and accepting what her fingers told her and what the web described through her comp. She glanced up at his face.

His expression was a mix of fury, frustration, and arousal. Then he wiped it clean and smiled at her, far too agreeably. "Would you believe me if I said no?" he teased.

"Would you, in my shoes?"

"No," he acknowledged, those blue eyes almost incandescent as he watched her. She strolled her fingertips down the curve of his buttock and he shuddered. His cock began to swell again.

Cream warmed between her legs in anticipation. But best to get certain formalities out of the way first. "So try to escape."

"There's no need to play such tricks on me."

She shrugged. "It's an honest offer," she corrected him. "You won't believe you have to come to an agreement with me until you understand you can't escape."

"I could kill you, if I get out of this." He was studying her closely, still looking for the trap.

"You can try. But you'll have no more luck at that than you'll have escaping from my web." And I won't free you until you're sated and willing to do anything, swear anything, for a repeat of the same ecstasy. *"Go on; try it."*

Lindstrom hesitated then reached up and gripped the closest strands. He yanked hard, in a move that would have ripped a crowd control mesh to pieces. But Arachne's Web stayed immobile.

Growling a curse, he studied the web and its anchors closely. Then he filled his hands with the strands, catching more than half of those hanging from the ceiling. He braced his feet and pulled, muscles heaving. Arachne's Web was unimpressed. Lindstrom released the strands slowly, breathing heavily. He growled as he studied the recalcitrant mesh. He was starting to show his true colors.

"Hardrada augmentations?" Elizabeth asked casually and went to the refreshment center.

"Yes, damn you," he spat. "I can kick through this cruiser's decking and I can bloody well rip this web apart." Roaring a wordless shout of determination, he tried again. Veins bulged as he strained. His chest heaved. He was beautiful beyond belief.

But finally, he slumped in defeat. He closed his eyes and fought for breath as sweat streamed down him. Arachne's Web adjusted at her silent command, thickening the undersides of his bonds to support him. She offered him a cup with a straw. "Drink this."

His eyes opened slowly but he didn't move.

"It's not drugged," she reassured him. "I want your brain as much as your body."

"Why doesn't that reassure me?"

"It shouldn't."

He hesitated then stretched forward. She brought the straw to his mouth and he drank thirstily. "My men?" he asked, when he finally finished.

"Well enough for now. You know the custom; you've practiced it often enough. Primarily carnal usage, no permanent damage to either the body or psyche."

His eyes probed hers before he relaxed. "Fair enough."

Elizabeth ran her finger lightly up his arm, from hand to shoulder, exploring the bristle of fine hair, the heat of his muscles. He jerked briefly, watched her warily. "Dammit, Nakamura, what the hell are you planning?"

She curved her hand around his biceps, enjoying the contrast between her slender white fingers and his tanned strength. He must do his fitness training the old way, naked under a solar light. What a delight it would be to watch him.

His cock jerked, brushing her hip. "Thor's Hammer, do you mean to skin me alive, as Pym did to the Skagerrak Mob?"

"I am not Admiral Pym and you will do well to remember that," Elizabeth bit out, whirling to face him. "Do keep it in mind that he was drawn and quartered for that crime."

His eyes narrowed, assessing her response, then he inclined his head in a slight apology.

"No, I intend to have your service as my altrama, Lindstrom. Your complete, willing submission to me as your tuismitheoir, bound to my service for the rest of your life. Sexual service and anything else I want."

"A very flattering offer," he smiled and inclined his head. His feet pushed against the web, striving to unobtrusively break free.

"If you serve me as my altrama," Elizabeth continued imperturbably, "you have my word of honor that I will claim your remaining crewmen in uchtaigh. They will live out their lives in my household, under my protection. I am the only one aboard this ship with the naval and political standing to pull that off."

He froze. Those thick, long, golden lashes lifted and he stared at her, a fierce hope glimmering in the blue depths. His great chest heaved. "You wouldn't."

"I give you my word. But only if I have your full submission. And I must warn you: I'm a level five dominant in the Amber Society."

"So you're a top flight domina." He shrugged impatiently. His cock twitched and began to rise again. Interesting; his instincts might crave sexual submission. That could simplify matters. "You have a reputation for keeping the highest standards of honor, Nakamura. Your crew is astonishingly loyal to you; no pirate has ever successfully bribed one. What the hell do your bedroom tastes count, when compared to that?"

"They matter a great deal when you're the one responsible for satisfying them." She twisted his nipple harshly, deliberately halting his slide into sensuality. He winced and his eyes flashed to meet hers, anger flaring briefly in the vivid depths before he mastered himself.

"Remember that my altrama is mine, whether in the bedroom or the council chamber," Elizabeth went on, delicately fondling his abused nipple. Contrasting the present pleasure to the past pain, beginning the linkage of pleasure and pain granted by her, in his body and mind. "I will own every inch of you—not just as a pleasant game in private, but everywhere, at every time. If I tell you to kill a stranger in a public restaurant, you will do so without hesitation, secure in the knowledge that I will deal with any consequences. If I tell you to suck one of my sentries, you will drop to your knees in thanks for the opportunity to please me."

"Nakamura, that's not necessary. I'll serve you so that my men can live."

"I must trust you, Lindstrom, body and soul, before I claim you as my altrama and bring you closer than my shadow. If I don't trust you and don't claim you, your crew will die on the gallows of New Hebrides."

He swallowed hard, stubbornness graven on his face under the overly pleasant mask. "I have given you my submission, Nakamura."

"Then I will test it, Lindstrom." She leaned forward and swirled her tongue over his ruby-red nipple. He gasped and his back bowed. Excellent, both his taste and his reaction. She set to work on both his nipples, enjoying how pleasure lanced her core every time he cursed or moaned. She cupped his balls gently, a promise of greater delights to come. His hips jerked forward, striving for more. She petted him lightly, never touching his cock nor letting his arousal grow too fast. She'd permit him an orgasm only when she was certain it would overwhelm him.

She sent the comp another command. Arachne's Web obediently rearranged itself and sent a delicate, well-greased probe, warmed to match her skin temperature, toward his most hidden of entrances. The fingers of her hand delicately rubbed the thick rib of flesh and nerves running between his legs. Perineum, or taint in Old English. Extremely sensitive and responsive by any name. His reaction was everything she could have wished. Gasping, shuddering, rocking his hips to meet every one of her movements.

Then he groaned and rose up, arching his back. "What the hell—"

The probe had slipped inside his ass. Elizabeth flexed her index finger and tilted her head back to watch him. Arachne's Web answered her command, echoing her movements within him, like the touch of her little finger on his most hidden flesh. He moaned involuntarily as his eyes widened. "Thor's Hammer, what is that thing?"

"Arachne's Web, an erotic version of the crowd control mesh you've obviously met before. It can hold three Imperial Marines against their will."

"Odin's Wolf," he muttered. "Three Imperial Marines?" He shuddered again and his channel relaxed for her, just a little. The probe slipped deeper inside, gently rubbing him. He was so very hot and tight here, almost certainly a virgin.

Elizabeth bit back a moan of her own and continued to talk, all the while lightly stroking his perineum. "It's linked to my internal comp and can reconfigure itself to any shape I choose. Pseudopods are usually the same size and shape as one or more of my fingers, which is how it relays feedback to me."

The Switch

"So you can feel me." He took a deep, shaken breath and the probe delved farther. Just a little more and she could fondle his prostate.

"Very well." Too well, judging by the hot ache in her breasts and the knot in her belly. But if she pleasured herself with his cock too soon, she wouldn't gain the submission needed for uchtaigh.

"Nakamura . . ." His head fell back. A spot of blood showed where he'd bitten his lip. The probe eased deeper a fraction and found the smooth, rounded nodule that marked his most sensitive spot. Elizabeth rubbed it gently. He trembled, waves running through his entire body. His cock was hard, rearing up like a Yamato gun. She brought him almost to the brink, then stopped.

He moaned. His channel tried to clamp down, to force the probe to give him more sensation. But inexperienced as he was, he couldn't act quickly enough to trap the suddenly narrower probe, which slipped free. He groaned something wordless and desperate. Beautiful. He was so damn beautiful when he was entirely a sexual animal. But that wasn't enough for her, not when she'd have to protect him and his men as their tuismitheoir.

Elizabeth waited, hands tense against the need to hold him. Ignoring, with the icy discipline gained during years of training, her body's desperate need to claim satisfaction from him.

Arousal decreasing, her comp reported. Tactfully not saying exactly whose excitement was fading. The probe faded back into the web.

Harsh lines bracketed his mouth when he opened his eyes. "What do you want of me, Nakamura?" he demanded, staring at her. "Another minute and I'd have begged you for sex."

"That's not enough, not for a lifetime together. I want everything from you. Obedience to my will. Your mind and body, your pleasure and pain. Service for my needs, whether carnal or chaste."

"Chaste?"

"Mopping the floor. Taking my grandmother shopping. Plotting fleet maneuvers with me."

He considered this. His brain was working again, not his sexual instincts. But he'd fall victim to arousal faster the next time she handled him, thanks to coming so close this time. "Plus obedience."

"Submission to my will, to my initiative, in everything," she agreed. Her comp overlaid his image with a map of his most easily excited spots.

"Unnecessary," he shrugged.

Her mouth curved wryly. "So you say. And as I told you before, without it, your men will die."

"You offer a harsh bargain, Nakamura." His eyes measured the distance between them, as if longing to strike a blow.

"You're a very stubborn pirate, Lindstrom." She sent a command to Arachne's Web. It formed fringes, feathers, tendrils on the strands near his shoulders and neck. She cupped her hands and they flowed forward to delicately stroke the strong tendons and sensitive skin. Another set rubbed his arms, like an expert masseuse's reassurance.

He jerked but couldn't escape the tentacles' attentions. "Damn you, not again, Nakamura," he growled. "You can't keep teasing me like this. I told you—"

"I'll do whatever I want and you'll obey. Now relax." She iced her voice, as demanding as if she stood on Tsushima's bridge. Her hand curved and set a black pseudopod curling around his chest. It encircled his nipple and began to squeeze and release lightly, like a lover's first explorations.

"Thor's Hammer," he growled, then closed his eyes. He shook when he breathed but he obeyed. His chest tightened, highlighting his hard nipples. His cock, which had never fully lost its erection, hardened *again.* Another tendril slithered over his chest and began to toy with his other nipple. He hissed, his jaw tight as if striving not to yield command of his body.

Elizabeth licked lips gone very dry. Her voice was a little rough when she spoke. "Well done, Lindstrom. Soon you'll beg for a session with Arachne's Web."

"Never," he gritted. His body betrayed his words, with a flex of his hips and a delicious quiver under the black tentacles' blandishments.

"Foolish pirate." Elizabeth chuckled at his ongoing defiance and kissed him. He answered immediately, displaying all the skill claimed for him. But he had the wits—or the discipline—not to force the pace and try to take control. Instead, he gave her the initiative. Let her explore his mouth, his taste, the shape of his lips, the flex of his tongue. Learn how to make his breathing turn ragged and unsteady, as her mouth enjoyed his. She squeezed his cock and he groaned, his urgency increasing. But he still waited on her unspoken commands, even when he gasped as she played with his nipples.

Somewhere in the back of her head, she wondered how she could still stand upright when her pussy was so hot and swollen and dripping with cream. She broke free of him, forcing her breathing to stay even. His eyes were very dazed and very blue as he watched her. "More trials," he muttered, his cock brilliantly crimson and hard.

He was thinking again, dammit, and too damn quickly. But what else could she expect from a pirate who'd successfully dominated—and seduced—hard-nosed corporate executives into his harem? A dominant's calm finally embraced her, giving her the discipline needed to capture his heart and mind. Her body's hungers could—and would—wait.

"More trials," she agreed calmly. His eyes narrowed at her tone and he started to say something.

Then a series of commands to Arachne's Web sent more black tendrils around him, even as the probe slipped back into his depths. The tentacles flowed to his front and reformed there, until his face was pressed to the web rather than his back. A single long, narrow tendril stretched up from the quivering probe and settled around his hips, like a thong.

His eyes widened and fine tremors ran through him as he saw the tentacles glide over his golden skin. Good, he hadn't panicked. Best to reward him a bit.

Elizabeth eased his cock through an opening in the web, toying with his foreskin. He arched his back, blatantly enjoying her ministrations. He groaned as his hips rolled in eagerness. "Thor's Hammer, what now?"

It wasn't quite a question but she answered it. "Look down, Lindstrom."

Arachne's Web formed fringe, feathers, tendrils on the strands surrounding his cock. Elizabeth cupped her hands and they flowed forward to delicately fondle his cock. Another set cupped his balls, warm and reassuring to a man who'd never experienced the web but less so for someone with more experience. Lindstrom was imprisoned more completely than if he'd stood in Tsushima's brig. But he needed no carnal encouragement, judging by his jutting nipples and jerking cock. He forced a yawn. "Really, Nakamura, your quarters are not very well equipped, compared to my harem. Perhaps I can give you some pointers, as soon as you let me down."

Elizabeth's eyebrows lifted in amusement. A slight waggle of her index finger set a black strand to dragging his foreskin up the crimson length of his cock. His cock hardened still further. Oozed a slender thread of pre-come, which the tentacles smoothly polished away while working his foreskin.

He hissed, his jaw tight as if striving not to yield. He groaned and

162

clenched his hands around the web, closing his eyes as if withstanding the web's blandishments demanded all of his senses.

Damn, but his backside was beautiful. The broad shoulders, wide enough to fill a doorway. The great sweep of muscle from the deep furrow of his spine to his shoulders. The irresistible elegance of his ass. The heavy muscles of his thighs and calves narrowing to his knees. The sharp line of his Achilles tendon and the solidity of his ankle meeting the ground. Lovely.

She fanned her fingers over the marvelously irregular pair of dimples just above his buttocks, her thumbs resting lightly just above his asshole. The probe's vibrations sang through her fingers, heating her as it did him.

He shuddered slightly and involuntarily arched his back toward her. "Odin's Wolf, are you trying to drive me insane?" he gritted through his teeth. "Can't we just fuck?"

"Don't try to be calm," she countered. "Trust me with your sanity, as with everything else."

"Like hell," he snorted and choked when she squeezed his buttock hard. She began to stroke him restlessly, exploring all that strength and beauty. He twisted under her touch, muttered something about Thor as he pushed against her. Her breasts tightened, heat rose in her veins, sank into her bones. She rubbed herself lasciviously against his back, smiling at how her body armor transmitted the flow of his slabs of muscle to her nipples. He groaned, writhing. Irresistible.

She wrapped her leg over his hip and stretched up, so she could open herself to him, bring the curve of his buttock against her pussy through her armor's synthleather. She rubbed herself over him like a cat and found every contour, every prickle of hair. He gasped her name and bucked back against her. Pre-come dripped from his cock, scenting the room.

She kissed his shoulder. Licked him. Tasted him. Scraped her teeth over him, discovering the heat and strength of muscle under silky skin. He groaned again and again, pushing against her. But he hadn't begged for orgasm.

She bit his shoulder, hard enough to draw a few drops of blood. Lindstrom gasped, jerked and rose up on his toes, then pushed back against her. Arousal flared, bright as a nova, in her sensors' vision.

Ah, so he'd finally started to savor pain. Just another sensation, a harsher one that his increased excitement could embrace, rather than flinch from. Something she was obviously the first to give him, judging from his surprise. Excellent.

She scraped her teeth over him. Bit him again, this time on the strong tendon at the base of his neck. He threw back his head and gasped her name. His hips rolled, began to buck rhythmically. When she glanced down, his cock was a curving crimson bar rearing up to his belly. He sobbed her name again, his eyes falling shut.

She stepped away and let him calm down a trifle. Bring him down from the peak, but not completely. Peaks and valleys of arousal in a cycle, each valley a little higher than the one before and each building to a greater peak than its predecessor. When she finally permitted him to climax, it would be a greater magnitude than he'd ever experienced. It had to be; that was the only way to overwhelm both his mind and senses, to bind him to her for a lifetime.

She moved to his front and began to nuzzle his chest. Licked it, lapping and swirling, building a moist heat. His eyes blinked open, focused on her. "Nakamura?"

"Have you ever used a stim whip, Lindstrom?" She scraped her teeth over one hard nipple, nipped it lightly, then looked up at him.

"Are you crazy? You can kill people with one of those." He was white

under his tan as he searched her eyes. Comprehension dawned. "You've got one, don't you? With a bill of attainder over my head, you'd be well within your rights, as Tsushima's commander, to use it on me."

"True. Then I could claim your next in command and force him to submit to me." She kept her expression serene and implacable, as close as possible to a battle goddess. "This is not your game or your harem, Lindstrom. It's mine and you enter on my terms, no one else's."

His lips thinned. "True submission. Regardless of my sexual satisfaction."

She shrugged and pinched his other nipple. He choked, flinched. His hips jerked forward.

"You must learn that this is about what I want. That I will do what I please, how I please, when I please. Your reward is anticipating and increasing my pleasure, not your own. If you don't—can't—do that, then I cannot trust you as my altrama and will walk away from you."

"But if I do, then you will accept me under uchtaigh and my men will live." He curled his lip, as if the proposed bargain was acid on his tongue.

She bowed formally, honoring his comprehension. "You are entirely correct, Lindstrom. I also promise to stretch your boundaries, to teach you things about yourself that you never knew, to make you stronger." She sent a command to Arachne's Web.

"But that's so much unnecessary work for you, Nakamura, to teach me all that, when we could be fucking." His voice was etched with stubbornness under the polite surface. Even this close to orgasm's madness, he was still fighting. The web gripped his cock and began to rub, masturbating him ruthlessly in the same rhythm his hips pulsed in. He growled and surged against the black tentacles.

She bowed again, amused by his reaction. Another order flashed to the web. It began to roll his balls against each other, toying with the exquisitely sensitive orbs. His head fell back as his back arched.

"I have your understanding, Lindstrom. Will you give me your trust?"

"You're not asking for consent, are you?" His voice was rough and uneven. His hips began to rock steadily. He shifted, as if trying to find a safe place to stand.

She snorted, unwilling to dignify that idiocy with an answer.

He blew out a breath and closed his eyes, harsh lines bracketing his mouth. Then his fiery blue eyes lifted to hers. "Very well, I trust you. I believe that you will not kill me without good reason."

Elizabeth raised an eyebrow, considering his refractory tone. He still sounded more like someone negotiating a truce, not a surrender.

He spoke again, through clenched teeth. Her comp reported his arousal was decreasing. "You captured me, so I will serve you for the rest of my life."

She smiled at him sweetly, an expression that would set any of her crew trembling if aimed at them. Silently, she commanded and the web went back to work on his cock. Her toy chest rose out of the deck and waited for the order to open itself. "Now, Lindstrom, why do I think you're just speaking pretty words to save your men? And planning to keep your brain entirely separate from whatever your body does? Why does that not sound like complete submission to me?"

His eyes flashed for a moment before golden lashes shielded them. His diplomatic words were honey sweet, but his tone was edged. His hands restlessly clenched the web's strands. "Nakamura, your pleasure is the lode star of my being. I will dedicate my life to keeping you happy."

"Especially if I finally grant you that orgasm you want?"

"Yes, dammit, especially then!" Blue eyes flared as brilliant as a

Yamato gun's barrage. He glared at her, then bit out ungraciously, "Please."

"Then you won't mind if I give you to my Marines for the night. I'm sure they'll have some excellent ideas on how to induce an orgasm." She turned toward the door, sending another command to the chest. Arachne's Web answered to another order, becoming as narrow as a pillar.

The toy chest obediently opened.

"Fuck you!" he roared and spat at her, ignoring the web's changes.

Elizabeth immediately whirled, snatched up the proffered stim whip from the chest, and brought it down across his shoulder. He howled a curse and tried to lunge for her. Another step and she was in position for another blow. Crack! The stim whip laid a trail of fire down the nerves of his other shoulder. Her sensors showed his nerves sparking like fireworks.

"Vidar's Boot, Nakamura, I'll kill you for this!"

She was barely breathing hard as she came into position behind him. Her eyes flickered—and her comp promptly showed her his previously identified arousal pattern. While her comp and sensors could show how he felt, only her skill could lay the stim whip in exactly the right spot.

Arachne's Web began to fondle his cock again, binding pleasure and pain and obedience. The probe in his ass shifted gears, gently urging his prostate to remember what delight could be. Two neural paths that orgasm could follow; she would excite both of them, while the whip summoned his endorphins.

Her third blow was lighter, finding an area that preferred softer caresses. Endorphins bloomed under the stim whip's touch. His earlier arousal had warmed him up enough to accept its harsher, sharper stimulation. To unconsciously revel in his nerves' increased excitement.

The fourth blow—and he gasped her name. A golden line marked the strike to her sensors; his skin showed only a light red arc, as if he'd leaned against a hard edge for a few minutes. Elizabeth reset the whip's controls. He was too new to this, and too responsive, for its typical severity. Best to keep this light by aficionado standards so there'd be no risk of driving him insane with sensory overload.

Then she set herself to seducing him. The whip caressed him, blazed into him. Learned his strengths and weaknesses, how his broad shoulders arched and opened under the whip's figure-eight pattern. Brushed his ass and flowed over his thighs. Tantalized him and streaked into him like torpedoes from a squadron of fast destroyers.

He moaned, cursed, flung his head back. His hips jerked, rocked. Moving from side to side behind him to vary her angle, she paid still more attention to his most sensitive points, until his back and sides were a fiery blaze to her sensors. And all the while, Arachne's Web made love to his cock and ass in a manner calculated to drive any man wild.

"Fuck, fuck, fuck!" He screamed in pain and pleasure as his voice grew hoarse. His crimson cock gleamed like an iron bar in the blacksmith's forge under its steady flow of pre-come.

Orgasm imminent, *her comp reported.*

He danced for her whip like a Denebian bacchante now, totally absorbed in the madness she'd brought him. The crimson stripes on his back were a solid stretch of blazing heat, the same scarlet as his tumescent cock.

Elizabeth petted his scalding skin, licked his sweat, tasted the wild tremors running through his muscles. She gloried in her sensors' picture of him. The stim whip's path etched in gold as his deepest nerves fired convulsively, the heat of his arousal a brilliant scarlet, his dazzled eyes an incandescent blue. Beautiful and rare, a delight to treasure. His hunger was a sweeter wine than anything served from her family's cellars.

Another blow, watching for his reaction. His hips speeded up their frantic jerks.

Another blow, very carefully placed. His head was arched back, desperation blatant in his clenched teeth and jaw.

"Now, Lindstrom. Come now," she ordered, her tone as irresistible as Tsushima's batteries.

One more touch of the stim whip, delicately placed across the top of his buttocks. It caught him perfectly, sending a shockwave through the intimate muscle that linked his cock and asshole.

He reared up onto his toes, howling, and exploded into orgasm. Ecstasy blazed through his every muscle, her sensors showing her its rocket-bright path through his body. Savaging blood and muscle and nerves with its power. Jet after thick jet of semen shot across the chamber, ribbons of white against the brilliant carpets. He shouted again and again, spending himself extravagantly, utterly. "Fuck, fuck, fuck—"

She watched and waited. Would this be enough to capture his stubborn brain?

He finally finished and sagged bonelessly in his bonds. Arachne's Web obediently guided him to the floor and released him, letting him crumple into a sated heap on the crimson silk carpets.

Elizabeth took a step forward to assist him but he moved toward her. One arm reached out, then another. She stilled, wondering what he'd do. He had no defenses left to fight her with.

Lindstrom wrapped himself around her, shuddering. His lungs heaved to drag in air. Slowly, almost reverently, he kissed her boot. "I surrender, Nakamura. You have me, body and soul, for life."

She stooped down and gently stroked his golden hair back from his *face, searching his expression. His blue eyes blinked up at her, dazed and sleepy. "Anything you want," he said carefully, working to form the words. "Any time, any place, I will do for you."*

At last, the complete, achingly sweet submission of a strong man. "You're finally speaking the truth, Lindstrom. Good man. Now go to sleep." She kissed her fingers and touched them to his forehead.

"Thank you, Nakamura," he murmured. "Thank you." And he was asleep.

Elizabeth petted him for a long time before she stood up. They'd make love later. For now, it was more than enough to know that she'd finally captured her golden pirate.

Beth pulled herself back to the present with a jerk. She'd love to be ferocious with Sean, roar like a tigress as easily as she purred like a kitten. But he was so new to the scene that she had to go gently with him. He was so definitely submissive, with his quick obedience. He only took the initiative with her permission and to please her sexually.

She had a great deal of responsibility to protect him. So she'd never frighten or scare him, never risk his future happiness with someone else. Best to focus on basics, like introducing him to the simplest of tactile pleasures.

She ran her finger lightly around the rim of her glass, thinking about the clothes chosen for Sean. He'd looked like a Viking just now, wearing a thick cable-knit sweater over jeans and boots. Silk would frame his delicious attributes marvelously.

Would he be uncomfortable in the unaccustomed confinement of underclothes, especially a silk thong? If he fidgeted, she'd just have to stroke that beautiful ass of his. Perhaps she'd calm him down, but then again, perhaps not.

Finally she walked into the jazz club, raincoat over her arm, and saw him immediately. His face brightened and he came over to her. Beth leaned up for his kiss, deliberately deepening it, when he would have kept the contact light enough for a public setting. He groaned and gathered her close against his big hard body. Finally, she pulled her head back.

She wiped lipstick off his mouth carefully, delicately emphasizing her possession of him. His hand ran down over her back, lightly exploring the red silk shirt and black wool trousers under her matching cashmere jacket, before dropping away.

"Let's go sit down, darling," Beth purred and Sean nodded. A few words to the hostess later, Sean and Beth followed the woman past the dance floor to a small, secluded booth. Beth slid in first and Sean sat down next to her.

She let the silence hold for a moment, relishing his tension, then turned to him. Why on earth had he worn something that hid his beautiful forearms? She'd have happily settled for a flannel shirt with the sleeves rolled up.

"Ready for inspection?" she asked. He nodded, looking slightly bewildered. She ran her fingertips along his jaw, testing for the facial. Lovely smooth skin greeted her, above the strong bones.

Sean watched her, frozen in place like a new recruit. Had he worn a similar look of disbelief during his first inspection at West Point?

"Hands?"

Sean promptly gave her his hands. Beth lifted one and studied the fingernails. She dropped a quick kiss on a scarred knuckle before releasing him. She gave his other hand the same scrutiny, but lightly sucked a fingertip before releasing him. His quick intake of breath was clearly audible in the confined space.

"The scarf?"

Beth held out her palm for it and Sean offered the small bag he carried. Inside, she found the scarf, carefully bundled in protective tissue. She closed the bag and set it aside. "Very good, Sean. Have you been celibate for the past twenty-four hours?"

She ran her hand up his thigh and rested her fingers lightly over his fly. His hips jerked under the almost imperceptible touch.

"Yes, ma'am," he gritted.

Beth tapped the hard ridge once then rested her hand on his thigh, a few inches below that bulging crotch. "I can see that you're telling the truth."

Sean draped his arm around her shoulders and relaxed slowly, visibly relieved—and frustrated. Beth could have purred.

The waiter appeared quickly and she ordered a club soda and lime, plus the same for Sean. His eyes widened a bit, when she ordered for him, but he didn't object.

"How is your son?" Beth asked quietly, enjoying making him wait.

"Uh, Mike's doing well. His team won the game tonight. Did I tell you that he's the varsity quarterback for his high school?"

"Congratulations! You must be very proud of him."

Sean pulled his wallet out to show his prized cache of photos. A few moments later, Beth was studying pictures of a young man who looked remarkably like his father.

"Mike's everything a fellow could hope for in his son," Sean said quietly. He looked down at her and went on, encouraged by her evident interest. "I'm very lucky to have him. He plans to go to West Point and I think he'll make it."

"West Point?" Beth was genuinely surprised. "Why? Because you went there?"

"I was released at the end of my first year when my girlfriend got pregnant."

"Did you regret being released? Sorry, I'm prying." She tried to shrug off the question. Why had she asked it? She didn't need to know that before spending a weekend with him. A voice in her head reminded her that her father liked to know career plans, past and present, of potential spouses for his children.

"I can talk about it if you want," he said easily. "I wasn't a good enough wrestler in high school to get a full scholarship anywhere, while the service academies would pay me to attend. My grandfather had been a Ranger during World War II and my father was one in Vietnam. I chose West Point so I could follow them into the Army. As for being released, I got a son and a career out of it. I felt at home as a Ranger sergeant, more so than at West Point, so everything worked out."

"You were very lucky," she murmured and changed the subject to something less emotional. "That was a very nice bookstore where we met. Do you rent to other businesses like that or a variety of industries?"

He raised an eyebrow at her but followed her conversational lead. "I own over a dozen commercial properties, all of which are currently rented. There's only the one bookstore that you saw. The rest are different companies, including some small offices and a couple of restaurants."

The waiter put their drinks down and disappeared silently. Beth slid a twenty-dollar bill onto the table and studied Sean again.

"How did you move to real estate from the Army?" She delicately scraped her fingernails over his thigh, enjoying the hard muscle under the denim. Social niceties were all well and good, but it was time for a reminder of the weekend's agenda.

His answering quiver was delicious. Sean gulped a bit but answered. "A buddy of mine, Adam . . ." He lifted his wrist and the black bracelet burdening it, so she could see the lettering. "I wear his bracelet in memory of him, ever since he died in the Mog. In Somalia, I mean."

"I've heard about the Rangers in Somalia, Sean. He must have been a magnificent soldier to be remembered so honorably," Beth offered.

Sean's eyes flared in surprise. "You remember it! It was on and off the air so damn fast, most folks have forgotten," he breathed, before resuming his story. "Yeah, Adam was a great guy. He left the business to me, along with his life insurance and a small house in West Seattle. Then my wife died almost six months later, leaving me to raise Mike. That's when her folks filed the first lawsuit and I got a hardship discharge."

Beth frowned, surprised that a family member would attack him.

Sean went on, more slowly now as he reached the more private topics.

"Tiffany's dad threw her out when she got pregnant with Mike and wouldn't have anything to do with her, or Mike, afterward. I notified him, of course, when Tiffany died."

"Of course," Beth agreed, both her Japanese and Scottish instincts insisting on the importance of family ties.

"When he heard that Tiffany was gone, he filed suit for sole custody of Mike. Said that I wasn't fit to raise a son and that he could do better, being a lay minister and so on. And Mike was pretty wild then. Tiffany couldn't give him as much attention as he needed, with her strokes and paralysis and so on. I swear Mike knew every cop within ten miles."

Sean sipped his drink as he looked back, old agonies cutting deep into his face.

"I couldn't counter the lawsuit very well, not as a Ranger who had to be free to deploy at any time. I had friends who'd watch Mike while I was gone, but the judge wasn't impressed by that. He gave me two weeks to make better arrangements. So I left the Army and came here."

He stopped, seemingly embarrassed by his long speech. Beth patted his leg gently in reassurance. He gathered himself to go on.

"Real estate has been a very good business for me. It pays enough to support the two of us and the hours are pretty much whatever I want. I've been able to spend all the time I want with Mike." He smiled, his eyes lost in happier memories.

"And Mike's grandfather dropped the lawsuit," Beth concluded.

"Not until Mike turned eighteen this year," Sean snorted. "The old fool even refused to see Mike if he couldn't have custody. He's missing out on a grandson, just because of stubborn pride."

Beth sipped her club soda, fighting the urge to reassure him. Dear heaven, the pain he must have known in his life. She wanted to hug him and promise him he'd never be hurt again. She felt his body's heat flowing into her.

"What about you? What do you do when you're not browsing in bookstores?" Sean asked, pulling himself out of his reverie with an appreciable snap.

"Well, I was a currency trader for three years after I graduated from Harvard. Now I help the Treasury oversee that business." She kept the conversation to her work, as he had, rather than mentioning any hobbies.

"Currency trading? Is that like commodities trading? Where you bet on what the price of what stuff will be?" He shifted on the leather seat uneasily, probably trying to relieve his pants' tightness. Hmmm, he must be fantasizing about tonight.

Beth chuckled at his predicament and happily teased him by continuing their conversation. "Yes, currency trading is a lot like that. My first boss called it high-stakes gambling. I enjoyed it for a while, but now I like having a different view."

Sean started to ask other questions, but she put her finger to his mouth. She needed to touch him, if only the minimum contact allowed by a public place. "Let's dance. It'd be a shame to miss out on a good band."

Sean opened his mouth to say something but stopped, his eyes wide before he controlled himself. How many times had he danced with a woman?

Still, he led her to the dance floor with an elegant courtesy that pleased her greatly. Beth would bet his mother had taught him manners, along with morals. She immediately moved into his arms and they began to sway with the music.

She slid closer to Sean until her nipples brushed his chest and his leg was between hers. She could feel his erection and she leaned against it, enjoying how her slow dance movements caressed him. Her nipples were quite hard and she turned her face into his chest, tucking herself neatly under his chin. She stood eye-to-eye with most men, but she felt like a little girl in Sean's arms. She purred as his hands stroked her back and ass.

The music changed. Beth blinked, looking at her watch. "We'd better get going," she said regretfully.

"Whatever you say, ma'am," Sean said. "Although I could have stayed here a while longer."

Beth chuckled at that, enjoying how he'd changed his mind about dancing. "But wouldn't you rather go someplace private? Hmmm?"

She laughed at the look on his face as he steered her back to their booth, so they could retrieve their belongings.

The chauffeur was standing by the limousine and held the door for them to enter. Sean hesitated but recovered quickly, following her inside as if he rode in limos every day. He openly studied the interior as the driver pulled out onto the road, his eyes finding every high-tech gadget. Beth ran her hand up his leg, deliberately distracting him, and rubbed his crotch seam, following it as it rose to meet the zipper.

Sean caught his breath and stared at her. She caressed his jaw, then moved in for a kiss. Their hands fed on each other as much as their mouths did, seeking skin to fondle and heat.

Sean made a wordless sound when his fingers cupped her breast. Her nipple tightened under the touch, stabbing his hand directly. He unbuttoned her shirt and Beth arched her back, silently encouraging him to look his fill. He cupped her breasts, rubbing his thumbs over the velvety nipples. "No bra?"

"No underthings," Beth corrected.

"Shit." He closed his eyes for a moment and she waited eagerly. Then he bent his head to her throat.

"Very nice," she approved, tilting her head back for him. His hands moved over her and Beth gasped, startled by how much he remembered of Wednesday's explorations. She moaned when he moved his mouth farther down, tasting and teasing her until she was on fire.

"Please, Sean, do it!" she begged.

"No, not until we're someplace private." His eyes were fierce with the effort to control his own hunger.

She nodded slowly. There were hours yet to come, when they could play all they wanted. Then she could bend his self-control to suit her.

Sean smiled slowly at her acquiescence, then kissed her on the mouth, backing away from the previous urgency but still keeping her excited with hands and mouth. This kiss lasted for a very long time.

Eventually, there was a polite tap on the window and Sean lifted his head from Beth's breast. His blush was visible even in the dim light. She stroked his back for a moment longer then sat up, buttoning her blouse quickly. Sean's condition appeared more respectable than hers, once he fastened his shirt. At least he looked respectable above the waist; behind his zipper was another matter.

He left the limousine and froze, staring at the small private jet in front of him. Beth patted his ass. "Come on, darling," she urged, smiling at his shock.

"Currency trading must have paid very well." Sean got out.

Beth laughed out loud, pleased at having surprised him. "Oh, it did, Sean, it truly did." Millions of dollars in commission, in fact.

Moments later, they were aboard the jet and had settled into their seats. Beth glanced around, satisfied by what she saw. The plane was even more luxurious, with its rare woods and fine upholstery, than she had requested. The steward offered drinks, but she motioned him away. Once they were in the air, she unbuckled her seat belt and stood up. "Let's go explore the rest of this plane, darling."

She headed back and found the stateroom easily. Once inside, Beth ran her hand appreciatively over the silk coverlet on the enormous bed, its various shades of gold glowing against the wood paneling. That color combination was why she'd picked this particular jet: it should frame Sean's magnificent body like an altar cloth. A small display next to the door showed cruising speed and altitude.

She looked back at him where he braced himself in the doorway, eyes hot but body still leashed. "Come on in, lover, and close the door. Don't you want to join the Mile High Club?"

His eyes blazed and he kicked the door shut. He dived onto the bed, pulling her down with him. Beth laughed and caught his head in her hands as he leaned over her.

"You big beautiful Viking, you," she purred and arched against him. He caught her mouth with his and came down on top of her. Their tongues danced and dueled together, as they relearned each other's taste. Beth caressed his neck, enjoying the strong cord of muscle and bone below those sensitive points.

Sean changed his angle and kissed her face, attending to her forehead, her cheeks, her chin. His tongue circled and explored her ears until she shivered and purred under the onslaught. He went lower still to mark the pulse points on her neck, exciting the sensitive points until she begged for mercy. Whatever else he did or didn't know, he was a genius at foreplay.

He rubbed her breasts through the thin silk, tugging at her nipples as they hardened. Then he licked them, until the silk became a wet circle marking her body's need for him. Beth watched him, twisting restlessly as she tried to catch her breath.

He suckled her hard enough to pull much of her breast into his mouth. Beth choked at the hot, wet cavern he created and closed her eyes. She tugged at the bottom of his sweater, anxious to feel skin.

Sean straightened up, pulled the sweater over his head and tossed it aside.

"Shirt, too," Beth panted as she sat up, peeling her jacket off with more haste than art.

"Okay but not yours."

"What?"

"Everything else, but not your shirt." Sean paused to glare at her. "Understand?"

Just a red silk shirt? Her eyes lit at the possibilities. "Yes, sir."

She began to shed the rest of her attire as quickly as possible. A big arm wrapped around her and pulled her back across him, stretching her across the bed, just as she toed off her last shoe.

"Sean!" she protested laughing. "My trousers!"

"I'll show you how to take off trousers." He shoved his hand inside the waistband and down between her legs, forcing his way until his finger met her clit. She jumped and giggled, wriggling as he fingered her into a frenzy.

When he had her writhing on top of him and almost incoherent, he quickly pulled his hand out and unbuttoned her trousers. Two seconds later, they were on the opposite side of the stateroom together with his clothes. A quick roll put her under him on the big bed and he grinned in triumph.

"Is that how they taught you to wrestle in high school?" Beth gasped.

Sean laughed. "No, but it sure would have been nice to know how to do this back then."

"Care to show me a few more wrestling moves?" she invited.

"Sure thing, ma'am," Sean agreed. "But maybe we should start with some cowboy moves, like how to ride a bucking bronc."

"I don't see any horses in here." Beth tried to be obtuse but her dancing eyes gave her away. "Maybe we should ask the pilot to land and fetch us some."

"Like hell! I'm sure we can find us some. Just have to know where to look. Like here, perhaps." He fondled her breast.

"Surely not there," Beth choked and gasped in earnest, when his head dropped down to follow his hand. Her breasts quickly remembered all he had done before and became one giant, throbbing ache.

"Condoms in the nightstand," she moaned, just before his hand found her clit again and destroyed any pretense of conversation.

"Good girl," he praised, then brought her off hard and fast. Twice.

Beth opened her eyes, trying to recover. When was he going to put himself into her? His hand was nice enough but she wanted that big cock.

She found him standing by the bed, rolling on a condom with rather more skill than he'd shown before. Sweet baby, had he been practicing? Still, she liked his focus on the basics. Get her satiated and relaxed enough to take a cock of his size, then sheathe himself quickly before entering. Considerate to the end, that was Sean.

He blushed and shrugged when he caught her watching.

She smiled up at him, letting her genuine fondness show through, as he knelt between her legs. "Lift my legs up with your arms, darling, until they reach your shoulders."

"Can you do that?"

"I didn't learn yoga just to make conversation."

He grinned back at her and followed her suggestion. He pushed into her quickly this time, watching her face. Beth sighed as he reached even deeper than before.

"Very nice," she praised, settling herself around him for a welcoming wriggle. His eyes widened and he hissed at the sensation. "But I think we need one thing more."

"What else could there be?"

"What's the highest you've ever ridden a bucking bronc? Six thousand, eight thousand, maybe ten thousand feet? Think we can do better now?"

He caught the reference immediately and looked over his shoulder at the instrument panel.

"Welcome to the Mile High Club, cowboy," Beth purred.

"You are a wicked woman, ma'am," Sean drawled, his eyes alight. "Guess this cowboy will just have to show you how to ride a bucking bronc, no matter where it is." He circled his hips, pressing deeper inside her. Her eyes half-closed.

"Better teach me well, cowboy," Beth managed before he rode her in earnest. He dropped all pretense as soon as he started moving, thrusting into her as if heaven could only be found somewhere deep inside her.

The thought slid away from her, as his body demanded her full attention. She watched the muscles rippling in his strong belly, as his hips thrust and released. The strong shoulders and arms, beaded with sweat as they strained above her. The magnificent forearms, with the elegant twisting veins standing out in fine relief, so close to her. The beautiful mouth, tight now in concentration, as he fought his instincts for a few minutes longer.

But his eyes trapped her. Those incredible blue eyes, half-veiled by long golden lashes, blazed down at her and held her. She caught fire from his need and became achingly conscious of just how much she wanted this man. Cream gushed forth, welcoming him, as her body transformed itself into an instrument focused solely on carnal satisfaction.

"That's it, honey," he grunted. "Come for me. Fuck, honey, come!"

She obeyed him, her hand dropping to rub herself. Her eyes locked on his, as the first pulses rolled through her body. Fierce satisfaction lit his face.

"Fuck!" he shouted, then again as he freed himself into orgasm. She locked herself around him, relishing his climax as if it were her own.

He collapsed afterward but managed to roll, so that they lay side by side, his cock still throbbing inside her.

"Got any other wrestling moves, cowboy?" Beth managed. Best to keep this light.

"All the wrestling moves you want." To her shock, he stirred inside her. Dear heavens, he wasn't joking.

Hours later, Beth saw that the cruising altitude was dropping. Silently cursing the passage of time, she leaned up on one elbow and looked down at Sean. His white skin glowed against the gold silk sheets, and she twined a lock of his hair around her finger. That golden pelt on his chest even looked magnificent when it was sweaty.

Sean's eyes opened slowly. He watched her for a moment then gently caressed her throat. Beth tilted her head, opening her neck to his touch.

"Ten minutes until landing, Ms. Nakamura," said a disembodied voice.

Beth closed her eyes. "Damn," she murmured.

Sean kissed the nape of her neck and sat up to start getting dressed.

The steward imperturbably helped them strap into their seats in the main cabin, calmly ignoring their barely respectable condition. Sean flushed a little, at the conclusions that the steward had obviously drawn, but stayed quiet.

Beth patted his leg after the steward left. "Look out the window. Recognize where we are?"

He leaned over her and gazed out. Blazing lights danced in the darkness beyond. A single beam of light pointed straight up to the sky. "Las Vegas?"

Beth nodded.

"You flew us to Las Vegas for the weekend?" Sean's voice roughened in astonishment.

"Sure did. It seemed like a good place to have fun with a beautiful man," she purred and stroked his arm. She smiled at his astonishment but remained silent while they landed, letting Sean watch the sights.

Another limousine was waiting when the jet taxied to a stop. The chauffeur touched his hat and held the door for them to enter, which Sean didn't quite flinch at. They drove down the Strip and Beth opened the sunroof, so Sean could see all the hotels' neon lights. He stayed silent, keeping his thoughts to himself.

The limousine turned off the Strip and down a wide, curving drive, before coming to a stop under a large portico. A uniformed bellman rushed forward to open the door and two men in suits, both slender and fit, followed him.

"Welcome back, Ms. Nakamura," said the taller of the two men, wearing a very expensive gray suit. "This is your butler, Gianni Caraballo."

Gianni bowed, looking composed and elegant in his formal black suit.

"It's a pleasure to see you again," Beth said politely. "Sean, this is Paul Graziano, our host here. Paul, this is Sean Lindstrom, my guest."

Another round of handshakes followed before the men focused again on Beth, leaving Sean isolated on the periphery.

The two men kept up a steady stream of chatter as they led Beth and Sean to a private elevator, which deposited the party in an elegant foyer with only a few doors visible. Graziano opened the most distant door and ushered Beth and Sean in.

The suite was huge and incredibly opulent, with gold brocade and marble. Another hotel's lights gleamed outside the windows, with the desert sands and a mountain range shining beyond. Beth noticed that Sean had frozen beside her when he saw the room, but she said nothing to him.

Gianni Caraballo, the butler, gave them a brief tour, emphasizing the amenities in the living room, master bedroom, and bathroom. He assured Beth that the suitcases had been unpacked and everything was exactly as she had ordered.

Beth nodded and agreed that everything looked perfect, then showed the hotel's representatives to the door. She closed the door behind them and locked it, grateful for the silence. She stayed still for a moment, trying to gather herself before dominating Sean again.

"Strip," snarled a deep voice from directly behind her.

Beth choked and tried to turn.

A man's body immediately pressed her into the door and a single huge hand caught her wrists high above her head. She shook her head and he leaned into her harder, until she couldn't move. After a few minutes, he shifted and quickly turned her to face him, still gripping her hands. His leg shoved between hers, opening her wide for him, while pinning her to the door.

Beth stared at him, startled and a bit frightened by his change in behavior. Sean was an imposing figure, almost barbaric in his rough-edged simplicity against the intense adornment around him. He looked like a Viking taking stock of a palace and its ladies before ransacking it. A jolt of lust ran through Beth as she saw her fantasy come to life. Finally, some high-handed dominance from him.

"No . . ." she managed to get out, as the dream demanded.

"Hell, yes, foreign witch," he rumbled. Then he caught the front of her blouse and ripped it open. He shoved her shirt and jacket down her back so they trapped her hands behind her. Beth quivered as his fingers squeezed and stroked her breasts, then ran lower. He grabbed her hips and pulled her higher on his thigh. Her head fell back helplessly, offering herself to him.

Sean took advantage of the invitation and bent his head. Beth trembled when he nipped her. He lifted his head and surveyed her, his mouth curved in a cruel smile.

She stared back at him, seeing the hard line of his mouth marked by a single drop of crimson.

Very deliberately his tongue slid out and tasted her blood.

She swallowed convulsively. "Please," she moaned.

His eyes flashed and he let her slide down his leg, until she rested against the door. She stared at him helplessly, ensnared by his leashed violence.

He bent and tore open her trousers. Another grab pulled them down to her ankles. Then he picked her up over his shoulder and started to walk. Beth struggled to get free, frightened and excited by his deliberate violence.

He dumped her on the big bed and she gulped for breath, her face pressed into the heavy brocade coverlet. She froze as a finger traced her spine lightly.

"Foreign witch, do you want to be a barbarian's plaything?" he growled. He pulled the clothing away from her wrists and his finger continued down, ending between her legs. She shuddered as it explored her slowly, before another finger came to bathe in her cream. Then both fingers found their way inside her and she rocked against their pressure.

A moment's pause, then he pushed more strongly. How many fingers would her body welcome? She groaned again at her body's answer: four.

"Please, master," she choked as his hand shoved at her. Her muscles flexed and yielded to his demands.

Suddenly he ripped off her trousers, overcoming the slight resistance of her shoes by a stronger yank. Beth heard a zipper's metallic snarl before his weight came down on her. She gasped, crushed between the harsh brocade coverlet rasping against her breasts and his fur-shrouded muscles. She tossed her head, gripping the coverlet, as she writhed under him.

"Do you want it, little witch? Do you want this big cock of mine?" Her hair rippled under his breath.

"Please, just take me!"

Sean's weight shifted and she shuddered as his teeth sank into the nape of her neck. He held her like that for a long minute, a tigress pinned for mating. Then he slammed into her to begin a long, hard ride.

She climaxed almost immediately but he ignored her stifled cry. He continued to pump her, pulling almost all the way out, then pounding his great length into her with all the force of his iron-hard body. He grunted rhythmically as he worked her cunt, angling his thrusts until he found exactly the right spot inside her.

Beth gasped and bucked against him, fighting for more.

"Fuck, fuck, fuck . . ." His words beat in her blood like the force of his cock savaging her womb. They drove thought out of her, to be replaced by animal need. She gripped and squeezed him, striving to keep him inside her.

He bit her shoulder hard and she screamed, the sharp pain triggering ecstasy throughout her body. She shattered around him, every bone and muscle convulsing in an orgasm such as she'd never known before.

She heard him shout her name as he too found his release. Then she collapsed into unconsciousness under him.

Beth woke to see the sun peeping in past the curtains. She stretched slowly, feeling the answering soreness. Sean's body was like a furnace against hers, a welcome source of nighttime heat for a Viking's woman. His torso showed touches of red where she'd bitten and clawed him in passion. She purred at the memory of his response to those love marks.

His cock was warm against her, where it lay nestled between them. She petted it idly, comparing how cuddly it looked now to how ferociously it had stood the night before. Memories flowed stronger and she bent her head over him, laving it with her tongue before sucking gently. Its quick rise to greet her surprised her, given how hard and how often he had used it. She began to caress it more intensely, as she remembered her plans for the coming night.

She squeaked when Sean suddenly pulled her up. A quick roll trapped her under him, and he gripped her wrists in one big hand. The other found a condom in the litter on the nightstand.

"Witch," he muttered as he ripped the condom open with his teeth.

Beth sighed happily and twined a leg around him. How delicious; a display of dominance to match his previous submission. But was it just a reaction to being slighted so consistently at the hotel, a demand for after-care by a bruised ego?

And would he—could he—be dominant when more than sex was involved? Power exchange was too deep in her bones to be satisfied only in the bedroom. But this was not the time to worry about the issues of a long-term relationship. Sean was a weekend's delight, no more.

Eight

Sean woke up when Beth touched his shoulder. She kissed him lightly on the mouth then moved away slightly. "Time to get up, sleepy head. Your bath is ready."

He blinked then shut his mouth. He'd hoped for a shower together, but he quite possibly couldn't have taken full advantage of it, especially since his cock was rather sore at the moment. Beth undoubtedly had the experience to know when a man needed to soak his aches. But she also had an excellent eye for fun. Even breakfast that morning had turned into a sexual delight with her. This weekend was turning out to be an even bigger adventure than he'd hoped.

The Switch

The bathroom was dimly lit by a single light, over the tub itself, and a few candles clustered at the tub's corners. Sean sniffed, trying to decide what smelled so good. It didn't smell like any of the few scented candles he'd encountered before or anything at the spa.

Shrugging, he got into the bath. It was very warm and slightly oily, lightly scented to match the candles. His muscles began to relax and he slid down into the Japanese soaking tub, which was big enough to hold him comfortably.

He was drowsy again within minutes, wondering what Mike was doing now, before pulling his thoughts away. His son would be fine. He had to start building a life without Mike around all the time.

The water rolled against him and he opened his eyes to see Beth getting into the tub. Sean's eyes widened, but he quickly shifted to make room for her.

"Just get comfortable, Sean. I'm going to wash you."

Sean nodded and tried not to fidget. A woman hadn't bathed him since he was a child. For Beth to do this, now, was something he had no idea how to deal with. What was she planning?

"What are the candles scented with?" he asked, trying to find a distraction from his discomfort.

"Sandalwood, frankincense, bergamot. It's a blend of relaxants and aphrodisiacs I ordered just for us."

Sean's brain stopped working at the mention of aphrodisiacs.

Beth's mouth twitched at the look on his face. "Take it easy, darling. These are relaxants, too."

Sean nodded slowly and closed his eyes again. Aphrodisiacs? Don't think about it.

Beth lathered a sponge and knelt beside his hip. She circled his shoulder slowly, watching how the soap clung to his skin. Then she lifted his hand and cleaned his entire arm, in a spiral movement flowing down from his shoulder to his fingernails. She carefully separated his fingers and made sure that every inch was quite clean.

"Why are you washing me like this?"

Beth paused, still holding the tip of his thumb. "What's the matter? Don't you like it?"

"Well, yes. But it's not like a regular bath." Sean's hand twisted under hers. She tightened her grip and he went still.

"Why should it be? I'm enjoying it," she answered calmly. Her eyes softened. "Just go with the flow and I promise that everything will work out."

"Okay, then," Sean agreed, still puzzled but not inclined to argue more.

She rinsed out the sponge, applied more soap, and cleaned first one leg then the other. Sean could only shudder when she attended to the crease between his torso and thigh. He looked away from her breasts, so enticingly close, and caught sight of her beautiful back in the mirrors, flexing as she worked over him.

She attended to his other arm before washing his face and chest. Sean felt the slow drag of the sponge through the thick hair and his nipples' rise to follow the motion. The sponge moved farther down to where his cock reared in welcome.

He was slightly disappointed, but said nothing, when she washed it carefully. Repeatedly soaping, rubbing, and rinsing until every fold and wrinkle, every hard line, glowed clean and sweet. He tried some breathing exercises to control himself, until he could lie acquiescent under her hand. He didn't dare look at her reflection.

"Roll over, darling. That's right. You have to kneel, so I can wash your backside." Her voice was very gentle.

Sean closed his eyes and obeyed, praying he wouldn't disgrace himself.

She started at the nape of his neck and worked down, attending to all the places hidden before. The sponge felt rougher now, or perhaps he was more aware of its feel.

He bucked then steadied himself, when her sponge first traveled from his spine to between his buttocks. She held it there for a minute; he shivered at the contrasting feelings of slickness and teasing roughness. When he had relaxed a bit, she spread his buttocks with one hand. His head snapped around at that: holy shit, she was studying him.

His breath sighed out at her intent look. He nearly climaxed when her tongue tasted her lips. Then she cleaned him there, too, handling every hidden inch with the same steady caresses she'd used on his cock. Fuck.

Beth wrung out the sponge and dropped it aside. She pulled out the small shower attachment and turned it on, testing its temperature, before meeting his eyes in the mirror with a smile. "Time for some cooler temperatures, darling."

Sean could only shrug in agreement.

She rinsed him easily, keeping the water barely warm enough to maintain his mood, while still slowing him down. After she stepped out, she held a big bath towel for him to step into. Before he had time to even pat himself dry, she'd headed back into the bedroom. She beckoned him to follow and he went, fascinated, willing, and confused.

The bedroom was now dim as well, lit only by a few of the same scented candles. A single stick of incense sent lazy tendrils into the air. A futon was spread out on the floor to make a low, flat bed, with cushions, sheets, and towels scattered around. Small bunches of fresh flowers gleamed from vases around the room, while a piano's notes ran through the room like a mountain stream. The room was warmer than before so he felt hot in the towel.

"Lie down on the mat, Sean, on your back. I'm going to give you a massage."

Sean laid down immediately, a little surprised and confused but definitely hopeful. Maybe now she'd bring him off with her hand.

She knelt next to him and removed the towel around his waist. His hand went to catch it but stopped. Naked was good. Naked could be very useful for fucking.

She placed cushions under his neck and knees. He relaxed, feeling secure and comfortable as he waited for her first move.

"Straighten your legs and relax your back. Very good." She knelt behind his head and began to gently pinch the skin on his face.

Sean closed his eyes, trying to understand what she intended. This felt like how his gym's masseuse worked out muscle tension. Not like the start of bedplay. Surely, he shouldn't be getting aroused.

She worked down the front of his body to his hips and then sat back. "Now roll over slowly and lie face-down."

Beth readjusted the pillows and quietly sat next to Sean's hips. He turned his head to watch her, still surprised by her ease with her own nudity. She looked like the goddess's handmaiden in an Eastern temple.

She poured some oil into her hand from a small jar and rubbed it into her hands. She rested one hand between Sean's shoulder blades, feeling warm like the heat from a baker's oven, before she slowly began to rub his back. She wasn't trying to excite him or release tension now, more as if she was just exploring the muscles in his body. He twitched and rearranged his legs, trying to find a position that gave his rapidly hardening cock some ease. "Beth, please, can't you move a little faster?"

"No, darling. I'll move to the tempo I want."

She rubbed his back a little more. He couldn't imagine what she intended. He squirmed under her hands, trying to find a position that felt productive. He really, really wanted to just roll over and grab her. But he couldn't; she hadn't said yes. "Beth, what the hell are you doing? I can't lie here like this while you just, just, play with me."

"What's the matter, Sean? Can't you let me have control?" Her voice was quiet and reasonable.

"It's not that! It's just that . . . Well, how about letting me do something? I could rub your back instead. Or your breasts or . . ."

"Isn't control the problem? I am enjoying touching you." Her hands stopped. Beth looked down at him, her face very serious. "We agreed you'd do anything I want this weekend. So what is your objection?"

He came up to his knees in a fury, his cock achingly hard. She watched him, entirely unruffled.

"What are you trying to do here? It'd be great if you were getting off, but you're not. And I'm not getting off either!"

"I told you my reasons: I am having a good time. That is all you need to know, in order to obey me." His dangerous lady looked straight back at him, as implacable as a samurai sword.

He glared, his fingers digging into the futon. For the first time in his life, he understood forcing a woman who'd said no.

She raised the stakes. "Are you saying no, here at the first step on the road that I have asked you to follow? If you are saying no, then leave now. Forever. I have no need of your company on this road."

"I can't do this!" he roared. "There's no point! I want to fuck, goddammit!" He started to sit back on his haunches.

"When you submitted to me before, it was because the sex was good. And maybe because you enjoyed dealing with a woman who knows what she wants and doesn't hesitate to reach out and take it. Correct?"

"Yes." He waited tensely, trying to understand her logic.

"But this time isn't about sex. In fact, you don't know what the purpose is, except to please me. You feel awkward and stupid, beset by a host of activities you have no control over and don't understand."

"I haven't felt this clumsy and useless since my first week at West Point," Sean admitted slowly. At least now, he wasn't feeling every pulse of blood moving into his aching cock.

"So use your brain this time, too, and not your cock," she snarled. "You've had to trust your leaders before, when the going was rough and the goal nowhere in sight. Sex alone isn't enough to keep me interested, Sean. You have to let me into your head. You must prove that I can trust you, even when it's not to your best advantage, or I'll leave. Do you understand me?"

"Yes. But, damn, it feels like my guts are being torn apart, to yield control and relax. Not to have you."

"Think like a Ranger and follow me. I'll never lead you astray and I'll fight to keep you safe." She slipped into the Ranger creed, her voice sharp as a sword leaving its scabbard. "Readily will I display the intestinal fortitude required to fight on to the Ranger objective and complete the mission though I be the lone survivor."

He froze. How many times before had he heard that? How many times had he sworn he wouldn't give up, no matter what it took? But this was different, harder than ever before. This time he had to yield, without taking action, even though he didn't know where matters were leading.

Sean closed his eyes, shaking. He took a very deep breath before he lay back down on the futon. He relaxed cautiously, one reluctant muscle at a time, long slow breaths until his cock sulked and softened. It was a difficult fight to calm his angry, whirling mind, which insisted on asking why he couldn't do something else. But if he was to stay with Beth, the woman who looked at him as if she couldn't have enough of him, he had to trust her.

He shivered once, when a draft touched his cooling body. Beth draped a towel over him and he steadily warmed up again, reassured by how she cared for his comfort.

"Concentrate on your breathing, darling," she whispered. She stroked him lightly, her fingers barely touching him, until he lay docile under her touch.

Then she began the massage again. This time, he focused on her hands as they moved smoothly over him. The pattern was different than anything he'd experienced before, whether from a masseuse or a lover. Gradually, he realized she was awakening his body, building a current that passed from her hands through his skin, before diving into his bones. It was a dance of energy between them, which gave everything and asked nothing except enjoyment of the moment. He was drawn steadily into a world of sensuality. His breathing deepened, as time ceased to exist.

She worked his spine thoroughly, pressing and stroking, sometimes just keeping her hand still. Sean began to feel both incredibly happy and relaxed at the same time. Strength flowed through him and he became more aroused. He heard himself purring like a cat.

Beth started to pound lightly on his spine, emphasizing different points as she worked. Heat built up and desire started to intensify. Then she stroked the length of his back, rocking Sean toward and then away from her. He shuddered when she reached the base of his spine.

"Relax, Sean. The massage is a gift for your sexual pleasure. All you have to do is enjoy."

He began to moan as his excitement built, but he stayed receptive to her movements as she taught him the sexual potential of his entire body. He had always focused primarily on his cock, sometimes on his nipples and anus. He had never imagined there could be so much sensation found elsewhere.

Her hands circled his back several times, before coming to rest at the top of his thighs. Then she rubbed his legs and buttocks until Sean's hips rocked.

Her hands left him briefly and he heard a packet rip. He lifted heavy eyelids and saw her pulling on a glove slowly, smoothing it down past her wrist with an elegant, fluid sensuality.

"Gloves?" he whispered. She turned back to him, and he shifted toward her hopefully.

She chuckled softly. "Take it easy, darling. I think you'll like this."

Her hands repeated their work on his legs, moving up to his buttocks until his hips repeated their earlier pleas. He needed more, and this time she gave him the additional stimulus he craved. Her gloved finger circled his asshole, in an erotic dance that echoed through his body.

His hips swayed eagerly, intent on gaining more attention to this most neglected of erogenous areas. Would his lady accept him here, too? His body shuddered in welcome and her finger slipped inside.

Taken at last by his dangerous lady.

He thought she groaned something, but hearing was the least important sense at that moment. His previous experiences with his fingers or stolid sex toys were no match for this reality. Every fiber was concentrated on her single finger, so warm and supple, slender and elegant as she teased him. By the time it left, his hips were rolling against the futon and he could have screamed with lust.

Her strokes changed to a harsher movement, which pushed away sensuality. Her hands lifted briefly and the glove snapped as it came off, triggering a hot flash of disappointment.

Sean took a calmer breath as his arousal eased slightly. If this was the first step on the road, would he survive the rest?

"Roll over, Sean."

He obeyed, as if in a trance.

Beth placed her hand gently on his chest and simply kept it there for a long moment. Sean yielded to his trust in her and closed his eyes.

Beth showed the same skill and loving care on the front of his body that she had given his back. Chest, arms, legs, groin were all massaged. She dragged her palm over his body, toward his cock but never quite touching it, slowly marking all the points of the compass on his straining torso. He couldn't have spoken, as his life force centered under her hands.

Then she worked over his cock, using strokes that built energy and trapped it, repeating the pattern until he thrashed below her. She pressed hard between his legs, and the surge stopped. He dragged oxygen into his lungs, trying to prepare for whatever came next.

Then she began again but, this time, her hands demanded that he climax. He erupted like a geyser, thrusting his hips up between her hands, screaming her name, rockets firing behind his eyes.

He recovered his senses to find her smoothing his face in a light massage. Then a large warm towel floated down over him, and he mumbled his thanks before falling asleep in her arms.

"Wake up, Sean. It's time for dinner."

Beth lightly ran her fingers through Sean's hair as he blinked up at her. His eyes traveled downward and he stared in shock at her attire. She was wearing a short black velvet dress that emphasized every line of her delicious body. The cloth wrapped around her neck and left her shoulders and back bare. He was acutely aware of her breasts moving behind the single layer of fabric.

Beth chuckled softly and stood up. "Your clothes are laid out on the bed. I'll wait for you in the living room."

He dressed very slowly. The first item was a black silk thong, soft as a lady's undergarments. He held it in the air studying it, recognizing it as something he'd never thought to wear. A suspicious sniff identified the same scent as the candles and massage oil. Finally he put it on, fussing and twitching until everything was in place, or at least as much in place as possible, given the size of what the thong was supposed to contain.

When he stared at himself in the mirror, he blushed at the emphasis on his sexuality. He almost looked like one of those male strippers, except none of them were as big and hairy as he was. Eventually he slowly reached for the other items.

When he was done, Sean scrutinized himself in the mirror for a long minute. The single-breasted black suit, with its Italian label, was cut from the finest wool he'd ever seen. The matching vest framed the white shirt and the narrow line of black silk tie. Even the shoes fit perfectly in their glove-soft leather. Money whispered from the beautiful cut and fabric, as well as the monogrammed gold cuff links and the gold watch on his wrist.

He tugged at the tie, very aware of the unfamiliar constriction. He felt as if he'd been tied up. Silly thought, considering that this was less restrictive than his uniform had been. He was flying in some pretty high circles with his dangerous lady.

All of his embarrassment was wiped away by the look on Beth's face when she saw him.

"You look wonderful, Sean. Even sexier than I'd hoped." She leaned up and kissed him on the cheek. "Let's go have some dinner."

He offered her his arm and led her out, caressing her hand as it rested in the crook of his elbow. They strolled slowly through the casino, glancing at the gamblers' restless attentions to the garish slot machines. A few people were playing blackjack and roulette.

"Crowds look pretty good tonight. I guess tourism seems to be coming back," Beth remarked.

"If you say so, honey. I've never been here before." Sean was much more interested in the slow rub of Beth's dress, and the heat of her skin, coming through his fine clothes.

The restaurant was small and exclusive, looking more like a private house than a large hotel. Oil paintings lined the walls, gleaming against silk wallpaper.

A waiter approached and asked for their drink order. Sean looked at Beth, waiting for her response. Was this behavior what she wanted?

She asked for the wine list and the waiter departed. He returned with another gentleman, who was introduced as the sommelier. The sommelier and Beth engaged in a lengthy conversation regarding the merits of various wines. The gentleman left, clutching the wine list and looking very pleased with Beth's decisions.

Sean sipped the chosen wine slowly, savoring the taste. He'd tried wine in Germany but only rarely. This was both light and complex at the same time, satisfying in its own right even as it hinted at complementing foods.

"I thought you didn't like drinking, Beth," he remarked, glancing at her.

She raised an eyebrow at him. "I believe in moderation, Sean. It's best to be aware of what our bodies feel, not the chemicals in our blood. But one drink tonight, especially of wine, should be just enough to help set the mood." Her eyes caressed his body for a moment, and he blushed. She smiled and patted his hand on the table. "Relax, Sean. Dinner and a little gambling will be fun."

He nodded and smiled back at her. Beth began to talk to him about his son, drawing out stories of Mike. Sean lost himself in recounting adventures and successes, paying little attention to the excellent food that she selected.

Beth told a few stories of her own childhood, lingering on her nieces and nephews' escapades. He laughed out loud over a tale of her nephew's misadventures at a Japanese kindergarten and answered with a story of his own days at West Point.

Finally Beth ran her fingers gently over his hand.

"Do you know how to shoot craps?" she asked. He nodded.

"Then let's go. You can show me how it's done." She rose to leave. The waiter bid them farewell, including a wish that they would look him up when they came back. Sean suspected that Beth had left a tip large enough to attract attention, even in this jaded town.

The casino was more crowded now, as they walked slowly through it, dodging other gamblers along the way. Beth attracted many envious stares as they went, and Sean swelled with pride and possession. She led the way to a craps table, in the middle of the high-stakes area.

Sean's eyes swept the room, managing not to stare at the intimate surroundings and exquisite décor. He watched the action at the table for a few minutes, matching the behavior here with what he'd known in Army barracks. Matters were fairly quiet, as the players spent more time joking with the dealer than rolling the dice. "Have you ever played craps before, Beth?"

"Once with my brother Jason, years ago. Neither of us knew what we were doing." She glanced over her shoulder and nodded to their host at the casino, who'd come up beside them unobtrusively. "Hello, Paul."

"Your usual stake, Ms. Nakamura. Is that enough?"

"Yes, that'll do for a start." She passed the chips over to Sean and signed the receipt quickly. He looked the chips over casually, then froze when he read the denomination. A thousand dollars per chip? He started to hand them back when she straightened up, but she refused them. "Use these to start with, Sean."

"Yes, ma'am," he responded, recognizing an order, however soft-spoken. He could follow her commands in this. He might not know how to read a fancy menu, but he'd played craps more than once. He sent up a quick prayer that Lady Luck would ride his shoulder tonight, as long as his dangerous lady was on his arm.

He began to bet on the action. His pile of chips grew quickly and he took over the dice, when the current shooter bowed out of the game. Beth slid closer to him, near enough he could smell her exotic perfume even in the crowd. He began to sweat but kept rolling the dice and winning, even while acutely aware of Beth's warmth and her bare back. He wrapped his arm around her, pulling her even closer, and grinned down at her.

"You're bringing me luck, lady!" he exulted and she laughed with him, her eyes dancing with excitement. A tremor slid through him, echoing her obvious delight in his actions.

The crowd kept building around them and Beth rubbed against him, her body plastered to his. Sean managed to pay enough attention to the game that his bets made sense to the dealer, even as his head spun with her nearness. Her hand rested in the small of his back, lightly caressing while she cheered him on.

Other people shouted and laughed around them, cheered and cursed the dice. Sean was only conscious of Beth and the dice as they rattled across the table.

Finally the pile of chips was a mountain in front of her, and his cock was threatening to come out of that silk thong. Sean leaned down to Beth and kissed her on the cheek.

"Let's go, lady. It's time to play another game," he pleaded.

She kissed his mouth hard and fast, then drew back smiling. "Okay, Sean, let's find something else," she agreed.

He gathered up the chips and they moved away from the table, leaving a trail of laughter and envious comments behind.

He offered the chips to her but she shook her head, rejecting them. She scanned the room quickly and the host appeared next to her. "You might enjoy the far table, Ms. Nakamura. The Chinese gentleman there is an excellent baccarat player," he suggested quietly.

"Thank you, Paul." Beth slid into the only available chair at that table and Sean took up position behind her. Graziano produced more chips for her, before disappearing into the crowd.

The play began within moments and Beth focused strictly on the game. Sean watched her, admiring her coolness and command of herself. His arousal ebbed, replaced by pride in her ability to beat the other players at the game. Chips accumulated in front of her, always neatly stacked by her elegant fingers.

Finally there was only the Chinese gentleman playing against her, the table surrounded by a circle of quiet whispers. Sean tried very hard not to see the chips' denominations. The watchers' demeanor was more than enough to convince him that a large sum of money was at stake.

The final hand was dealt and played. The Chinese gentleman bowed in defeat and Beth bowed deeply in return. Both players rose from the table and Beth turned to Sean. "Did you enjoy watching, Sean?"

"Yes, ma'am. It looked a bit like James Bond at the end though."

Beth smiled at his reference to the most famous baccarat player on film and kissed his cheek.

"Let's go then," she smiled. "Paul, will you cash our chips in, please?"

Paul took the proffered chips with a murmur of congratulations, which Beth acknowledged. She took Sean's arm and wandered toward the main casino area, glancing at other gamblers as she went. Sean resolved not to learn how much money had been at stake.

Paul caught up with them as they idly watched a roulette game and discreetly passed a stack of bills to Beth, which she promptly buried in her purse. Another stack went quietly to Sean. He glanced at Beth and she nodded approval. He slid the bills into his pocket, resolving to give them to her later. A cordial good-bye followed and they strolled once again through the casino.

Beth stopped at the elevators and turned to face Sean. "Sean, I need a copy of the *Financial Times*, an English newspaper. Bring it up to the suite in thirty minutes, won't you?" It was an order, not a request, although her voice was very unruffled.

"I'll bring it to you in thirty minutes, ma'am," Sean answered, wondering where he would find an English newspaper on a Saturday night.

Beth patted his cheek. "Empty yourself before returning, Sean. Can't have any distractions," she murmured and entered an open elevator.

Sean stared at the closing doors and swallowed hard. Then he started hunting for the newspaper.

Sean got off the elevator twenty-seven minutes after leaving Beth, newspaper in hand. He walked down the hallway and checked his watch, catching a whiff of that enticing scent from his cuff. Adam's bracelet rubbed his arm under the fine cotton. For a moment, he saw Adam's eyes as they had been on that last night. *"Do it for both of us!"*

He snapped off a salute in response, promising silently, *"For both of us."*

He knocked briefly on the door, precisely thirty minutes after leaving her and entered at her assent. But he stopped dead in his tracks, at what lay inside.

The suite was now lit entirely by a few candles, with curtains drawn against the neon lights beyond. A blaze of light came from a room on the far side, past a door that had always been locked before. Exotic music spilled out, evoking ancient passions with a woman's voice and drums. Indian music, perhaps. The aphrodisiacs' now familiar scent caressed him.

Beth watched him from the distant room, surrounded by light.

Scarlet silk caressed her body like a lover, leaving one shoulder bare and showing a gleam of ivory leg. Her hair was twisted at the back of her head and secured by gold combs. More gold hung from her neck and wrists, delicate chains with hanging jade charms.

Sean's breath caught in his throat with a rasp.

"I am a priestess of the goddess Ishtar," she announced calmly. "And I embody the goddess on earth at this moment. You are a warrior who has done well in the past. Now you must leave the mundane world behind, with its petty quarrels and dangers. Here you will be tested for your suitability to celebrate life with the goddess."

Sean nodded, overwhelmed by the appearance of his fantasy. The twentieth century disappeared and he became entirely a servant of the goddess, trusting the priestess to lead the way to fulfillment. The newspaper dropped unheeded to the floor.

"You will call me ma'am at all times. I will call you Ranger."

"Yes, ma'am."

"Strip to the skin, Ranger, and place your clothes neatly on the closest table."

Sean obeyed promptly, the elegant suit, silken underclothes, and expensive accessories discarded without a second thought. All his blood seemed to be flowing to his crotch.

"You may approach me now, Ranger."

Sean marched into the far room, careful to maintain a steady pace and keep his eyes in front. Old skills awoke and he observed as much as he could of his surroundings, without turning his head.

It had been a bedroom once but was now an exotic nest. Incense and red and white candles blazed, all casting the odors of musk and exotic flowers into the air, together with their light. Red and white roses spilled across the bed and every other surface.

A dagger almost as long as his forearm lay, cradled in blood-red roses, on the table next to her. Candlelight danced along its slender, rippling blade, emphasizing the cruel edge. Was it there for appearance? What if she used it to taste his blood?

Heat pooled in his groin at the thought.

"You are a warrior and must have a care for yourself, Ranger, that you may serve the goddess again in the future."

Sean concentrated hard. What was she leading up to?

"If anything occurs to sound an alarm, then you must speak immediately, Ranger. When you say the word *alarm*, I will stop your test and consider how best to proceed."

Safeword? Was she offering him a chance to stop fulfilling his fantasy?

"Do you understand me, Ranger?"

"Yes, ma'am." He saw no chance for opting out, not with Beth. She was too skilled and considerate for him to worry about harm.

"Listen up, Ranger!" she growled and he came fully alert, to meet her admonition. "You have a duty to the goddess to speak, if there is any chance of physical or emotional damage. A good warrior always warns of a threat. Stay silent and you will have failed. Do you understand me, Ranger?"

"Yes, ma'am," he responded contritely.

"Now tell me how you will sound an alert, Ranger."

"*Alarm*, ma'am."

"Very good." Beth pointed a finger at the floor in front of her. Sean promptly knelt at her feet, bowing his head to the ground, thankful his years of martial arts training made this movement easy.

"Sit up, Ranger, so that you may be attired suitably to serve."

He sat back on his heels but kept his eyes straight ahead, reflecting the attitude learned in the Army.

Beth held up a scarf for him to see and nodded approvingly, when recognition lit his eyes. It was the scarf she had worn into the bookstore, which had pleasured them both. She wrapped it around his neck, then tied it carefully in front with the knot against his Adam's apple. The soft silk caressed his throat from chin to collarbone, with the golden ends brushing his chest.

Then she tied a red and gold scarf around each of his upper arms. They hung down, stroking his arms, while the delicate tips danced against his wrists.

"Now kneel down with your hips up in the air. Keep your knees spread."

She walked slowly around Sean then knelt down behind him. She caressed him slowly, stroking his legs. Her touch traveled to the inside of his thighs. He choked back a gasp at a particularly intense sensation.

"Do not keep the sounds of your pleasure from the goddess, Ranger," Beth snapped.

"Yes, ma'am," Sean answered, then sighed when her fingers stroked him again. He knelt in a trance of utter pleasure, as her hand explored him, gliding forward to tickle his balls from underneath.

He shivered when a single oily finger prowled down his spine. A long, slow pressure followed and he yielded readily to the finger's gentle foray into his insides. It felt even better than it had the first time.

"Tell me if anything hurts, Ranger. This should only feel good."

More? Was she going to give him more fingers to twine inside him? He murmured an assent, focused only on the delights her hands were teaching. He groaned a welcome to the second finger and quickly adapted to its additional pressure.

"Beautifully taken, Ranger. You did well," she assured him. He murmured something in response, more concerned with her touch than the words' meaning.

He stretched eagerly for the third finger, savoring the hot, flexible pressure against his core. He rocked peacefully against their slow massage, savoring the slow pulses flowing from his prostate into his balls. How many times had he beat off, as he imagined being possessed by his woman in this way?

A brisk buzz stroked him and he pushed back against the steady vibration, circling near the fingers caressing his insides. Her hand slipped out and the vibrator slid into his anus on the same beat. It nestled against his spine, smaller than many in his collection at home, and its base settled neatly into the cleft of his buttocks. A butt plug, with a vibrator singing inside it.

"Thank you, ma'am," he groaned in welcome, as her hand rested reassuringly on his hip. He felt stuffed with sensuality, as if she'd gifted him with a key that could unlock marvels. This game would be played out with a living woman who wanted him, in the bright light of an open room. Not in the dark behind a locked door, with only his books and his two hands.

"Stand up, Ranger, and face me."

Sean came to his feet carefully, acutely conscious of the effect his movements had on the throbbing pressure deep inside him. His erection was enormous, reflecting his body's enjoyment of that internal pressure.

He caught sight of the waiting dagger as he moved, and hair lifted from his skin. He almost laughed at the familiar rush of adrenaline. This game would be played out in sensuality, in climaxes that racked his body to the bone. Not in blood or injury. This tide meant life, not death, to a warrior.

"Excellent. You look magnificent, Ranger." Her low voice was husky and fired his veins like whiskey.

She began to wrap lengths of black velvet ribbon around him, first around his waist then between his legs, to secure the butt plug. A few loops caught his cock and balls, lifting and separating them for display even while controlling them. A quick knot at the waist followed, leaving the ribbon's ends to float against his groin, every touch a reminder of her control.

His eyelids drooped with pleasure as he gave himself to her handling. A single twist of her fingers left the vibrator silent. Sean mourned the lost stimulus, even as he anticipated the slow buildup possible in its absence.

"See yourself in the mirror, Ranger," Beth said quietly and stepped aside so he could look.

His body surged in response to the carnal image of himself, packaged and waiting for his woman's pleasure. He caught sight of Beth watching him, the dagger next to her hand and her eyes full of yearning. Something deep inside him snarled in triumph.

Nine

Beth stared at Sean, hungering to taste him. He was magnificent, a pagan in silks that only emphasized his masculinity. The narrow lines of ribbon called attention to his engorged cock, standing up proudly against his white groin.

She took a deep breath and savored the flow of energy that this scene was releasing, beginning when her first words had snatched Sean into his fantasy's embodiment. He'd yielded himself readily to the plug's penetration, symbolizing her dominance while pleasuring him. Now he was dressed, with his cock standing at attention and a vibrator waiting inside him. Already the most enticing male sub she'd ever seen, he'd be irresistible once he was fully, carefully trained. Not her dream of a switch but perfect for this moment.

Her terror at playing the scene well dissolved, leaving her free to concentrate on the rich chemistry between them.

She regally seated herself again in the big armchair. "You may give me a footbath now, Ranger. You will find everything necessary through that door." She nodded her head toward the bathroom and waited.

Sean's first steps were hesitant, clearly responding to the dildo shifting inside him, before he found a steady pace. Beth bit her lip against a smile as he disappeared. He returned carrying a silver tray, holding basins and small jars, with several towels neatly draped over his arm. He knelt silently in front of her, set the tray next to him, and took her shoes off.

She sighed happily when he eased her feet carefully into the hot water. He slowly bathed each foot and rubbed it with the oil provided, which was similar to that used for his massage. His inexperience showed, but so did his absolute absorption in the task as he carefully polished every inch. His cock hardened further as he labored.

Beth leaned back in the chair, letting her eyes drift shut. She spoke when he hesitated at her knees.

"Work up my legs, then attend to my womanhood. Use your hands and mouth, Ranger." The order sounded like the soft growl of a tigress in a temple courtyard.

Sean's eyes widened for a moment before he bowed his head in acknowledgment. "Yes, ma'am," he rumbled.

He kissed her feet, following the trail he had laid down in oil earlier. Then he moved up her legs with his hands first, closely followed by his mouth.

Beth closed her eyes in rapture. Tense muscles relaxed under the insistent caresses of his mouth and fell deeper into bliss with every soft brush of his hair between her thighs. Her legs fell open, inviting him closer. Her hips moved forward on the chair, seeking contact with his mouth.

She hummed when she smelled her own arousal. He answered with a delighted murmur, as his tongue first tasted her secrets. Tonight only they wouldn't use barriers during this climactic fantasy, given that they were both clean. Not even later to prevent pregnancy, thanks to her being on birth control.

His attentions were slow and insistent as he pleasured her, taking her to multiple climaxes. Beth's hands moved in his hair, enjoying its feel against her skin, as her clitoris shivered and danced under his teeth and tongue. But a corner of her mind kept touch with reality, while her body melted for him.

Finally she pulled his hair abruptly. She needed to fulfill his fantasy, not lose herself in her own pleasure. "You have acknowledged the goddess well, Ranger. Now you must be tested before true service can begin."

Sean bowed to the floor, then stayed kneeling with his head bent.

"Sit up, Ranger, and look at me." Beth studied him, seeing the slow swirl of desire in his blue eyes. She took an item from a box next to her and held it out toward him. "Do you know what this is, Ranger?"

Sean stared at the small piece of metal, its narrow curves glittering in the light. Somewhere a drum pounded and tambourines danced. Recognition burned but he shook his head slowly. "Please explain to me, ma'am."

"It's a nipple clamp. It will test you with pain, Ranger, even as it adorns your beauty."

Sean looked at the small object for another moment then bent his head. A drop of sweat trickled down the center of his chest from under the scarf. Another drop echoed it from the tip of his cock.

Beth leaned forward and stroked his chest slowly, centering his blood and attentions where she wished. She put the clamp on carefully, watching his face. Sean closed his eyes but remained silent when the pain hit him. His breathing steadied after a moment and Beth took her hands away.

The other clamp went on with equal ease. Sean groaned softly and his breathing stayed slow. Beth relaxed, certain now that he could tolerate the small pain. His cock gleamed as a thin trail of moisture slid down it. "Close your eyes."

Sean complied immediately and she blindfolded him with a black silk scarf. He turned his head from side to side then stayed still. His mouth worked slowly then relaxed, as he accepted the loss of sight.

Beth stood up and took his hand.

"Come with me, Ranger, and lie down on the bed." The scent of roses came strongly when he sat down on the bed, crushing the delicate petals under his body.

"Put your hands over your head and spread them wide. Place your fingertips against the headboard, Ranger."

She guided his hands into position, making sure each finger touched the bed. Muscles and tendons stood out in sharp relief, as his arms stretched and twisted to achieve the desired position.

"Very good, Ranger. Now bend your knees and place your feet flat on the bed. Keep your legs spread wide. Lift your hips." She slid a pillow under him so that the soft skin between his legs was completely exposed. "Excellent."

She stepped back and studied him. His body lay like a banquet in front of her, with its most sensitive areas fully exposed for her handling. The tension necessary to maintain this position emphasized his muscles and made him look even more masculine. Astoundingly beautiful.

"Now hear the rules of your test, Ranger."

Sean's head turned toward her voice and his breathing seemed to stop.

"I will tease you with three fabrics. You must keep your fingertips and feet pressed firmly against the bed at all times, Ranger. You will receive ten blows for every time your fingertips or feet fail to touch the bed. The goddess wishes you to move the rest of your body often. Do you understand?"

"Yes, ma'am." Sean's voice was very steady.

She looked him over again and reached for the first fabric.

A long strip of silk velvet glided over his face, before sliding down to caress his shoulders. It traveled slowly across him, taking special delight in seeking out hidden places.

"One," came the count, when it slipped under his arm and he shuddered, as it found his pulse there.

The velvet embraced his nipples and danced with his navel. It sank against his ankles before sliding underneath his thighs. It melted against the ribbons where they bound his balls. He choked and shivered.

"Two."

It flirted with the plug's base. He trembled.

"Ma'am, please, oh, Christ!"

"Three."

"Fuck!" he swore, hips jerking wildly.

"Four," as another tremor rocked his body. He grunted and bit his lip until blood dripped, as he mastered himself.

Finally the velvet moved away from him.

Beth explored Sean slowly with the Venice lace. It was soft, textured, and seemed particularly good at lifting hairs away from his body.

He twitched when it dropped on his cock like a delicate hammer blow. "Shit," he hissed.

"Five."

Finally she dragged metallic tulle across him. It looked like a fine golden net, every wire standing in clear contrast to his white skin. It scratched him lightly, a harsher sensation that he welcomed in his growing excitement. His cock stood stronger and his breathing deepened, when she rubbed around his nipples, his shoulders twisting to follow her hand.

"Six."

She slapped his cock lightly with the tulle, and he bucked hard.

"Seven."

His hips writhed as they followed the tulle's path. The scent of his musk came clearly over the incense. He kept his fingertips and feet in the required position, despite the tulle's teasing. She finally lifted the bright web from his sweating skin, acknowledging that he'd signaled how many strokes he wanted from the spanking. "At ease, Ranger."

Sean collapsed onto the bed and groaned softly. Beth gently stroked his arms and legs, helping his circulation return.

Then she snatched off one clamp, giving her warrior a faster release than normal. He yelped at the agony, as blood rushed into his nipple. She bent her head and licked it carefully, covering the pain with pleasure.

Sean groaned and tossed his head from side to side. "Ma'am, please, oh, ma'am, more, please," he begged. The tulle had verified his checklist's claim: he liked strong sensation. She could give him what he wanted.

Beth removed the remaining clamp with equal speed and suckled him, binding the clamp's harshness to the wet heat of her mouth. He moaned happily and arched his back, shamelessly seeking more.

She lingered over his chest for long minutes, adorning the strong muscular curves with soft laving caresses, before sucking and nipping his nipples. They shone brilliantly red against his golden pelt, when she lifted her head. He was truly beautiful, flushed with heat in such delightful areas, as he quivered against the coverlet's golden silk.

Her hand covered his face for a moment, warning him of the changed focus, before she pulled the blindfold over his head.

Sean squeezed his eyes shut and opened them slowly. He shuddered slightly and ran his tongue slowly over his lips, then straightened to his full length.

Beth seated herself in the armchair again, very pleased with her warrior. He could have wriggled less often, if he wanted fewer blows. "Fetch me the gloves from the table, Ranger."

He found a pair of fingerless, black leather gloves where she indicated. He bowed in front of her and lifted the gloves to her, spread across his hands. Beth accepted them and pulled each one on slowly. Sean watched her, spellbound and speechless. An occasional fine spasm ran through his body.

"Turn around, Ranger, so you may be bound for your ordeal."

Sean spun in a single clean movement that screamed eagerness and Beth purred softly. "Right hand first, Ranger. Now the left." She efficiently wrapped black velvet ribbon around his wrists just above his wrist bone, so that each hand rested against the opposing forearm. He would be able to stay bound like this for a long time.

"Well done, Ranger," she praised his acquiescence and he bowed his head in acknowledgment. "Now kneel down and bend over the bed, Ranger, to receive your punishment."

Sean dropped to his knees smoothly and bent over as directed, quivering when her leather-clad hands caught and steadied him.

"You will keep your legs together at all times, Ranger. It's the best way to protect your balls."

He flinched briefly. "Yes, ma'am."

"How do you give the warning, Ranger?"

"I sound out the word, *alarm*, ma'am."

"Good lad." Her voice was a bit abstracted. She slipped a pillow under his chest for his comfort and stood back to consider his position. Long tremors flowed over him, as he waited for her next move.

"May I speak, ma'am?"

"You have not been commanded to silence, Ranger," Beth corrected him, dragging a fingernail down his spine in emphasis. He choked back a gasp and took a minute before talking again, turning his head against the golden silk to watch her.

"I would like to ask that you only count the good strokes, ma'am."

Beth's eyebrow lifted, considering his request. He wanted all seventy strokes to be heavy sensation? His eyes burned bright blue as he stared at her, silently begging.

"You have done well so far, Ranger, and the goddess is pleased with you. You may have this boon."

"Thank you, ma'am!"

Seventy strokes, or more than an hour's worth. Quite doable, but she was still very glad for her years of practice and hours in a gym, strengthening her back and shoulders. Her old swimming coach would grin at this use of his conditioning regimen.

Beth trailed her fingers over one shoulder and down Sean's arm to his palm, enjoying the shudder that flowed through him in response. She acquainted herself with his other arm in the same way, reminding him of the pleasure her hands could bring. She visited his shoulders and spine, then his thighs, until he sighed and twisted under her touch.

Once she had returned him to sexual expectations, her hand dealt the first blow so it fell light as a raindrop. He hummed softly and waited patiently.

Beth smiled wryly. He would learn soon enough, especially when the plug started rocking between his tailbone and prostate, and sent each swat dancing into his groin. How much of a sensual spanking would he enjoy? Would he still be so willing when the seventieth blow fell?

She built the blows up slowly, always watching for his reaction to each increase in intensity. She stroked him where the blows landed, massaging the sensation into a broader area of skin as she kept him eager. She varied the rhythm, building his anticipation—and allowing her body to recover and prepare for the next round.

His arousal built, as his skin heated and his hips began to twist and writhe. She dealt different types of swats, usually with the flat of her hand, but sometimes only with her fingertips. She laid the blows evenly across his buttocks and emphasized the sweet spot above his thighs, where each contact sent a wave of pleasure through his pelvis and up his spine. She dealt a few swats to his shoulders, sending blood there to prepare him for the future.

She sharpened the tempo, pushing him to a higher level, and his arousal followed her lead. He moaned and wriggled under her hand, his ass clenching as the red heat built under his skin.

She smacked the plug lightly and he quivered in response before he begged her for more, pushing his hips up to meet her hand.

Her hand burned, matching his skin. The leather spread the blaze to every pore it touched, whether or not they'd felt his ass. She ran her hands down his back, driven to bring his heat into herself. He growled softly and arched against her palms, welcoming every touch. He was well started and now it was time to aim for more.

Beth found a soft deerskin flogger among her toys and came back to him. She laid the flogger against his back and slowly rubbed the soft leather tails against him, letting him feel the flogger first as part of her.

"Please, ma'am. Flog me, please," he sighed, his eyes drooping shut.

She dragged the tails over him until he hummed and twisted to follow the caress. Then she tapped him lightly, teaching him how a soft thud felt. He moaned happily and arched under the different sensation. She landed a stronger blow and he stayed with her easily, as she built the intensity. It was the smoothest dance she'd ever had with a submissive.

After landing a few blows with real force, she ran an ice cube over his skin. He yelped in surprise but soon started purring, as the ice eased the pain. She trailed ice over all of his shoulders and buttocks, letting him enjoy the contrasting sensations. The ice's meltwater carried subsequent blows' impact across still more skin, building bliss. He began to rub his cock against the bed, seeking more stimulation.

She paused to admire him, licking her lips at his strong body twisting and bucking, displaying him in a frenzied ecstasy. His beautiful ass was as urgently colored as his cock before an eruption. He danced under her hand readily, erasing her anxiety at initiating a rookie and filling her with pride.

She dragged the overheated air into her lungs, letting his musk and sweat fill her nostrils like the blood pounding through his veins from her touch. It was all she could do not to roll him on the floor and take him.

She took another ragged breath and dropped her hand on him again, fiercely claiming him. He jerked, then thrust himself up, wordlessly pleading for another touch of her hand. She caressed him again and again, his bliss sinking into her while she focused on his sexual pleasure. Over an hour had passed since the first swat had fallen.

"Ma'am, please, more . . . ma'am," he growled, making his desires quite clear.

Beth fetched her favorite Jay Marston flogger, present now thanks to Jenn's preparations for this night, and fondled it, as she considered where to strike first. It was heavier and broader than the last and would make the remaining blows fall stronger and firmer into Sean's rapturous body. She didn't think of it as Dennis's gift, from when she first learned to dominate a man. It was simply her most familiar friend, come to help her take Sean as high as possible.

She ran the tails over Sean's back and he sighed ecstatically, shifting himself to follow the new touch.

"Hell, yes, ma'am. More, oh, damn, yes," he sobbed. An electric current ran through her at the rapture in his voice.

The last ten blows were the strongest, but Sean was delighted. He pushed his hips back for each blow and laughed ecstatically, when they fell. His cock was rich with blood, still lifting eagerly against his belly.

Beth tossed the flogger aside when she finished, shaking slightly. She caressed and kissed his back, feeding on his excitement until she wanted to sink her fingers into his bones to join them. He was well-marked but not bloody; he certainly wouldn't be able to sit down comfortably for a few days.

"Well done, Ranger!" she praised him. "You mastered your ordeal like a veteran. The goddess is very pleased with you."

Sean laughed and looked up at her, his eyes bright as an archer's after winning the Olympics. "Thank you, ma'am, thank you!" he sang out. "Damn but I needed that!"

Beth chuckled softly, letting out the reins on her excitement. "Lie down on the bed, Ranger. On your back."

Sean stood up jerkily, obviously fighting for self-control. He stretched himself across the silk, displaying himself in a silent demand to be taken.

"Shit," he cursed softly as his weight pressed his sensitized back against the rough silk. He groaned again and let out a long slow breath. His cock shuddered under the black velvet web. Heavy lids half-veiled the need burning in his eyes. His gaze lanced through her and shredded her self-control.

Experience meant nothing to her now, only the urgency to join him. But she had to play the game out and stay within his fantasy. She closed her eyes, building a priestess's command to a warrior.

"You did well, Ranger, and have earned a reward. You will be permitted to celebrate life in the goddess's service."

Beth lifted the dagger from the table and held it up, letting the candlelight light flames in it.

Sean froze immediately, eyes wide and staring at the blade. He slowly dragged in first one breath then another. His eyes lifted to meet hers, and his mouth curled in the hard smile of a warrior eager to enter the mêlée. "Take me, ma'am," he growled. "Let my blood flow like the roses. I will celebrate life in any way you command."

Beth inclined her head and glided toward the bed. She took a few minutes more to center herself, until her hands were rock-steady. He watched her eyes throughout, full of the same clean-edged calm that had doubtless faced guns and missiles before.

"On your side, Ranger, so your back faces me."

Sean's bound hands pushed hard against the soft bed and he arched into a roll, hips first. She caught him with her free hand and steadied him. She slid the dagger gently up his forearm until the tip caught under a ribbon. He stayed completely still as he waited for her, although she could feel his hammering pulse.

Beth eased the sharp edge farther up his arm until the black velvet fell away soundlessly. He hissed at the returning sensation but didn't move. She rubbed his wrists quietly until he relaxed, while still sneaking in some caresses to his beautiful backside. He jerked when the vibrator began to sing again, against his inner pleasure points.

"On your back, Ranger."

He hissed briefly but quickly assumed another wanton posture, flaunting his assets and his eagerness. Beth's mouth twitched. She laid the dagger along the vein in his groin, where the slightest pressure could kill or emasculate him. His heavy eyelids sank down for a long minute, but his breathing never faltered.

"I beg of you, ma'am," he started, then stopped. "Please touch me with the knife."

A predatory smile touched Beth's lips. She slid the dagger up and teased a line of black velvet from his waist. His cock swelled harder against its black velvet web. She pressed harder and the ribbon ends fell back against him, one strand gone. He moaned and his cock jerked against its bonds.

Beth cut the remaining ribbons away from him, with the same exquisite care she'd given the first strand. He watched every move, his eyelids drooping farther while his cock grew larger. She cupped his balls, her thumb rising up his shaft and over the fat glans, watching his pre-come and sweat gild his cock. He moaned, his hips thrust restlessly and his tongue traced his lips. His eyes memorized every move of her hand.

Beth stepped back from the bed. He snarled but managed not to form a protest. His eyelids fell then snapped up again, pleading with her.

She smiled, a very feminine promise of satisfaction. He shivered at the sight and his hands moved restlessly in the silk under him.

She slid the dress off her shoulder, letting the scarlet silk catch on her budded nipples. Her smile deepened when he hissed, his hips lifting as if to meet her. Her belly clenched as cream pooled between her thighs, ready to ease his way.

Then she slowly shimmied out of the dress, letting every wiggle reveal another taste of skin while pooling on another curve. His movements grew more and more restless, while his hands clenched and unclenched.

Finally, she wore only jade and golden chains to highlight her body's flushed eagerness.

"Please," he moaned, his eyes fixed on her and his body was nearly frantic, as it jerked restlessly. A continuous line of silver slid down his cock to brighten its crimson.

Beth knelt beside him on the bed, taking one last taste of his beauty before allowing herself to lose control. She straddled his hips, keeping her cleft just beyond his cock. Then she stretched herself upon him and let consciousness of his body seep into every cell of her being. His chest fur pricked her nipples while his heartbeat echoed in her bones. He smelled richly masculine, as the scent of musk, sweat, and aphrodisiacs enfolded her. Beth nuzzled his shoulder, inhaling him further, then licked him, swallowing his taste.

Sean growled at her possession of him, before relaxing slowly and yielding himself to her. He shuddered at the pressure of her body against his erection.

"Ma'am, please, have mercy and fuck me," he begged shamelessly. He twisted impatiently and yelped, when a particularly forceful move scratched his backside.

Beth settled deeper against him, deliberately reminding him of the marks she'd already left, and he gasped. The hard ridge between their bellies grew harder and hotter as his hips circled under her, intent on finding the ultimate satisfaction.

Beth caressed him restlessly, as her blood seemed to seek him out with every pulse. Her breasts were full and flushed, her nipples burning where his chest fur rubbed them. She sank her fingers into his shoulders and rubbed her hips against him, as cream came forth in a match to the surging blood in her veins. Her foot kneaded his calf, desperately seeking the rough tickle of his hair.

"Ma'am, please! I want to give, I need to . . ."

Now. She needed him now.

She came up to her knees above him, letting his cock stand proudly free.

"Look at yourself, Ranger. Your manhood is as naked as when it came from your mother's womb."

He moaned, his eyes seeking hers as his hips writhed.

"Now it will return to its rightful place inside a woman, cleansed by the proofs you have provided and tonight's ordeal." She wrapped her hand around his cock and squeezed it hard. He arched off the bed in response.

"Fuck," he groaned as more pre-come glided down the jutting length.

Beth smiled, a predator seeing the endgame at last.

"I demand all of you, Ranger! All your body, all your strength, now!" She rubbed the fat plum-shaped head through her folds until it gleamed.

"Fuck me," he groaned again as his head tossed. "Fuck . . ."

Beth leisurely claimed him, fiercely watching his eyes as he saw more and more of his cock vanish into her.

"Fuck," he mumbled, his eyes enormous as he stared. "Oh, fuck . . ."

She rolled her hips and sighed, when his balls rested hard against her cleft. Her vagina was so full of his big horse cock that she felt barely able to contain their combined life force. She felt the fine tremors running through him from the vibrator deep in his ass. He rumbled his wordless encouragement.

She rose up again until he almost left her. She knelt tall and powerful above him, as his hips pushed off the bed in a quest to regain her.

"No, please!" he begged.

She caressed her breasts, rubbing and plucking at the tightly furled buds of her nipples. Then she swooped down on him and filled herself again.

"Yes, goddammit, yes! Fuck me now!"

Beth groaned and slowed her thrusts, fighting to postpone her climax. He keened his hunger and grabbed the silk covers so tightly that his hands shone white. His cock traced circles inside her and she lost all sanity against his silent plea.

She moved faster and faster on him, seizing him ravenously. He matched her movements, hips pumping rapidly into her and his eyes shut. He yowled and hissed, snarled and grunted as he fought for more.

She twisted and danced above him, his vitality filling her. Pulses built in her, starting deep and low, pounding into her blood and bones. Her orgasm overwhelmed her and she abandoned herself to the flood, her senses tumbling into the light.

Sean's head snapped back as he finally launched himself into his own climax. He screamed her name over and over, as he pumped his life's essence into her.

Ten

Sean stared at himself in the big mirror over the sink. Another mirror in the opulent bathroom displayed his back, still marked by the night before. Bites and clawmarks showed clear against his skin, both in front and in back. Some of them—but not all—were from Friday night when he'd joined the Mile High Club.

Red stripes over his shoulders and lower asscheeks, with a few lines marking the flogger's fall. The real wonder was that none of them had hurt at the time. Shit, he distinctly recalled begging for more.

Three interlocked ruby circles, at the base of his cock and between his balls, showed where the black velvet had held him. He remembered clearly how she'd cut the ribbons off, using the dagger so very carefully.

Flogging—hell, even that little dagger she used, seemed damned unimportant now, after watching her come to the most spectacular climax he'd ever seen in his life. And she'd had it with him, nobody else.

He traced a particularly vivid scratch across his pecs and shivered. He'd enjoyed the creation of all those marks. He'd even bit Beth hard enough to mark her, a couple of times. She'd pulled his head closer and moaned when he did. And he'd laughed as he bent down to her again.

What the hell did that say about him?

Mrs. Wolcott had left marks on his ass after their night together, that had hurt like the devil for the first day. He'd wanted to go back to her bed but it had been simple to catch the bus, leaving her behind. He always knew she had no place in his future life, no matter how many times she walked in his fantasies.

Did he want to play like that again, make love so fiercely that pleasure and pain blended together into ecstasy? Or was it just for this one time only, to be remembered later in dreams? How would Beth treat him, now that she knew so much of his dark side?

Sunday morning and he had less than a day remaining with her. The center of the curtains glowed brightness where they didn't quite close, providing just enough light to make the golden bedspread gleam. Beth slept soundly under it, her hair scattered across the pillow. A little snore escaped her.

Sean smiled at the sound. His dangerous lady wasn't perfect and she was here with him now. This was real life and he'd best take what he could, while luck still favored him.

He slid silently back into the big bed and tucked her up close, careful not to wake her. Her nose twitched at the contact with his hairy chest and he froze. He calmed when she wrapped an arm around his waist and buried her face in his shoulder. No woman had ever trusted him enough to sleep with him the way Beth did.

A very old knot, too deep inside to be named, loosened and fell away.

He lay quietly and watched her sleep against him. He tucked a lock of raven hair back behind her ear and pulled the covers higher around her. His beautiful lady needed her rest, no matter what he wanted. A night like that one would wear anyone out.

She mumbled something and shifted closer. Her hand gently stroked his back and he pushed against it. A purr grew in his chest, as her hand slowly moved up and down his spine. She rubbed her face in the hair on his chest then nuzzled him, until she was delicately licking his nipple.

He choked but kissed her hair. His hands began to revisit her favorite spots. She stretched to suckle his other nipple and his hand pulled her head closer. He slid his leg between hers, as she reached up to meet his mouth.

"My turn," he murmured, tightening his fingers in her hair gently.

Beth looked up at him quizzically, with her mouth still wrapped around his nipple. Then she released him gently and leaned her head against his shoulder. He tilted her head farther back and began to kiss her slowly. Their mouths played with each other like children exploring an ice cream cone.

He ended it finally and began to gently work his way down her body. He cherished each bruise and mark with his mouth and hands, giving the softest of massages to ease her aches.

231

She stretched her head back and abandoned herself to him, trembling when he kissed the bite marks on her thigh. She twisted against his hands, as he lifted her hips to his mouth. She gripped his head to pull him closer and moaned, when his tongue slipped inside. He savored the taste of her, as she glided into her climax.

She stretched like a cat under him, as he propped himself up on his elbows to look at her. Her eyes had a faint touch of sadness. Then she blinked and smiled at him. "Care to bring that marvelous mouth up here, lover?" she invited.

Sean smiled and slid to kiss her mouth. She returned his kiss with interest, one leg wrapping around his waist as she welcomed him. The kiss was deep and slow, like an opium poppy or his hips' rhythm as he worked his way inside her. She was entirely open and willing, as her hands urged him on with soft strokes over his shoulders and down his back. Even his climax was strong and leisurely, as he lost himself in her.

A hunter's instinct stirred in the aftermath. She was still interested in him. It hadn't been an act, just to seduce him into letting her play games with him. What did that offer for the future?

Beth lightly ran a fingertip down a vein in his forearm. "You're a wonderful lover, Sean," she sighed.

Sean's mouth twitched but he kissed her forehead. "Maybe. Or maybe it's because you're such an inspiration."

"Maybe we should just agree that each other is incredible," Beth murmured and grinned up at him. Her stomach rumbled and she laughed openly. He joined in and hugged her, rolling across the bed.

"I ordered some breakfast for us, darling. It's waiting in the living room. Would you like a shower first?"

She blinked at him, clearly surprised he was taking charge of the arrangements, and relaxed. "Shower and breakfast would be very nice," she agreed. "What did you order for breakfast?"

"Healthy stuff, mostly. Yogurt, granola, fruit. But there's coffee and sweet breads too," Sean confessed.

She chuckled and patted his cheek. "I understand. Seattle boys need their coffee in the morning," she chuckled, and sat up.

He relaxed slightly, pleased that she had accepted his decisions.

They showered together, playing in the water like children. First came little splashes as they tried to get each other wet enough to lather up, then greater bursts as they rinsed the soap off. They managed to get the entire enormous shower stall wet, until streams flowed down from the very top. The sight brought even more merry peals and Beth threw her head back, laughing like a toddler.

Sean settled his hands on her sides, rubbing her up and down as he joined in her amusement. She arched back against his grip, wriggling happily as the water bounced off her breasts and against him. She shimmied and chortled, as she turned the shower into a fountain tumbling over him.

He laughed with her and shook himself like a dog, sending as much water back as he could. Drops fell from the tiled ceiling overhead, like a waterfall. One drop landed on his nose and he crossed his eyes at it.

She laughed so hard at the sight that she couldn't stand and had to lean back against the wall.

Sean frowned at her, in pretended hauteur, and she laughed louder. He pressed forward in a mock scolding, only to freeze when a drop fell down his forehead and into the corner of his eye.

She gulped back laughter and he advanced again, letting his own mirth ring out. She reached up and smoothed away the water above his eyes. He kissed her, sharing his enjoyment through the intimate touch of their mouths.

She drew him closer, wrapping her arms around his neck. Her leg slid up and down his before finally embracing his hip, in an echo of their tongues' dance.

He sighed happily and leaned against her, until the wet tile pressed her closer. She stretched up until her nether lips cradled his cock. He moaned and lifted her up, then slid her down onto him.

"Ooh, darling," she purred as he kissed her throat. "Damn but you feel good."

He rocked against her easily and slowly, memorizing the feel of her.

"*Kakko ii*," she breathed as his hands kneaded her ass. "You are so fine." She climaxed sweetly, her body rippling around him. He continued to thrust to the same slow, steady beat and felt her reach for another orgasm.

"Good girl," he praised, somehow keeping his breathing as regular as his thrusts. "Let's see how many climaxes you can have before breakfast."

She found three more before his body finally arrived at one. He came heavily in deep shuddering spurts that tugged at his heart as they pulled the last drops from deep in his balls.

Beth blinked up at him afterward then licked her lips daintily. "You really are fine, lover," she purred.

He blushed, his legs barely able to support them, and let her slide down.

Dressed at last, she looked over at him, where he sat peeling a banana and trying not to think about his sore backside. The remains of breakfast were scattered across the table. "That looks good, darling. Can I have some?"

"Sure." He started to reach out to her but she jumped out of her seat and came over to him.

"Now how can I sit on your lap, Sean, when you're up against the table like that?" she teased him.

He pushed back his chair and stood up. She cocked her head inquiringly but he caught her wrist. He towed her over to a big chair by the window and sat down, pulling her down into his lap. She promptly snuggled against him and he winced as her weight pressed him harder into the chair. But those marks would only be around for a few days to remind him of her.

He fed her pieces of banana, savoring the sweet warm weight of her while he still could. She rested comfortably against him, watching his face and the Vegas skyline. Sean listened to his heart pound against her warmth.

"Did you enjoy last night, Sean? Are you comfortable with everything that happened?" she asked quietly and twisted her head up to see his face.

"Comfortable? Are you kidding? Beth, that was the most fantastic night of my life! And you were great, better than any fantasy I'd ever had."

She smiled at his emphatic response and he kissed her hard on the mouth. Then his lips trailed over her face, as he tried to convince her of his sincerity. "Darling, I couldn't ask for anything more. But the best part was when you looked at me . . ." He stopped, overcome by the memory.

"What do you mean?"

"When you had the scarves on me and the ribbons . . . and the vibrator tickling my ass. I stood up and you looked at me, like I was the greatest thing you'd ever seen. As if you couldn't wait to touch me." He paused, choking on emotion. "Sweetheart, I'd do anything to have you look at me like that again. I'd like it to happen often." His eyes met hers earnestly.

Beth searched his eyes then closed hers. Had he frightened her? "Let's go spend some vanilla time together," she said and stood up.

"Honey?" Hell, what had he said? Six years a widower, twelve years celibate, and now lunging at the first woman in his bed? Cool down, Lindstrom, and think with your head for a change.

"We're only together for a weekend, remember? And neither of us is ready for a replay of last night. So let's just hang out together." Her eyes were deep and still, implacable.

He had committed only to a weekend. His hold loosened on her and she stood up.

Beth tossed a leather jacket at him from the closet. He caught it and pulled it on, his mouth quirking at yet another display of her moneyed tastes. He was wearing designer jeans and an incredibly soft turtleneck sweater, both of which outlined every muscle. She'd called the sweater's wool alpaca and said it came from South America. An exotic item from an exotic lady.

The red silk thong underneath reminded him of its twin from the night before. Red, dammit. Red silk where nobody would see. She'd wanted him to remember their passion, even while he looked as respectable as a banker.

Beth joined him, settling her own jacket around her shoulders. He purred to himself, as he saw how much they looked like a matched set. Where did that thought come from? Dammit, did he want to rearrange his life for a woman again? It had hardly worked out the last time, except for bringing Mike into his life.

Beth calmed down slightly once they were out of the room. She even slipped her hand into his in the elevator and leaned against him. He kissed the top of her head and followed her out when the doors opened.

They walked through the casino quickly, barely noticing the scattered gamblers. She led the way outside and waited for the light to change. Sean pulled her against him, automatically putting himself between her and the traffic. Beth glanced up at him but said nothing about his protectiveness.

They crossed the street and walked up the path, past towering palm trees and an immense fountain, into another casino, full of tropical plants and running water. They moved more slowly here, stopping often to compare it to where they were staying.

Beth was more relaxed now, talking easily of small things like the use of different color carpets to guide gamblers through the casino. They found a small set of shops that Sean eyed cautiously, wary of womankind's well-known urge to shop. The jewelry looked very expensive but no prices were visible. Still, he'd go in there with her if she wanted, even if a single item could easily cost as much as his pickup truck. Hell, most of the items probably cost more than his old Ford.

Beth moved past the shops without pausing and he allowed himself to start breathing again. He was even more relieved when they emerged outside.

An incredible swimming pool lay beyond, edged with bright umbrellas and centered on water flowing from rocks, someplace where you could play out fantasies for hours. They stood in silence, studying it. Sean felt Beth's hand caress his hip and he kissed the top of her head.

"Do you want to sit down here?" he asked.

"No, let's go on farther and look at the white tigers. I've never seen them before."

"Okay, honey," Sean said easily and moved on with her. Sean paid the admission fee at the tiger exhibit, stopping Beth's protest with a finger across her lips. "Let me pay for this one, darling."

She shook her head at him, then smiled ruefully. He dropped a quick kiss on her mouth, thankful she was willing to accept his money.

The white tigers and their companions were scattered along the winding paths, screened by chain-link fence, with few other people braving the brisk autumn air. Soon Sean and Beth found themselves alone at the end of a cul-de-sac, watching three young tigers sleep.

"They are so adorable, aren't they?" Beth murmured as one tiger rolled over on his tree branch, somehow managing to stay on. "They remind me of children."

Children. Permanent relationships have to consider children. Did he want more? His heart pounded and he couldn't speak, seeing her eyes soften as she watched the tigers. She'd look like that with her own baby.

He wanted her to look at his child that way. Jesus. He closed his eyes against terror. He'd been interested in dating, especially fucking, but not marriage.

"Yeah, they're sure cute," he managed to say, hoping he didn't sound as stunned as he felt. Mercifully, Beth paid more attention to the tigers than to him.

Finally, she put her hand on his elbow and started to stroll on. Sean stayed silent, watching her rather than the exotic animals behind the high fences. What the hell was he going to do?

She was quieter than usual; was she sad that this was their last day? Surely not. Her world was so much bigger and brighter than his, with lots of handsome young men begging her for a chance to worship at her feet.

He bit back a snarl at the thought.

They returned to the jewelry store but this time Beth stopped to glance at the display. Sean looked for the prices this time, considering what her toys had cost. What would it feel like, to buy something just because it felt good and you could afford it?

What the hell could he offer that might make her stay with him? He had money but not as much as the men she was used to. He tried to think of things he could do, put them together in a pretty speech.

They wandered silently through the casino with their arms around each other, barely making it back in time to meet the limousine. He raised an eyebrow at the two neat suitcases, obviously packed by the butler. But that fellow had probably made a lot of other things possible this weekend.

In comparison, the private jet was nothing new, just the same plane they'd flown down in. Sean followed Beth up the stairs and buckled in silently. Then he looked around the cabin, trying to memorize every detail for the long nights ahead. It had been a great weekend but there would be other chances with other women, women who would fit into his workaholic Seattle world. Yeah, right.

Finally, the seat belt sign clicked off and Beth unfastened hers impatiently. She stood up and held her hand out to Sean. "Come on, Sean, let's go back and lie down."

His breath caught and he followed her quickly. She kicked off her shoes in the stateroom and lay down on the bed. He followed her lead and was rewarded, when she came straight into his arms. He cuddled her, building memories in this refuge against the outside world. Her breath warmed his heart and he nuzzled her hair, catching her scent and holding it.

They lay like that for a long time, holding each other like two children afraid of the dark. Then she kissed his shoulder and rested her head against his arm. His mouth traveled through the heavy black silk of her hair. She turned to meet his kiss.

They kissed for a long time, trading touches and sighs like the air they needed to live. Contentment built into a smoldering flame and Sean left her lips to explore her face. He caressed her with his nose and tongue as much as his mouth.

Beth murmured something, maybe in Japanese, and opened herself to him, kissing him whenever his mouth came near. She slid her hand under his sweater and stroked his waist, in a sweet echo of his caresses. His hand slid down her hip and back again, so that his fingers tucked themselves comfortably into the small of her back. At some point, first one sweater and then another became too hot and had to be eased off, with many kisses and murmurs of appreciation for the skin revealed.

Sean forgot who touched whom, as he sank further into her passionate welcome. He explored her body and tried to memorize every aspect, with every sense he possessed, so he would remember her on all the long, cold nights to come. She was still his to enjoy and to pleasure, until the clock struck ten.

Beth encouraged him with throaty little whispers that sent shivers running through him. She rippled her body to beg for his caresses and filled the air with the heady delight of her musk. Her skin was softer than her silk scarf, ivory behind the rose of her arousal, as she fondled him. He opened himself up for her bold touch and she purred, cupping his balls as if they were the greatest prize in the world. He groaned and stretched, his sore back forgotten, watching her with heavy-lidded eyes, as she fondled him. She leaned down to kiss him, and his hand came up to guide her home to his mouth.

They found many excuses to linger and pause on the slow climb to the top, both showing reluctance to end this moment. But finally the time came when he rolled a condom down his shaft, while Beth watched avidly. A barrier between them now, symbol of their coming good-bye.

"You're so beautiful," she murmured.

He looked up at her quizzically, as he finished adjusting the latex. "Women are beautiful. Sunsets are beautiful. I'm not," he corrected her.

"Yes, you are," she said, her eyes bright with a suspicious wetness. "I hate losing sight of you for one instant to that latex, let alone the touch of you. But . . ." She swallowed and went on more brightly. "On the other hand, seeing the latex means that party time is here." She slid her fingers up his straining cock, playing him like a fiddle.

He choked but soon laughed. "Maybe I am beautiful, if it makes you touch me like that." He bit off the last word as her thumb rolled over his cock's head and circled the shaft.

"Hell, woman!" he growled and pulled her on to him. She came willingly and he rolled, settling her under him. She smoothed his head and smiled wistfully, as his mouth found her again.

They kissed desperately this time and urgency built. He raised himself over her and entered her, watching every small twitch of her body as she accepted him. Christ, he felt like he'd come home.

He thrust hard and soon lost the errant thought in a haze of hormones. Their lovemaking was fierce now, and wild. His climax seized him like lion taking a gazelle, leaving him spent afterward as small tremblers continued to course through him.

How could he leave her? Giving up moments like this was hell. Never hearing her laugh again or talking to her about books felt like a prescription for loneliness.

A soft tap on the door sounded as he was trying to find words to what he wanted.

"We'd better get up and get dressed," Beth said quietly. She started to find her clothes without saying another word.

She'd never said she wanted to stay. Time to keep the bargain they'd made, build a life without her.

"Here's the scarf, Sean. Keep it in remembrance." She held it out. His gut clenched. This scrap of black and gold silk was all he'd have of her tomorrow.

"Thanks." He tucked it into his pants pocket, hiding it like everything else that had captured his heart, except Mike.

The same limo and driver met them at the airport. But this time, Sean and Beth sat at opposite ends of the back seat, as separate as their universes.

He shoved his hands in his pockets, angry with himself for being dissatisfied with his world. It was a good life, with a fine son and good friends. More than enough money, too, even if not as much as she was used to.

And no one who lit up like a firecracker when he walked into the room, as she had on Saturday night.

The scarf smoothed his fingertips. He squeezed it into a ball and made up his mind. Dammit, he couldn't let her go.

"Do you like children, Beth?" Sean asked, beginning his campaign with the basics.

"I love children and I'd like to have some of my own," Beth admitted, turning to face him. He gently brushed a lock of hair away from her mouth.

"I'd like more children, too. But I'd like most of all to have a good marriage." He watched her cautiously. "A good, loving, committed relationship with the woman I adore." He took a deep breath then laid all his cards on the table. "I love you, Beth. I know that now. I want to build a long-term relationship with you."

Her jaw dropped and she stared at him. "Sean, darling, you don't know me," she protested. "We haven't even known each other a week. Okay, so we had some great sex but that's not everything."

"No, it's not a guarantee but it's a damn good start, Beth. I'm willing to take the chance and work on it with you."

She started to speak, but the rest of his speech kept tumbling out. Maybe he couldn't keep her in luxury, but he could at least show her he cared by being with her.

"I'd be glad to move to Washington, D.C., to be with you. I can't do it until Mike graduates, but then I'd move immediately. And in the meantime, I'd fly out every chance I could to be with you. And there's e-mail and phones to help us keep in touch."

"Sean, please calm down." She patted his knee like a maiden aunt. "We've had a great time playing together, but that's all. You need to look for someone around here, someone who'll fit in your world and be a great wife for you."

"Is it the money?" He hated asking, feared hearing that the problem was something he couldn't counter, but he needed to know for sure.

"What?" Beth stared at him. "No, of course, not! I earned my money and I honor people who do the same." She was so emphatic that he believed her. She'd never lied to him and she wouldn't start now.

Sean tried to imagine what she objected to. If it wasn't his money, then what did she want? "What do you mean by fit in my world?"

"Sean, you don't need me. You can get involved with the local scene in Seattle. Maybe pay a fem domme to spank you or tie you up. Keep it as private as you like. Not everyone tells their spouse, so you don't have to. You can even find a nice vanilla wife, who'll adore you . . ." Her voice tightened and she broke off, blinking rapidly, her eyes suspiciously bright.

Sean frowned at her, trying hard to understand. Why was she talking about his sexual tastes? He tried to bring the conversation back to basics. "I hid everything I thought and felt from Tiffany, and I'm not going through that again. I can tell you anything, and I'd trust you with everything. It's a good start on a marriage, Beth. So will you let me see you again?"

"That would be very unwise, Sean." Tears choked her voice and she hunted for a tissue in the limousine's capacious cabinets.

Oh Christ, was she going to cry? What the hell did he do now? He tried again, more cautiously. "Why not? What do you want, Beth? I'll give it to you. I swear I'll go out and get it. Anything you want, just name it."

"Sean!" Beth wailed and stopped. Driven by an instinct beyond thought, he reached out for her. She came easily, not seeking him but not fighting him either. She lay against him, shaking but silent, and he clumsily patted her back. He had no idea what to say.

He'd kill any man who'd done this to her, but the fault was his. He was the one who had upset this dangerous lady. He felt like the lowest scum in the universe.

She sat up finally. Their eyes met and he remembered Tiffany's doctor at Walter Reed Hospital, talking about the blood vessels in Tiffany's brain that could rupture and kill her at any time. That man had worn the same sorrowful, resigned look that Beth had now.

Sean waited for her to speak, truly frightened now. He hadn't been this cold inside before, even when he waited to jump onto that heavily-defended Panamian airfield from less than five hundred feet.

"Sean, what I want isn't something you can obtain. You either have it or you don't."

"Beth, honey, just tell me." He kept his voice low and soothing.

"You're a damn fine submissive male, Sean. Masculine and challenging. You're going to be a splendid sensation slut, devouring every impulse that comes in from your five senses, and turning it to sexual gold. But that's not enough."

She swallowed hard before she continued.

"I want . . . No, *need* a switch. Someone who can do either dominance or submission. Someone who enjoys taking, just as much as being taken, just at different times."

He saw her face clearly in the reflected light from a street lamp. Her eyes were implacable above the glimmering tracks of her tears.

"You're not a switch, Sean. You're marvelous, magnificent, superb. Some other woman will be very lucky to have you. But I'm not going to lie to myself again, as I did with Genichi, and say that only one side of my personality needs to be happy. I can't play the dominant all the time, even for you. Please forgive me for saying this; I don't want to hurt you. But you're a submissive male, not a switch."

The last words hit him like bullets. His eyes narrowed. He'd never given up without a fight before. He damn well wasn't walking away this time, not when it mattered more than life.

"I can take you. Remember the first night in Vegas?" Jeez, they fit together so well, no matter what they did. He'd had plenty of experience in the Army with teams that worked and ones that didn't. He'd seen the results of both, often enough to know how rare and priceless the right team was. Beth was the one woman for his future.

"Did you do that because you wanted to? Or because I goaded you into it, by flaunting my wealth and importance?"

"Does that matter?" He answered her question with another.

"I need a man who dominates me sometimes, just because he wants to. Not because he's trying to please me. Do you understand the difference?"

"Yes." He cursed his inability to make a pretty speech to a civilian, now when it mattered so much. He'd always been better at actions. Hell, she probably took his silence as consent. His brain whirled, while she went on. Christ, how could he convince her?

"Even my ancestors are divided on which road to choose. My Japanese side says that a woman should always follow her man. My Scottish side says that a strong woman can be a partner and even take the lead."

The limo pulled to a stop and the driver got out. The clock said ten PM.

"Beth, we can work it out. I've mastered harder situations than this. I know we care about each other." He took her by the shoulders, willing her to trust him and his belief in the future.

"That's why we should say good-bye now, while we're still friends. I'm sure you'll have a great life without me." Her voice broke a little on the last two words.

The chauffeur opened the door and Sean shook her a little, desperate to crack her resolve.

"I don't know everything about you and you don't know everything about me. But you never do know everything about the other person! I'm sure that I can be the man you need."

"You haven't shown me that, Sean. The only time you ever showed the smallest bit of ferocity was just after you'd been thoroughly belittled by the hotel. You didn't do it when you felt comfortable and strong, so it never felt like a true expression of your soul." Her eyes, deep wells of anguish, searched his in the misty light. He couldn't hide his understanding of her estimate.

"I'm sorry, truly I am!" she continued. "I wish I believed you were a switch. But you're not. So if you want to do something for me, then find somebody else and be happy. Have that nice wife and children. And if you still need a woman to pay attention, help you stretch your sexual boundaries, then spend a little time with a professional. Please."

She put a finger over his mouth, stopping any words that he might find. Her throat worked convulsively before she went on. "Let's just call it quits before anyone really gets hurt. Now I'm going to visit my parents and you're going back to your son. You'll be happy, I know you will." She held out her hand, completely ignoring his fingers biting into her shoulders. "Good-bye, Sean."

"I love you." The words came without thought, blazing against the despairing agony that racked him. He'd been lonely for years and survived. He couldn't go back to that, now that he'd lived with true companionship.

She flinched, her hand falling back. She removed herself to the other end of the seat. He saw his future sliding out of his hands. "That's what you think now, but you'll forget about me. You have to, Sean."

Sean looked into Beth's eyes one more time. He'd lost the opening salvo but the campaign had only just begun. "Just remember that Rangers never quit."

Sean let go of her and climbed out of the limo. He turned back for a few last words from the sidewalk.

"I won't say good-bye, Beth, because I'll be seeing you again soon." He was more certain of that, than what he'd do when they met. "Just, good night and sleep well."

She flinched then held out her hand to him. "Do please take care of yourself, Sean."

He kissed her hand, pressing a soft nip against the vulnerable pulse on her wrist, and released her. The wind rustled down the sidewalk and brushed against him, its harsh cold a reminder of Alaska and his bleak future without her.

The driver closed the door and touched his cap to Sean. "Good luck, man," he offered. "Better get going. It's due to start raining again, anytime now."

"Thanks," Sean responded. He watched, hoping against hope, as the limo pulled away from the curb, just in case she changed her mind at the last minute. Then it turned a corner and she was gone.

He rocked back and forth on his heels briefly, considering his options. What the hell was he going to do now?

His pickup waited patiently across the street, its battered skin an emblem of what his life looked like. He frowned, then turned his back on it and started walking.

First, he'd buy that Range Rover. Something tangible, shiny and new like a future with Beth.

Second, he had to convince her that he was a switch. So he had to dominate her sexually. How? Whatever he did had to be something that would turn her on. He couldn't be a medieval knight, like that fantasy of hers. So what else?

She'd fantasized about him playing the barbarian and they'd done that in Vegas. It hadn't convinced her he was the right man, so he needed something else, something stronger and more aggressive. The only other submissive fantasy she'd mentioned was being kidnapped and interrogated by the French Resistance. That was a lot easier to pull off than a scene involving a castle and horses.

Okay, he'd become a Frenchman. She'd given few details of exactly how it happened, so he'd have to figure it out on his own. He could take cues from that space opera of hers. Turn the tables and dominate her as emphatically—and protectively—as Nakamura had dommed Lindstrom. Damn, but he'd enjoyed that fantasy of hers— both angles, as Lindstrom and as Nakamura. And the times he'd fantasized about being Lindstrom with a captive Nakamura . . . Guess he was a switch, if he reacted that strongly to both sides of that fantasy. But he still had to convince Beth.

What if he got it wrong? Well, at least he had her checklist, telling him what sorts of things she did or did not want to do. Christ, what if he did them wrong?

He shuddered at the thought. It was several minutes before he moved again, turning into the wind as he went forward.

Nothing ventured, nothing gained. This was the best chance to win Beth and he'd take it. She'd responded when he'd grabbed and kissed her in the bookstore, so there was at least a chance she'd like being dominated by him.

That settled, Sean started considering what he needed. Someplace to enact her fantasy, of course. Someplace private near Berkeley. He knew a commercial real estate broker in northern California, who had a brochure of old warehouses. Maybe one of them would do.

What equipment did he need? There were all the things locked up in his bedroom, which he'd never shown anyone before. What else had he played with, that could appear in daylight without notice? She liked leather, so that was a good starting point.

Sean kept walking, as he worked out the details of exactly how to kidnap Beth and enact her fantasy. He instinctively became a Ranger again as he did so, writing an operation order as he had so many times before in the Army.

Situation. Enemy: Beth's belief that he's strictly a submissive, not a switch. Friendly: California real estate broker, his collection of sex toys, her checklist.

Mission. Obtain a commitment from Beth Nakamura to a long-term relationship.

Execution. Concept of operations: convince Beth that he's a switch by dominating her during an enactment of her French Resistance fantasy. Scheme of maneuver . . .

Rain splattered against his jacket as he finished the remaining sections: service and support, command, and signal. A few standard operating procedures mentioned anywhere.

Then he started to test his operation order for flaws and found a big one.

He came to a full stop and stared ahead. He had reached an old commercial district leading down to the docks. Puget Sound lay ahead, whipped to a frenzy by the wind, with the lights of West Seattle beyond. His home was over there, keeping Mike safe and warm.

If anything went wrong, he could be arrested and sent to prison for kidnapping. He'd never harm her but that didn't matter, not if the law found out. The world would know all about him.

He shuddered in horror but kept thinking. He had to bring Beth to him; she wasn't going to seek him out. He couldn't believe love letters would succeed better than action in convincing her, even if he thought he could write them. The kidnapping and interrogation scene offered the best chance of impressing her.

Christ, he was cold with a chill that began deep inside. He recognized it as an old friend that he'd met before, the mind-numbing terror that comes just prior to combat. He fought it back as he had then: reminded himself of the objective, analyzed the plan, and tried to minimize the risks.

Beth was worth any risk. He had a chance of winning her, given the way she'd cried. His dangerous lady wouldn't break down if she didn't care. Was he being a stalker? No, he'd stop immediately if she demanded it, after he'd tried to enact one of her fantasies.

The plan could easily go wrong but it was his best hope.

Now, reconsider the worst case: the world would know and Mike would know. Mike would believe that his father was a criminal jerk.

Oh, shit, not that. Maybe he shouldn't try for Beth, not if it would cost him Mike.

But not having Beth around. Not laughing with her or kissing her or cuddling when she was sad . . . He couldn't do that either.

Mike was eighteen and he'd be out of the house in less than a year. Maybe he wouldn't be too upset, since he wouldn't have to live with the scandal for very long. Maybe Mike was enough of an adult now, that he could understand grown men sometimes have to do things that sound foolish to an outsider. Maybe.

So the absolute foulest situation was having neither Beth nor Mike in his life.

The wind bit into his face but he didn't hide from it.

Finally, he turned around and started walking back to his pickup.

Sean walked into the house at midnight and dropped his portfolio on the table, with its penciled ops plan inside. Dudley clattered down the stairs and woofed softly in greeting. Sean squatted down and hugged his old friend. "Hello, Dudley. Did you have a good time in Portland?"

Dudley's brown eyes softened at Sean's tone. He licked Sean's face and pushed closer. Sean choked then turned his face into the golden fur. Dudley always knew when a human needed comfort.

Mike's arrival was quieter, especially since he kept his mouth shut, even when he stood motionless on the threshold. Sean stood up smoothly and acknowledged Dudley's help with a pat, ready to move into action. "Hi, Mike. Have fun in Portland?"

"Yeah, it was decent. Tracy really liked the bed and sent a thank-you note." He came into the kitchen cautiously, clearly trying to act as if his father always blinked back tears.

"Care for a soda?" Sean invited, opening the fridge. This might be easier if it was framed as a man-to-man discussion.

"Sure. What's the occasion?" Mike sat down at the table and Dudley settled happily next to him.

"No celebration. Not yet anyway. Just wanted to say a couple of things and might as well do it tonight, since you're up." And while he still had the courage. Damn, he'd rather face a Somali mob again, alone and unarmed, than do this.

He tossed a soda can to Mike and straddled a chair, opening another for himself.

"Shoot." Mike was now openly curious. He rocked back, lifting the chair's front two legs off the floor.

"First, please tell Bill that I'm not interested in his uncle's Range Rover." Start with the easy stuff first.

"Sure. Any particular reason?"

"I'm buying a new one for myself."

Mike's eyes widened. "What kind? A Discovery?"

If he was going to do this, then he sure as hell wasn't going cheap. Well, as cheap as a Land Rover came, anyway.

"A Range Rover 4.6HSE. Black, of course." The Range Rover of his dreams would be a good symbol of his future with Beth.

"Tight! That's really tight. When?" Mike almost bounced in his seat and the chair wobbled.

"Tomorrow."

Mike lifted his drink in salute and Sean matched the gesture, then drained his dry.

"So we'll have it for the Thanksgiving hunting trip."

"Yes, we should be able to drive it off the lot." The Thanksgiving that he might be celebrating from a jail cell. Hell, Beth was worth the risk.

Mike caught his mood and waited.

"Second, I may be going to jail."

Mike's chair thudded into place as he spewed soda across the table. He coughed and choked, but his words were still intelligible. "Like hell you will! You'd never do anything illegal."

"FBI might not see it like that."

"No way. I'm the one who did all that shit until you straightened me out. I know you." His eyes blazed angrily as he wiped up the sticky froth. He looked dangerous and years older than his age.

His son's faith warmed him but Mike needed to understand all the details.

"Mike, I met a lady but she's not ready to think about marrying me. She could get upset by my methods of persuasion and call the police."

The teenager snorted and relaxed a little. "Your lady? Any woman who can catch your eye is smart and tough. Not the type to call the cops."

"She likes playing games." Sean hesitated, uncertain how to describe the way he'd spent the weekend.

"BDSM, right?" Mike tossed his can into the recycling bin.

"What?" Sean's world spun and he set his drink down slowly; this wasn't the time for confusing his brain with caffeine. He'd always done everything possible to ensure that first Tiffany, and later Mike, wouldn't know what really turned him on, all the things that the big world disapproved of but he found exciting.

"You know, sex and power. Role playing, power exchange . . ." Mike shrugged, looking as casual as if he was trying to find words for the latest TV show. He looked straight into his father's eyes. "Dad, I know what kind of books and videos you've got hidden away. It just makes sense that this lady likes the same stuff." He shrugged again, nervously. "I didn't mean to snoop in your stuff but I was looking for some of your old films from Ranger School. When I saw your cabinet was unlocked for once, I thought the movies might be in there. Kept locked up from Mom since she hated everything to do with the Army, except the NCO Club and pensions. I'm sorry if you think I was spying but—"

"You wouldn't," Sean reassured him. "I know you didn't break into any of my things. You could have done so years ago, if you'd wanted to." Mike had been quite a burglar before Tiffany's death, breaking into houses but never stealing more than trifles, just enough to prove that he'd been there. It had ended surprisingly easily, after Sean's discharge and the move to Seattle. The police and courts had been right; Mike had needed consistent love and discipline to feel safe. He'd become a son to be proud of.

Mike relaxed with a sigh of relief, then stood up to fetch a clean glass from the cupboard.

"How long have you known?" Sean returned to his main concern, as he tried to absorb the implications of his son's awareness. Mike knew and wasn't disgusted by Sean's sexual interests, even though they were outside the usual run of things. He still cared about his father.

"A year, maybe." He poured himself a glass of water from the fridge, avoiding the soda like someone who needed to keep a clear head. "You keep it locked up pretty well."

"That long," Sean muttered. He hadn't seen any signs of a changed attitude in the kid. He really did respect his father, no matter what Sean kept hidden.

"So what are you planning?" Mike straddled his chair, facing his father as an equal.

"None of your business. No need for you to go to jail." Sean's decision was firm.

"Dad, nobody's going to do jail time." Mike was patient and reassuring, as befitted a veteran of close encounters with the law.

"Worst case, the police find out. I won't have you involved so you don't need to know anything. Things go badly, you'd lose your shot at West Point and the Army." He stated the indisputable facts one more time.

"The Army doesn't matter, not if it means you're in trouble." Mike's voice was dead calm, as if he stated a fundamental truth.

"Mike, dammit, you've always wanted to be in the Army." Sean tried again to reach him.

Mike's eyes never flickered, his face set stone cold. He looked full grown, almost a combat veteran. "Family is more important than the Army. You proved that when you took that hardship discharge. I'll find something else, the way you did."

Christ, Mike was willing to give his dreams up for his father.

Sean shook his head. "No way I'll let that happen."

Mike pondered, swirling his water in the glass. Sean waited for him to try a different angle of persuasion. Mike was clever and charismatic; he'd be deadly as an officer. But the old man could usually still outsmart him.

"You know, Carol's uncle is a big-time stuntman in Hollywood. Arranges complicated stunts all the time. He's even directed a couple of cheap movies."

"So?" Where was this going?

"I talked to him some on Saturday night, while the ladies were getting dressed for the big dinner."

Sean nodded, waiting for Mike's real pitch.

"He said that he's helped couples pull off stunts that'd normally get them arrested. Things they both wanted to do but outsiders wouldn't understand. Like kidnapping."

Sean came to attention, considering the possibilities. Somebody who could provide a good cover story might make this much less dangerous. "How?"

"He tells questioners it's for a movie. Just need to have somebody around with a camera and the right permits. He bragged about how fast he can get a permit, especially when it's a student film."

"Perfect." Any amount of foolishness went on in the movies, so pretending to perform a scene from World War II shouldn't worry the police at all.

"When did you want to do this? He's only in town for a little longer."

"She's in Berkeley this week."

"Sounds like time's short, so you'll need both Carol's uncle and me." Sean slammed his fist down on the table. "Hell, no!"

"Dad, getting a filming permit usually takes time, but it's faster for student permits. We can do it, if you bring me in."

"Mike, we're talking serious jail time here. I wouldn't be a father if I let you anywhere near this."

"You got a student ID?" Now, Mike sounded like the one who'd thought things through.

"No! But you're too young to be involved." Sean fell back on the most basic fact, the one he'd built his life around. Mike was his son and under his protection.

"You need my help, Dad. You've always done everything for me, no matter what it cost you."

"You don't need to pay me back, Mike. This is about me and you're better off staying out of it." Sean's voice was softer now, but still firm. Mike had always been too old for his years, even when he was dealing with all those cops.

"I want to do this for you, Dad, as a present. It's something only I can do. You don't get many chances to give something really unique." He leaned forward, willing his father to understand.

Sean hesitated, startled by the naked love in Mike's voice. Neither of them had ever much mentioned their feelings for each other, of course. How could he refuse a gift from his son, given in full knowledge of the risks? He tried once again.

"Mike, I really don't think you need to. I'll be okay."

"Dad, we're doing this together. If you don't want to think of it as a gift, then just see it as the two Lindstrom men standing together, no matter what the odds. Okay?"

Sean froze, trapped by the old saying he'd first used when Mike was four. The two Lindstrom men always stood together, no matter what. He had no counter for this argument.

He glared across the table at the man sitting there, the adult he'd been privileged to sire. Then Sean laughed and held out his hand for a high five. Mike had won by turning Sean's weapons against him.

The two Lindstrom men were going into battle together.

Eleven

Slightly apart from the rest of her family, Beth waited patiently for her parents to clear customs. Everyone was there: her three older brothers, their wives, and all seven of their children. Even Kasey, Jason's very pregnant wife, had come to welcome her in-laws. Everyone carried a gift, flowers and balloons mostly. Beth had a box of her mother's favorite Belgian chocolates, miraculously produced by the concierge at her hotel. She was such a coward about seeing her parents again that she'd actually gotten a hotel room.

She hadn't slept the night before. In fact, she'd spent most of the night pacing her room. It had seemed a better option than tossing and turning, crying in a lonely bed. Sean was the finest submissive man she'd ever played with. But she couldn't lie to herself again and say that only one side of her needed to be happy.

Little Hiroki, her nephew, who considered himself a conqueror at not quite two, hurtled across the lounge toward the door. His father, Conal, broke off his discussion of the latest artificial heart technology and scooped up the toddler, just before the door swung open and passengers began to come through. Sean would have moved as fast to rescue a child.

Tears welled up at the image. She needed to find something else to think about, something that wouldn't bring her lost man to mind.

Suddenly the flow of bodies through the door opened up, showing her parents, Hiroki and Catriona Nakamura, walking hand-in-hand, behind a porter pushing a heavily loaded luggage cart.

The Nakamura clan burst into action, as everyone hurried forward. All was pandemonium as greetings were exchanged, children exclaimed over, and gifts given. Beth hugged her mother briefly and stepped aside quickly, as little Hiroki demanded attention from his favorite grandmother. She would have liked to linger a bit longer near her mother, who was always ready to reassure and defend her children.

Somehow Beth found herself in the back of Jason's minivan with her father, heading toward the family home in Berkeley. Catriona was in the middle row, catching up on the latest news of Kasey's condition.

Beth tuned the conversation out. All her brothers' wives wanted to talk about their pregnancies with Catriona, since she was an obstetrical surgeon. What would it be like to talk about her pregnancy with her mother?

"Your grandmother sends her congratulations, Beth."

Beth snapped her attention back to her father. "Forgive me, Father. My attention was wandering."

Hiroki's eyes searched hers briefly, seeing every detail. He patted her hand. "I mentioned to her that you have achieved career status with the American government."

Beth nodded, trying to see where this was going. She now had a permanent job with the government, not something that could be ended at its convenience. But to have Father brag about her to his mother, after not publicly defending her a year ago, made her heart clench. It sounded like he'd undertaken a quiet campaign to recover Beth's status.

"The Nakamura clan is very proud of your achievements, Beth. My mother sends this in token of her regard."

He offered Beth a beautifully wrapped box, which she opened carefully. Inside the elegant wooden box, lay a magnificent pearl necklace, composed of perfectly matched, graduated, large white South Sea pearls.

"The necklace was a personal gift to her from her grandmother, upon her graduation from college, the first woman in her family to achieve that. Now you are the first to serve the American government, a great honor for our family."

Beth's mouth worked but no words came out past the knot in her throat. Father had prevailed on his mother, the irascible matriarch, to bring her back into the clan again. She managed to smile at him.

He slid his arm around her shoulders and hugged her.

"I am so very glad to have you as my daughter," he said softly in Japanese and kissed her on the cheek. "You have always been everything and more than I hoped."

"Oh, Father!" Beth gulped and yielded to tears. He pulled her against him and she cried into his shoulder, finding the comfort she had needed from him a year ago. His arms continued to shelter her and she mourned the loss of Sean, even as she celebrated her reunion with her family.

The old pickup truck jerked to a stop. Beth was sprawled across the seat with her head in Sean's lap. The motion sent her feet to the floor, but her mouth never lost contact with his cock. She swirled her tongue up his shaft and opened her mouth to take him deep again.

He jerked her up by the shoulders. She caught a glimpse of the world outside for a moment. They seemed to be in the alley behind a lumber-yard. Not his house, not her hotel. That didn't matter; getting her hands on him was more important than finding a bed.

Then he dumped her onto the seat and came down on her. His tongue stabbed deep, claiming her. She responded fiercely, feeling teeth and lips grind as their tongues mated.

He growled and started fighting her pants' zipper. She lifted her hips for him, and he yanked the denim down past her knees. They fought the confined space as much as the cloth, as both lovers vied to overcome the jeans' barrier. Beth banged her wrist against the steering wheel but finally succeeded. Her shoes and trousers dropped onto the floor under the brake pedal.

A moment later Sean's hot body covered her again. She nipped his shoulder in welcome, even as he plunged inside her. Lights burst behind her eyelids as she convulsed.

* * *

The alarm went off at precisely six AM on Tuesday morning, as it had been told to. Time to rise so she could have breakfast with her father. Family togetherness time. Damn.

Beth rolled over and buried her face in the pillow. The dream had been so real she could still see Sean in the light from the lumberyard. She was wet between her thighs, and moved farther away from the matching spot in the sheets.

Reluctantly, she sat up and hugged her knees to her chest. She rested her cheek on the tight knot of her limbs and rocked slowly, curling to comfort herself as she remembered old challenges.

She had always wanted to be a Japanese lady, her head bent meekly as she followed her lord. But she didn't fit in Japan, either physically or emotionally, with her intense drive to reach the top and lead, both at work and in the bedroom. Genichi had been right about that, no matter how hurtful his words had been when she broke the engagement.

She had never wanted to be a Scottish lady, but she behaved more often than not as a strong, creative Scot. Was she asking too much for one man to be a switch, as Jenn said? Or was Sean right? Could he satisfy both sides of her dream?

No matter what she did, she kept thinking about him. He'd followed her into her sleep more than once. Even total exhaustion after playing with her horde of nieces and nephews hadn't kept him away. She felt like a teenager daydreaming about the man who'd showed her carnal pleasure for the first time. Had Mother felt like this after she met her future husband?

She sighed and sat up. Thinking didn't change the fact that she'd sent Sean away and lost him. No way he'd want to see her again, after she dismissed him so completely. At least she'd always respected his inexperience and gone very cautiously with him. She'd only done what his checklist had eagerly requested.

She came into the kitchen, after putting her sheets in the wash. The coffeepot was full and she checked the time in surprise. Her mother usually left for the hospital well before now, even on days when she wasn't performing surgeries. Beth filled the waiting thermos and started a fresh pot.

She sat on the chair, elbows on the counter, and contemplated the brewing coffee. She had never been a particular fan of the beverage, seeing it as a survival necessity in the workplace rather than a pleasure.

But now the smell reminded her of Sean. She smiled, remembering how he drank his coffee as if every drop was necessary for life. She wondered if he had a pickup truck.

A door closed upstairs and Beth jumped. She quickly popped a bagel into the toaster. "Good morning, Mother. Your bagel is almost ready and here's your thermos for the drive."

She noticed that her mother looked like the proverbial cat who'd caught the canary. And then spent the night playing with it.

For the first time, she wondered about her parents' sexual relationship. A quick glance at her father showed that he looked exhausted, sated, and very content.

She turned to give her mother a hug and flinched inwardly at her mother's surprise. Years of squabbles and subsequent distances couldn't be erased in a minute but she could start now.

She hugged her mother again, turning the casual greeting into something more significant. It almost felt like embracing her own twin, given their matching height and build. But Catriona had blonde hair and blue eyes, while Beth had the black hair and brown eyes of her father's family.

"Thanks, Beth, for looking after me. I don't know where the time went. Guess I must have overslept." Catriona's voice was a little hoarse at first but quickly recovered its usual lilt.

She kissed her daughter's cheek and Beth responded with a clumsy peck. She needed to do this more so she'd become less awkward. Her mother was gone within seconds, after a brief discussion of dinner plans.

"Would you like a cup of coffee, Father? Or would you prefer tea?" Beth offered, returning to their usual custom. She and her father always shared a cup in the morning on her trips home, before he departed for his lab at U.C. Berkeley.

"Coffee would be fine, thank you. Perhaps you will join me on the deck?"

Beth nodded her assent.

They sat outside silently, enjoying the mugs' warmth between their palms, while watching the morning sun burn through the fog. The Golden Gate Bridge would be visible later when the haze vanished.

But now the fog wrapped them intimately, even as it caressed the eucalyptus trees next to the deck. Hiroki Nakamura and his daughter sat in similar attitudes of contemplation, meditating on the scene before them.

"Father, may I ask you a question?"

He nodded calmly and waited, his expression open and relaxed.

"Were you surprised to fall in love with Mother?"

His eyes widened briefly at the question.

"Yes, I was very surprised to fall in love with Catriona. She was very different from what I'd ever considered finding in my life. But . . ." Never very articulate, he hunted for words to express himself. "She fulfills me. She fulfills needs I was unaware of. I knew within a day of our first meeting that I could not live without her. Knowing that made everything else easier to manage."

Beth nodded in understanding. Her parents' love and need for each other had been strong enough to build a good life together, despite the conflicts between their two totally different backgrounds. Two had become a strong whole. Could she build an equally satisfying world with Sean?

"Beth, life is not always what we want. It is often not what we would wish for our beloved daughter."

Beth smiled at him, misty-eyed. He had been so angry when Genichi had humiliated her, mincing no words in his denunciation of that dishonorable lout. Memory of that unexpected torrent now overshadowed his subsequent patience with his mother, when he waited for a better time to overcome his mother's angry disappointment.

He went on slowly. "I pray that your life has not left you too scarred to try again. I pray that you will take a chance again on a man that you can love."

Beth put out her hand and slipped it into her father's. Maybe he could comfort her now. "Father, I met someone that I'd like to tell you about."

Beth toppled her king, acknowledging another defeat at chess. Her father began to set up the pieces again, without looking at her, and she helped him, glad he didn't say anything about her lapsed concentration. If he did, she'd pretend she was thinking about her new assignment for the Treasury Department, which deserved more thought than she'd given it so far.

Thursday noon. Eighty-six hours without Sean—but who was counting?

"How are our birds doing?" her father asked as he set an ivory knight neatly into place.

"I don't know. I haven't been up to the park to watch them." She placed the ebony queen next to her king. The sunroom, with its walls of windows showing yet another storm coming in across the bay, felt like a prison.

"I thought of them while I traveled, every time someone mentioned the weather." He turned the ivory queen so she was aligned identically to her pale king.

"Perhaps I should go check on them and make sure the storms haven't disturbed them." And try to think about something other than the mistake she'd made with Sean.

"It is always good to know when loved ones are safe," her father agreed, moving pawns smoothly into position.

Beth stood up, then gave him a quick, fierce hug. His hand closed strongly on her arm, returning her affection. Then he patted her hand. "Take your time visiting our friends, Beth. I have much to catch up on at home, before your mother returns."

She started up the path with a hard stride, head up so she could taste the wind. She should be happy and excited to start her new assignment at work. Instead her thoughts revolved around a man that she'd left, quite deliberately, behind.

She turned past her parents' garden and up the hill, looking for the first vantage point where she could see the hilltop. The path to the park took almost two miles to climb, most of it spent skirting yards and cliffs. It crossed streets at only three points before it arrived at the grove.

Another bird watcher, a much more dedicated sort who kept his binoculars at the ready for minutes at a time, was visible from one of the few vantage points. He was a slender man, dark-haired, standing in the grove and sweeping the surrounding skies with his glasses.

Something in how he surveyed the scene reminded her of the bookstore clerk in Seattle, watching the sidewalk outside his store. What was his name? Gary, of course. Why did she remember him so easily? Was she fated to remember everyone and everything connected with Sean?

She shook herself into action and continued walking. She hit the next incline in a burst of action that sent sparrows flying. She moved with the speed of long-familiarity under the trees, glad they were recovering so well from the fire of a decade past.

She never saw Gary lower his binoculars, then speak quietly into a radio he produced from a pocket.

Beth paused at the first street, a narrow opening onto a cul-de-sac that seldom offered any traffic. It was busier than usual today, with an ancient truck rumbling in the middle, which looked old enough to have welcomed de Gaulle into Paris. One man was under the hood with only his hips and legs visible. Another sat behind the wheel with his head out the window, listening to the mechanic's instructions. The mechanic's backside was as fine as Sean's, even in a rough leather jacket and baggy pants.

Two men fussed over a big movie camera on a tripod, set up on the street corner yard. The one facing Beth was young and tall and blond; he might grow up to be as attractive as Sean one day. The other man seemed familiar, but he kept his back turned.

Beth swore silently. Was she doomed to look for Sean in every man she saw?

Time to go. There were two more streets, and another mile, before she'd reach the grove. She checked for traffic then stepped out into the street.

Things happened swiftly after that. One moment, she was crossing a strip of California road. The next moment, she was standing in the middle of the street, staring into Sean's wary but determined eyes under a black beret. It lay flat on his head in the French style, hiding his American haircut. Was that a Luger pistol in her ribs?

What the hell was going on?

"French bitch," he snarled. "Did you think your German friends would protect you?"

Beth stopped breathing as she recognized the question. It was the first line of the submissive fantasy she'd told Sean about. Then her belly tightened and her heart started pounding against her ribs. Was he going to dominate her?

"How dare . . ." She wet her lips and tried again. "How dare you stop me? You are a fool to challenge the Nazis, rulers of all Europe. Now go home and don't bother your betters."

The truck's hood slammed down. Beth glanced around Sean's arm and saw . . . Dave Hemmings as the second cameraman? He watched her from beyond the camera, his face neutral. Its young operator definitely looked like Sean's offspring, as he recorded her reactions.

She could ask Dave for help if she wanted to. Kidnappings were dangerous, with their open invitation for police involvement. Her skin ran cold and hot.

No. Dave Hemmings was her safety net; she could simply walk away with him and avoid any danger from Sean. If she didn't do that, then she consented to the fantasy being played here, taking the chance of submitting to Sean.

She would have no control once she left with Sean and would have to rely solely on him. She could be hurt physically or frustrated emotionally if he wasn't able to dominate her. She dismissed the first risk quickly. Sean would never harm her, although he must know she could enjoy pain's vivid stimulation.

The second risk was more real. He'd never proven he could top her in a way that placed his satisfaction before hers.

But this was her one opportunity to discover if Sean was a switch, capable of both taking and being taken. See if he really was the man of her dreams. Almost no chance but still, maybe it would work.

She looked back at Sean and swung her arm in a roundhouse swing at his face. "Imbécile!" she spat out the third line of her fantasy.

His eyes blazed down at her and he caught her hand, millimeters from his cheek. "Foolish wench," he laughed and she felt the scene's energy snap into place between them. Her breasts tightened and dew beaded between her legs.

The truck kicked into a smooth rumbling purr, just like all those old war movies. "Hurry up!" the driver called.

Sean twisted her arm behind her back and pushed her to the truck, the gun's barrel pressing into her back. Dave's face relaxed, and he gave her the smallest of thumbs-up signs.

Sean tossed her between the swaying canvas curtains, into the back, and followed her in a smooth dive. She found herself trapped between a blanket-covered hay bale and a very big man, who still had a gun in her ribs. There were apples in old-fashioned wooden crates toward the front.

She trembled and grew wetter. The hay rasped her nipples through the blanket and her heavy field jacket.

The truck's doors slammed shut, an instant before it pulled away from the curb. Beth didn't think of trying to guess its route or destination. This was now 1944 France and the Resistance would never let collaborators know their secrets. Her only hope was the man above her, with the hard ridge threatening to tunnel into her trousers.

He shifted himself, just enough to quickly buckle her hands into leather cuffs behind her back. Metal clanked and a chain slid against her palm. She tried to tug her wrists apart, but the leather and steel refused to yield more than a few inches. She couldn't possibly free herself.

She cursed him, angry and excited.

Then he pulled her head up and smoothly gagged her with a silk scarf, a knot in her mouth to keep her silent. Another silk scarf covered her eyes in a blindfold, and he tied her bootlaces together to hobble her.

Beth tossed her head from side to side, trying to orient herself in the new world composed only of sounds. The truck ran smoothly, taking the hills and curves easily if loudly. Its heavy engine sent a continuous vibration through its frame and into her body, triggering an answering throb from her shoulders to her hips. And into her core, which registered its opinions in the dampness of her panties. She could smell her musk beginning to rise over the masculine scents of hay and engine oil.

Sean yanked her onto her back and she tried to roll away. He grabbed the neck of her jacket, stopping her easily. Then he ripped open her jacket with one brutal tug, sending buttons flying. She tried to scream, even as her breasts firmed in anticipation.

He ripped open her broadcloth shirt quickly and easily. Beth twisted under him, too anxious to stay still. Her chest rose and fell with her rapid breathing, and her nipples were spikes of eager tension.

She froze when a knife slid up her bare midriff and teased her simple white silk bra. Her thighs tightened against her wetness. In the darkness behind the blindfold, his knife felt like an extension of his touch.

He cut the silk off her with a single smooth stroke, and she moaned when his hand cupped her. He kneaded her breast hard, lifting it toward him. He chuckled wickedly when her nipples tightened further. His other hand played similar games until both breasts were throbbing and heavy.

"Such tempting morsels," he rumbled, dropping his head. If his hands had been inviting, then his mouth was irresistible. She writhed under him, as incoherent pleas formed behind the gag. But she couldn't talk and she couldn't see. She was free to respond to him, without worrying how to please him.

The truck's motion sometimes sent her closer to him, but sometimes farther. The burlap was rough against her back, despite the protection of her remaining clothing, while the hay rustled with every movement. She could smell the hay's earthy scent and the apples' sweetness combining with her musk, as she grew wetter and wetter.

She tried to rub her legs together to relieve her tension, but he blocked that by shoving his knee between her legs. She pushed her hips against his knee, but his hands bit into her hips. She whimpered as she accepted his rules: he set the activities and the pace.

Thankfully, he returned to her breasts once her hips lay aquiescent against his leg. Perhaps soon he'd use his hand on her below her waist.

The truck stopped and he sat up. A whisper of cold air brushed her nipples, in stark contrast to his mouth's heated warmth. She listened hard, impatient for his return.

He cupped her breasts in his hands and she felt his avid gaze. She smiled under the gag when he pinched and twisted her nipples, enjoying the rapidly returning excitement. He focused his attention on one breast and its crowning bud, until she was frantic.

Then he slowly, cleverly claimed that nipple with a sharp stab of pain. She recognized a Japanese cloverleaf clamp's wicked touch immediately and gasped, adjusting herself. Soon only a hard ache remained.

She arched eagerly, when he rubbed cold metal over her other breast, and moaned when the second clamp took it. She would be very sensitive when he removed them.

Chain crackled, then lay across her belly like a lover, as he linked the clamps. She was held captive by him, at her breasts, wrists, and ankles.

He unzipped her trousers then yanked them down to her hips to free her mound. He cupped her, and she sighed at the welcome warmth after the cold air's snap. His fingers slid between her folds, and she tried to open herself farther, only to be stopped by the unyielding corduroy. A big finger stabbed into her, then another finger joined to screw into her.

Her belly tightened as her hips pushed up against him, desperate to find the climax he was lifting her toward.

"Now, woman! Come for me now," he snarled as a rough finger rubbed her clit in exactly the stroke she loved. Her body exploded, obediently and happily.

She gasped for breath afterward, feeling the last pulses die away.

Then his mouth closed over one breast, immediately returning it to a state of pure excitement. She grunted behind the gag when his hand delved between her legs. Soon he demanded another climax of her and she gave it willingly, spasming under his wicked touch.

The drive went on forever as he fucked her with his mouth and hands. Or was it only a few minutes? They left the hills and drove across a city full of dissonance, as the route turned senselessly. The truck bumped across bridges and railroad tracks more than once, producing a change in his hands' rhythm.

His breathing was occasionally ragged, but he never rubbed himself against her, never released his cock from its confinement into her welcoming warmth.

Sometimes his mouth used her breasts, but sometimes it traded places with his hands. Sometimes he led her slowly from orgasm to orgasm, but sometimes he took her at a gallop.

They stopped once, the truck idling while cars thundered overhead. He ran his hands over her, skimming from collarbone to pelvis as her body rippled in an echo of their passage. She hummed, trying to understand his new demands, as her body fell into a slower pulse of arousal. Then he circled her breasts until she sobbed her desperation. His hands cupped her nipples lightly, warming her as he hinted at his next move.

One hand delved below, gliding deep into her swollen folds. Her hips thrust into his touch as she obeyed his unspoken demand. Just before she eased into a new climax, he snatched one clamp off with practiced ease and simultaneously thumbed her clit with his other hand. She screamed soundlessly, as the two stimuli sent her body into a blinding orgasm.

She was still shaking when his mouth covered her other breast and his hand found her favorite pleasure point deep inside. He pressed firmly with his hand, while he simultaneously sucked her breast into his mouth. He repeated the two demands until her body throbbed in response, waves flowing from her breasts to her cunt and back again. Her body bent into a great bow of arousal, as it offered everything to him.

"Now, woman!" he snarled, snatched the last clamp off, and thrust his fingers deep inside her. His insistence was a rare hint to her effect on him. She came in a thundering rapture that ripped throughout her body, from both her clit and her cunt.

The truck rumbled back into life, while she was trying to catch her breath. Rain fell as they left the overhead highway's protection, first as a steady mist but soon as a downpour. He swirled his tongue over her, lapping at her enflamed nipples like a rare appetizer. The rain's drumming was an echo of her heartbeat as she satisfied yet another command to climax for him.

Finally the truck lurched its way down a railroad track and he stopped his assault on her senses, moving completely away from her. She was too sated to do more than shiver, as the cold air returned to her overheated body.

The truck bumped onto smoother pavement then stopped. Water poured over one side of the roof, indicating some shelter from the weather. The engine fell silent, as the Luger returned to her ribs. A door opened then slammed shut in the cab.

They had arrived. What did he plan now? Her pulse exploded into terror's trip-hammer beat. Or was it desire's rhythm? She struggled to think.

The truck's doors opened and the big man scrambled out, then turned to pull her after him. He yanked her trousers up to her waist and pulled her jacket back to her shoulders again. She was hot, wet, and swollen against the cloth's steady rub, and she twitched under the rough sensation.

He tossed her over his shoulder, paying no heed to her struggles, and ran into the building. An elevator—a freight elevator judging by the draughts brushing through it—lifted them higher and higher. Somewhere far below, the truck came alive again, before it faded into the distance.

He set her down on her feet, supporting her against his hard body. He unchained her cuffs then lifted first one wrist, then the other, shoulder high.

Each wrist was anchored before her head stopped spinning. Her hands instinctively grasped the metal bar that separated them. Four staccato clicks announced her legs' separation and their attachment to another metal rod, her feet firmly planted in her hiking boots against the floor. She could stand like this for a very long time.

He yanked the blindfold off so she could discover her new universe.

Beth blinked several times, as her eyes adjusted to the filtered light coming through banks of grimy windows and skylights. She stood in an enormous room in a brick building, furnished with a big wooden swivel chair, a table and a chest beside it, and two ancient wood stoves that heated their surroundings to almost tropical warmth. The floor had been swept to a warehouse's idea of clean. She was spread-eagled against a set of pipes, a relic of the room's manufacturing past.

She felt totally exposed and helpless, despite her heavy clothing. She was completely at the mercy of the big man watching her from across the room, his blue eyes considering her in a predator's level stare. He was ferociously calm, in contrast to her body's throbbing sensitivity.

She trembled, the motion traveling deep and ending in a slow burn in her gut. She gathered herself to fight. Oral sex was well and good, but she could find that with another partner, as could he.

"Are you going to tell me where the art is, beautiful bitch?" he purred, prowling toward her. His eyes stripped her remaining clothes in an unspoken promise. "As soon as you tell me where the Nazis hid our treasures, then I'll let you go."

She shook her head violently. Never, she mouthed against the gag. She would play this scene out to the end.

He held his knife before her eyes, a big, wickedly sharp dagger that he'd looted from an opera-bound Nazi general. She managed to sneer, even though she trembled and her breasts hardened under her shirt's remnants.

He rubbed the flat of the blade over her cheek. She remained motionless and stared back at him. What the hell was he going to do?

"You should never have left us, your true people, for foreign men," he remarked, teasing the gag's edge with the dagger's tip. The silk shredded slightly but didn't tear. "You should have stayed where you belonged, with those who love you."

His eyes burned into hers, but she managed to refuse again. Her insides were twisted together, while her cream now dripped onto her thigh. She tried to breathe.

"So you want to play this game, do you?" He caressed her neck with the dagger's sharp edge, so that her pulse beat frantically against it. "Then where is the art?"

In a move so fast that she had no time to respond, he cut the gag away and tossed it aside. "Tell me, or I'll pluck your clothes from you."

"No! You are nothing, compared to their mighty army." She found a laugh to throw at him. "They will hold Europe when you and your kind are long dead."

"Foolish woman, do you think you have experienced everything I can do to you?" He circled her, studying her closely. She snapped her head to follow him, growing more uneasy and excited with his every step.

He halted behind her and slid her hair away from her neck. He licked her nape and she jerked, then shrieked a little when he nipped her. He laved and nibbled on her sensitive points, until she trembled but remained stubbornly silent.

She was almost relieved when he left her and went to the table. But her eyes widened in shock when he returned with a pair of heavy scissors. "You wouldn't dare cut my clothes!"

"I find that I prefer your nakedness. It offers so many opportunities," he purred. Her blood ran cold and then heated as her breasts tightened again.

Still, she gasped in outrage, when he ran the scissors up her jacket and shirtsleeve to her neck. Now her only clothes above the waist hung by just one shoulder.

He stood back, savoring the view. She burst into a string of curses, railing at him for destroying her warmest coat. "How dare you cut it, you dirt-grubbing . . ."

He stopped her by the simple expedient of kissing her. She fought and tried to wrench her mouth away from him. He trapped her head between his two big paws and continued to kiss her until she yielded to him. Then his tongue roamed her mouth like a ravenous army, conquering everything it touched. His hands kneaded her breasts until she moaned and twisted.

"Where is the art?" he breathed against her cheek.

"No," she stammered, dragging her few remaining wits back. "No, the Nazis would kill me if I told you."

"Little fool," he rumbled, "do you really want me to question you until you beg for mercy? You know what I can do and how dangerous I am." His eyes gleamed, sapphire-bright but still controlled, above his flushed cheekbones. He paid no attention whatsoever to the bulge rearing behind his fly. He looked like a lion considering how best to spring upon a gazelle.

"I will never tell!" Beth cried out.

He cut the jacket and shirt off her other arm and tossed the remains under the table.

"How dare you! Do you think that is enough to make me talk?"

"You should have remained home," he remarked, his eyes never leaving her tightly furled nipples. Her breasts rose and fell frantically, while both her ruby-red nipples tightened.

Did he mean that she should have remained with him? Was he looking for a pledge from her?

"No! I, ah, oh!" she gasped as his mouth claimed her treacherous breasts. How could she resist him when her body reacted like this?

He suckled her strongly and she writhed, grasping the metal bar for support. "Damn you, how can you do this!"

His hand tugged at her other breast. She shrieked as he worked her breasts, using mouth and hands until every touch sent a jolt directly to her clit. He stroked her back and his hand soon traveled over her derriere, first over her trousers, then inside. Her head rolled back as he teased her. But the heavy corduroy trousers were too snug for the close contact he sought. He eased them open, while he marked her with small growls and nips.

She groaned when he rubbed her clit between her swollen folds. Her hips thrust convulsively, as she sought to follow his fingers' steady probes inside her. Then he lifted his mouth from hers and yanked her trousers down to her knees.

She squeaked and opened her eyes, shocked by the draft exploring her hot skin.

He walked around her again, studying every inch of her. She eyed him warily, starting to be very concerned about his plans. How far would he go to dominate her? The kind of oral sex they'd enjoyed in the truck should have been enough to make him use her like a ravenous stallion, leaving him spent and exhausted. Then she could have left him without promising any changes.

What had she said in that damn checklist that he could use on her now? She remembered mentioning nipple clamps, spanking, leather belt. . . . What else?

"Too many clothes," he remarked and brought back heavy scissors.

"You ruined them!" she protested, as two efficient cuts left the trousers lying on the floor at her feet.

"You're not showing me enough yet," he remarked. He ran a possessive hand up her leg and cupped her mound. She jerked, then rolled her pelvis into his grasp. "But you're starting to be wet enough."

She couldn't give him what he demanded. If she was right, then yielding would destroy them both in a failed union. The penalty for failure was huge.

She shuddered and tried to protest his hand's behavior, but soon lost the ability to form words. She grew flushed and faint, frantic with the need for more. But he wouldn't tell her to come and she hovered on the verge.

He smacked her hard on the butt. She jerked but it felt good, so good to have the harder sensation. He smacked her on the other cheek and she yelped. He rubbed the spot hard, before landing three more blows in quick sensation.

Beth cried out and wriggled as he fondled her. Had she mentioned spankings in that checklist? She tried to protest. "What are you doing?"

"You've been a very bad girl and you still haven't told me what I need to know. Now where is the art?"

"I'll never tell!" She didn't remember why not, just that she couldn't talk. So she added a few words about his ancestry in a tone that made his eyebrow lift.

He spanked her hard after that, blows and caresses mixed until her body writhed and her hips thrust into every touch. He visited much of her, including her throbbing, sensitive breasts, until she keened her desire. He paused from time to time, to fondle her or kiss her. Once his groin brushed her hip, with a hard ridge closely confined in his trousers.

But she never spoke of the art, or returning to her beloved home.

She hung on the bar, eyes shut as she gasped for breath during a respite. His hand gently teased her erect clit while the other fondled her fiery ass. She sighed her approval, before she registered the grease on the fingers sliding up and down the cleft between her buttocks. But its coolness felt so good.

A finger delicately teased her clit while another slipped into her ass. She welcomed both greedily, enjoying the lightly stretched feeling.

"Oh, yes, please. More please, oh, yes," she sighed, the first time she had begged.

He gave her more, gradually working more fingers into her until three very large masculine fingers stuffed her backside, while his other hand eased into her cunt. She rocked between his hands, moaning deep and low.

She floated in a haze when he left her, her eyes still shut. Then cold metal entered her ass and she shuddered at the size and weight. She'd taken jelly and silicone butt plugs before. But stainless steel? It was big, not the largest she'd ever carried, but enough to make her body stretch around it. And it was certainly the heaviest she'd ever known.

"What are you doing?" she whispered.

The big plug settled into place at last and her body clenched around the base, holding it close. Heat flowed between her breasts and her ass, encouraged by the finger circling her clit. She wouldn't be able to hold the weight long, but her body fought to continue the sensation for the moment.

"Where's the art?"

"I'll never tell," she managed, more faintly than before. He had far more imagination than she'd given him credit for, but she still couldn't take the chance.

"Little fool," he growled and pulled his belt free. Her mouth went dry at the familiar sound, and she stared longingly at the wide strip of flexible leather.

But this was Sean, who protected women. He wouldn't use that on her, even though she was so aroused she'd welcome it.

He doubled the belt and snapped it as a test. She shivered at the experience behind the casual motion.

"Talk to me, woman." His gaze was steady and controlled but her body heated under it.

She took a deep breath, fighting back the demand clamoring inside. She formed her answer very carefully. "No."

He brought the belt down unerringly on her ass. She shrieked and rose to her toes in response, before settling back. The blow ran through her body like a call to arms.

"No," she said again. But the word was now changing to another meaning.

"You need a damned good hiding," he muttered, "for all the trouble you're causing."

"No," she said again. And she meant yes.

He tanned her backside a dozen times with the leather, and she cried out in response every time. Heat rose through her like mercury in a thermometer. She lost the ability to form words when he rubbed the leather between her legs, then lightly tapped her pussy with it.

"No, please," she moaned then, uncaring what he thought. She needed this contact, the belt's hard touch setting an answering pulse through her body. She wanted more, needed more.

Beth floated in an ecstatic haze when he stopped, her body alive as never before. Somehow her body still embraced the butt plug, while her nipples throbbed. She was both grateful and achingly vulnerable to him.

She opened her eyes finally and looked for him. She found him standing naked in front of a stove, rolling a condom down his straining, vibrantly alive cock.

What was he going to do? She couldn't suck him, not when she was bound like this. And he wouldn't fit into her cunt, not in this position with that enormous plug filling her ass. But she couldn't bear not to hold every possible inch of him. She trembled with fear and arousal at the choices.

He looked back at her and smiled slowly, a curve of cruel masculine satisfaction, his eyes lighting in harsh triumph as he read her expression. "What do you think I'm going to do now?"

"I don't know," she whimpered.

"Yes, you do know," he corrected her. "Try again. What am *I* going to do? You said it once in that damn limo."

Beth sent her mind back to find the answer. "You're going to do exactly what you want, not what pleases me."

"Exactly right," he growled and came back to her. "What are *you* going to do?"

"*Whatever* pleases *you*," she gritted, fighting to enunciate the words against her body's cravings. Finally surrendering to him.

He probed her with the tip of his cock. She was wet, dripping with it. But how could she accommodate him and the plug?

"Ah, Sean," she moaned as his glans slid in, stretching her to the point of pain. He worked himself into her slowly and she yielded to him, easing her breathing so she relaxed enough to accept him. It was very difficult and she burned with pain, tight as a virgin in this position, with her legs spread just far enough to accept his hips.

She took a deep breath and filled herself with the scent of hungry male. Anything was worth it, if he was satisfied, even if she hadn't managed to accept every inch.

He stayed motionless, his eyes closed as if he were memorizing the feeling of her like this. Gradually she relaxed around him and softened in welcome.

"Oh, yes," he murmured. "That's it, woman. Open for me."

Beth trembled as her body did exactly that. He slid into her up to the hilt, filling her until she could barely breathe. His hot cock and the steel dildo in her ass occupying every inch, pressing against places she'd never known of, until she thought she'd go mad. Then he locked his arms around her and started to move.

He fucked her long and hard, in deep piston strokes that almost took him from her before plunging inside again, driven by the power of his muscled legs. Her inner muscles gripped him when they could, caressing him as her hands and legs couldn't. She nipped his shoulder, holding on to as much of him as possible. She arched herself, abandoning herself to being fucked by the one man in the world who really mattered.

"Fuck yes," he groaned when he found a slightly different nook inside her. "Perfect. Oh, fuck, fuck . . ."

His self-control vanished as he changed to swift strokes that pounded her deeply, without leaving her body. His voice deepened and roughened as it stopped forming words. She forgot everything except the magic of this moment.

He stabbed deeper and howled as his climax grabbed him. He yanked the plug out of her and a thrill blazed up her spine in response. Beth exploded into ecstasy, everything in her convulsing in an agony of satisfaction. A scintillating pinwheel of light burst behind her eyes and she lost consciousness, anchored only by him.

She came awake slowly and found herself still possessed by his cock. His hand ran down her back and one finger slipped possessively into her ass. Her eyes widened at his dominance.

"Say the words, Beth." He watched her calmly, then circled his finger inside her. Her hips quivered.

"Beth," he prodded, but didn't remove his finger.

Her mind stirred sluggishly before framing the truth. "I should never have left." She closed her eyes then forced them open. Time to yield, both in fantasy and real life. "Please, I'll tell you where the art is, if you'll just come back to me. I need you more than life, my marvelous switch."

Sean kissed her deeply then.

"We're going to get married," he said finally, producing a small jewelry box from his back pocket. "I don't care where and I don't care when, as long as we both agree we're engaged."

Beth stared as he slid an enormous square-cut sapphire ring on her finger. She couldn't run away, given that she was still bound hand and foot to the pipes.

"I don't even care how we get married, as long as it's legal in the United States."

"Okay," Beth murmured, still pondering the ring's promises.

"Is that all you have to say?"

She stirred at the stern note in his voice and met his eyes. Time to claim her future with him. "I love you, Sean."

"That's better." He kissed her, gently at first and mindful of her bruises, then more strongly as she welcomed him. "I love you. And you're going to dominate me again, you hear that?"

"When I want to," she shrugged, fighting to keep a straight face. He really was going to be a handful. Of course, she'd never wanted any other kind of man.

He eyed her suspiciously, then relaxed when he read her consent. "Good enough." He began to untie her wrists.

"Father gave you his blessing. Yesterday, when he went on campus," she remarked, just to confirm her guess. How else would Sean have known when she was outside the house?

He stilled, going a little white, then smiled at her. "Yes, he did. It felt real good to be accepted by your family. I didn't tell him everything I planned though." He gently rubbed her first freed hand.

Beth's mouth twitched at his concern. "Don't worry. You told him enough to make him happy or he'd never have helped you kidnap me."

"Yeah," Sean agreed and looked happier. "Yeah, you're right. He even welcomed me to the family."

Beth smiled, tears pricking at her eyes. Sean must have greatly impressed her father, if he said that much.

"Your mother packed some of her clothes for you. They're in the desk."

Both parents had helped Sean. Tears of joy swam in her eyes.

"Scotland at Christmas," she murmured, flexing her hand to help the returning circulation. Time to start talking about the future and make a gift to her mother.

"What?"

"My parents were married in a registry office, not a church. I'd like a big white wedding, like the ones my mother talks about. My family always spends the week between Christmas and New Year's in Scotland so we can get married then."

His face lit up and he kissed her again. "Hooah!"

"What?"

"Ranger talk. I'll teach you."

"Yes, dear." She rubbed his shoulder. "There is one catch though."

"Yes?" He went quite still as he watched and waited.

"You'll have to make the arrangements. I'm going to be very busy, moving from D.C. to Seattle and starting a new job."

"Yes!" He caught her against him and laughed. "Treasury, right? Hunting terrorist money?"

"Of course!" Beth laughed with him, especially when a tug reminded him that her ankles were still shackled. She giggled as she watched him bend to free her. "Can you manage my money, too? Heaven knows I barely have time now, before taking on you and my new job."

"Do you trust me with it?"

"With anything and everything, sweetheart."

The Seattle night was cold and clear, with a brisk wind blowing from the north, as Sean and Beth ran to the stadium from the parking lot. Mike had arrived earlier, at the time preferred by his coach. But they'd dallied in the new Range Rover until Sean's wristwatch sounded the alarm.

They reached the stadium just in time to stand at attention for the national anthem. Sean did so with the unself-conscious ease of long practice, while Beth settled beside him, feeling as if she'd always stood there.

Then whistles blew, cheerleaders yelled, and boys ran out on the field.

Beth touched Sean's neck where the black silk scarf barely showed above his parka. He smiled down at her.

"Come on, darling, let's sit down for the opening kickoff."

Dave Hemmings waved at them from the stands and pointed at the seats next to him, carefully marked by two very fancy stadium cushions, with pockets and back rests. They also looked brand-new.

Beth chuckled and started up the steps behind Sean. Their progress was slow as people brushed past, anxious to run just one more errand before the game started. Beth amused herself by rubbing Sean's ass whenever they had to stop.

One pause was especially long, while a woman standing in the aisle tried to get her daughter to decide which soft drink she wanted.

The girl looked to be of high school age, too old for such nonsense, while the woman had truly appalling taste in clothes. Beth considered memorizing the outfit, in order to tell Jenn you truly could mix four shades of green in one outfit for a bilious effect, but dismissed the idea as too painful.

She slid her hand inside Sean's jeans and petted him gently. Not too much really, since it would be hours before they could leave the stadium.

Then the woman saw Sean and her face brightened. She preened and shimmied toward him, bringing a stench of cheap perfume. He stiffened. Beth's hackles rose at the woman's possessive voice.

"Sean! Thank God you're back. When do you think we can get together?" Her voice died away as she stared.

Beth's left hand, with the enormous engagement ring on it, rested on Sean's shoulder. Her right hand gave his ass a firm squeeze, while she watched the woman coldly in a glare perfected by her grandmother, *Nakamurakou*. Centuries of noblewomen looked down her nose, while samurai loosened their swords in her eyes.

Sean choked. "Uh, ah, Jean." He stopped, appalled. "I'm sorry, Linda! I don't know how I could forget your name."

Linda looked ready to kill him. Dave Hemmings was trying hard to keep a straight face in the row beyond, while his wife was suffering a coughing fit. Beth smiled politely, too pleased with Sean to need any other triumph.

"Linda, this is my fiancée, Beth Nakamura. We're getting married next month," Sean managed. "Beth, darling, this is Linda Davison and her daughter, Jenny. Jenny is a senior here."

The women murmured polite nonsense before Linda produced a sickly grin.

"Sorry but I really do need to get drinks. Excuse me." She brushed past Sean and Beth and hurtled down the steps like a runaway car. Jenny watched her mother go and shrugged slightly, before turning her attention back to the pimply boy beside her.

Beth finally found herself seated next to Dave's wife, who he proudly introduced as Deirdre. Sean sat down beside her and produced a beautiful new blanket, which he carefully draped over their laps.

Beth wriggled slightly, testing the aftermath of Sean's courtship. Very little discomfort, really, so she'd be fine in another day or so. Hopefully, next time he'd go a little further.

Deirdre promptly demanded a close-up look at the engagement ring and Beth happily showed her.

"Beautiful!" Deirdre enthused. "It's just perfect for you. But I'd never have thought that Sean would spend—" She stopped, looking embarrassed.

Beth laughed. "Oh, Sean has surprising depths when you drag them out of him." She turned the conversation to an easier subject. "We're so glad you and your family can come to the wedding."

"Oh, we wouldn't miss it! Especially since Dave said you're chartering a plane?" Deirdre's voice trailed off expectantly.

"Yes, we thought that would be easier for our friends than to fly commercially right now. One plane from Seattle and another from Georgia, which will also stop in D.C.," Beth elaborated.

Deirdre started to ask another question but her attention shifted to the cheerleaders as they began to encourage the team.

Beth's hand ran up Sean's thigh, under the blanket, and cupped his balls gently. She stroked them possessively as she leaned against him. Mine, her touch said. All mine.

Sean froze in surprise then began to chuckle.

On the field, Mike gave him the thumbs-up sign. Sean returned it, grinning broadly, before putting his arm around Beth and pulling her closer.

"Uh . . . Gary called today," Sean remarked hoarsely. Beth glanced at him, a little surprised by the topic. "He said he just got in a new shipment of erotica. He's saved us some books."

Beth kissed Sean's cheek. "Maybe tomorrow, darling. Maybe tomorrow."

Epilogue

The last strains of the bagpipe died away outside, signaling that the last guests had arrived.

Sean marched to the front of the church, planted his toe as precisely as ever he'd done in the Army, and pivoted to face the assembled throng. Behind him, Mike matched every step exactly and lined up beside him. Sean was wearing his Army dress blues, with the scarf tucked in a pocket over his heart, while his son stood tall in a suit. A year from now, Mike would also be in uniform, thanks to his acceptance at West Point.

The Scottish cathedral was as big as Beth's mother had promised, old gray stones shining in the colored lights from the great stained glass windows. Christmas wreaths and garlands draped every conceivable surface, while white and gold roses and candles glowed for his wedding. People were packed into every corner, with uniforms more common than civilian suits, at least for the men. U.S. Army uniforms filled the pews on the groom's side and a flood of British Navy and Royal Marine Commando uniforms marked the bride's side. There were even kilts to be seen.

He was marrying the woman of his dreams, and all his friends had come to witness it. Gary Miller and his wife, Shannon, were in the front pew with Dave and Deirdre Hemmings and their daughters. His friends from Seattle, plus large contingents from posts across the U.S., and Beth's friends from Washington, D.C., had braved the uncertainties of air travel to celebrate his good fortune. Hell, a number of his long-time buddies had hitched rides on planes from Germany and points farther east, including the Gulf and Afghanistan, just to be here.

Just as important, all of Beth's family had come, too. Her Japanese grandmother—who had an aristocratic title, God help him— terrified him as badly as his Ranger instructors ever had. She'd brought heavy, formal wedding kimonos for both him and Beth and she'd looked just like a grandmother should at the Japanese wedding ceremony, shedding a quiet tear as he pledged himself to Beth. Then she'd given him a set of samurai swords, last owned by her naval hero uncle.

She was here now, sitting in the second pew with her sons and their wives, behind Beth's mother and all of Beth's brothers and their families. There were enough rich Japanese, mixed among Beth's Scots cousins, to alarm any edible fish. He thought the American ambassador was somewhere around, too. After the ceremony, they'd all march behind the bagpiper and a pair of ducks, in honor of Scottish and Japanese customs, to the castle a few blocks away and one hell of a banquet.

He'd come a long way from that orphan, in a one-cow South Dakota town, to the fellow with hundreds of friends gathered at his wedding. Now he was looking forward to a couple of years of getting to know his beloved wife better before they started the family they planned. "A Kind of Magic," as the Queen tune said.

The organ music gathered itself into a roar and all eyes turned to the door. Beth's friend Jenn smiled and started forward, wearing a long golden dress and carrying cream and gold flowers.

Sean saw her, looked past, and fixed his gaze on his woman. Beth was tall and beautiful in a figured, white silk dress, which hugged her curves like a lover, and her grandmother's lace veil. She saw him and immediately blazed with happiness, her delight surging across the big church and into his heart. Her smiling father patted her arm and they came down the aisle together, her dress swirling out behind her in a fan-shaped train.

Sean knew he was grinning like a fool and could not have cared less. He and his dangerous lady were about to become one, in the eyes of God and man. The dream he'd thought impossible had finally come true, and the future promised to be even better than his dream.